Will & Power: Inside the Living Library

By: Loan W

First Printing

ISBN-13:9781546972204

ISBN-10:154697220X

01) My Story's Beginnings

When I was a little girl, the adults of the crystal sky city often spoke to me about the many accomplishments of my father. Some would approach me in public and say things like, "Please tell your father our whole family sends our love and blessings." While many of them were genuine, I knew for certain some were fakes. When I would play with their kids on the playground, some would say things like, "My parents told me that your father is a blood thirsty monster and you're a half breed freak!" Once a little girl yelled, "My parents say that your father has a demon inside of him and you are contaminated with its evil!" Shortly after she screamed at me in front of everyone, my best friend asked me, "Is it true that he killed a bunch of people but everyone who saw it is dead?" Unfortunately for me, I never knew how to react, so I would just deny everything they said to defend my father and his honor.

Being a child I didn't know what to believe, leaving me very confused for many years. I dared not ask my father about it, for he was a large, intense looking man with a muscular frame covered in tattoos, a thick beard and a serious face, except when happy. His appearance alone was enough to make me wonder if he was who I thought he was; unfortunately it seemed no one in the world knew him the way I did. He was kind, patient, loving, trusting and devoted to bringing me up right. He listened to my every word, only offering advice when I asked for it and never once did he raise his hand at me. Somehow he always knew exactly what to say.

The rumors that the children were sharing may not have made any sense to me, but they did leave me curious about my father's past. So one day, when I was ten years old, I worked up the courage to ask him about the rumors while we both ate dinner at the long wooden table in front of our old fashioned brick fireplace.

"Dad?" I said.

"Yes Maria?" he replied, lifting his gaze from his soup with a raised eye brow.

"Why do the people in the village say mean things about you?" I asked, hoping he'd already know what was being said.

"What people sweetie? What are they saying?" he replied inquisitively.

"Some of the kids I play with say that their parents said you were a bad person before people lived in the crystal sky cities. That you have evil in you."

His face turned from amused to serious. "Those people know nothing of me or my past Maria. Pay them no mind sweetie." He continued eating his soup.

His response was not enough to satisfy my ten year old curiosity. So I pressed him for an answer "Then why do they say bad stuff about you? Why would they say such mean things like that?"

"I don't know sweetie. Maybe they are just mean. Now I don't want to hear anything more about it, okay?" He replied sternly.

"But why?" I asked in a whiney tone, "Is it true that you killed people before we lived..."

"Maria! Stop it!" He exclaimed, slamming his hand on the table. "I told you I don't want to hear anymore about it! Now go to your room!" He shouted pointing down the hallway to that led to our bedrooms.

His sudden burst of anger was abnormmal enough for me to know I pushed him too far, but still, I was heart broken for that was the first time he had yelled at me. I ran to my room crying, mumbling "I didn't even do anything..."

He soon came to see me crying on the bed with my face in the pillow. He sat down on the corner of the bed and sighed. He put his hand on my back and said "My dearest and only daughter, I love you with all of my heart and I apologize for raising my voice. I know you want to know the truth about what the people are saying, but I can't tell you right now sweetie. I just can't. You are only ten and that's too young to hear daddy's story about what really happened when he was a younger man."

"Why did you kill people?" I asked, lifting my mouth from the pillow.

He paused for a moment and tenderly said "People do die in daddy's story, yes. That's why it isn't for a child's ear to hear."

"Is how mommy died in your story?" I asked.

"Yes, what happened to mommy is a part of daddy's story." He replied with a sigh.

Still crying with my face in the pillow, I asked "Then why? Why can't you just tell me? I won't tell anyone! I promise!"

He rubbed my back and said "I am not worried you will tell someone sweetie. Daddy's story is scary; sometimes people get hurt, and it's got ghosts in it. My story would keep you up all night."

"Are there monsters in your story?" I asked, lifting my face from the pillow.

With a brief giggle, he replied "Yes. There are monsters in daddy's story."

"I wanna hear more! Tell me more!" I said, popping up with excitement.

He laughed and tickled me as he said "You sneaky little snake! I knew you were just trying to get me to tell you more!" We laughed and played until I lost memory of his loud reprimand, then he stopped tickling me, and kissed me on the head.

He was about to walk out when I said "Daddy?"

He stopped, looked at me and said "Yes sweetie?"

"When will I be old enough to hear your story?"

He scratched his head, closed his eyes, made a humming noise, then opened his eyes and said. "How about this: I promise I will not only tell you the story, I will show you my story in a very special way, but only after you have completed your planetary alignment ceremony at twenty-eight years old. Okay? But *you* have to promise *me* that you won't listen to the other kids on the playground and you won't to ask me to tell you my story until then, deal?"

"Deal!" I replied, sitting up smiling on the bed, putting my hand out. He smiled, walked up, shook my hand, looked me in the eye then rubbed my head and walked out of my room. After that discussion I paid the mean children on the playground no mind, and simply acknowledged the praise filled adults with a nod and a smile.

Later on, during my teenage years, I tried to live as normal of a life as I could while existing in a group of tall sun absorbing crystal sky scrapers floating on an antigravity bubble in the sky. Only, I never really fit in with the other kids. They seemed to avoid me when I attempted to engage conversation. This hurt my feelings quite a lot as I grew up and I came home crying many times to tell my father what happened. One day was worse than the rest however, I came storming in through the old fashioned wooden door my father put in our home instead of an automated electric door. I ran to my room as he was preparing food in the kitchen. He heard me and came in asking, "What happened sweetie?"

"This dumb popular girl at my school named Lilith walked by me at lunch and purposefully dropped her cup full of water all over my shirt, purse and the new book I was reading. Then everyone laughed at me, so I stood up and asked her what her problem was and she acted like she was gonna hit me. So I tried to block it and slipped in the water and hit my head on the table and everyone laughed at me again."

I started to cry even more and he took me into his arms. Gently he kissed me on the bump I had on my head and said, "Oh sweetie, Are you okay?"

"Yeah, but my head still hurts a little." I said, through my tears and mucus.

"Here let me help, okay?" he said gently.

"Okay." I replied.

As he hugged me and put his hands on my head, I felt the pain immediately subside. While he spoke, it lessened even more, "I am so sorry to hear that happened today sweetie! That Lilith girl sounds really mean! You know what though; I got picked on a lot in school too and when I grew up, I realized that all of the stuff in school really didn't matter when I became an adult. And anyone who was mean during those times, usually ended up regretting it when they got older and more mature. Besides, Lilith probably did it because you're so pretty and smart. Does she look like someone put lip stick and earrings on a pig wearing a wig?"

I thought about his remark and remembered that Lilith was kind of ugly and only popular because she slept with all of the popular guys. I started laughing and as I nodded, the pain in my head lessened even more. My father let go and I suddenly felt no more pain at all, then suddenly I was no longer upset at Lilith. I actually began to pity her for the deep insecurity she felt that made her behave that way.

My father looked at me as I stood there feeling compassion for her and said "There is the girl I know and love." Then he walked out the doorway and said, "I hope you are ready!"

"Ready for what?" I asked quickly.

"Ready to go to the Amazon Jungle, like I promised you!" he said, as he turned around to face me in the doorway.

I turned facing him and replied "You said that we would do that when I turned eighteen. I'm only sixteen, Dad."

"Are you really gonna fight me on this? I think now is a good time to go, maybe you can take some days off of school, and I could teach you a few things. I have many far more important things for you to learn than all that propaganda they feed you in school!"

"Are you serious dad? Or are you messing with me right now?" I said with a serious tone, looking him in the eye.

He smiled and said "I already packed the anti-gravity pod to camp out there for two-weeks. Now go and get whatever else you think you will wanna bring. But you can't take your eye lens; I want you to know the environment of earth without the use and ease of technology."

I squealed like a little girl, ran over and gave him a big hug, "Thank you dad! Thank you so much! Whatever you say, I can't wait to finally be out there!" I ran to my room, grabbed a few change of clothes and we left for the jungle.

After that trip to the Amazon, I became a loner at school. I missed classes, lost friends and stopped caring at all what my peers thought of me. My father and I often took trips down to the jungles, plains, oceans and forests of the planet in our own personal anti-gravity pod. We would collect food, medicinal plants, play in the rain and snow or just interact with the wildlife. He would take me to the ruins of the massive abandoned cities from his time and tell me of the world as it use to be, when he was a far younger man.

He also taught me so much about the earth, its countless plant remedies and food sources during our seemingly never-ending camping trips. His words could fill countless pages of text. He taught me how to hunt, use a bow and arrow, even prepare an animal for food. Despite the fact that physical violence is forbidden in the sky cities, he trained me in the ancient martial arts as well as the ways of alchemy. I learned how to forge a blade from smelted rock, make a home from mud and stone, even make pottery.

He assured me this knowledge was all necessary to know and understand. Despite its being considered outdated and archaic techniques by the people in the sky. On the rare occasion that people from the sky city venture to surface of Earth, they use an eye lens which allows them to know all of the animals and plants in a half mile radius as well as their distance, threat level and potential uses. This technology is so common place that it has become part of our fashion in the crystal cities. However, I was never allowed to use it in the wild when I went out with my father and I could never understand why. Whenever I asked, he would always reply the same way. He'd say, "To understand where you are, you must first know how you got there. To understand where you want to go, you must first understand where you have been."

On the eve of my twenty-eighth year, I completed my planetary alignment ceremony. And, like most single, pretty and intelligent woman in our sky city, I had several men ask me out to celebrate after the ceremony. However, I had more important plans than celebrating with strangers; my father's story was what I wanted for my birthday. Only he no longer lived in the sky cities. After I moved out of his crystal tower, he chose to live on the earth instead, a decision that no one had made in half a century. At dusk, I flew to his home in the Sonoran desert to ask about his story. He was atop the roof of his small dome shaped home made of obsidian glass. As I approached I saw he was meditating shirtless, wearing long black pants while looking into the setting sun. So, I walked up to its perimeter and shouted up to him.

"Dad?"

“Happy birthday!” He replied promptly.

“Thank you!” I said, “I just came from the temple after completing my planetary alignment ceremony. Do you remember what you promised when I was…”

He interrupted me with his hand rising from resting atop his knee and said “I know. I made you a promise eighteen years ago and I plan to keep it. There is no door. Climb the staircase; I will meet you in the ceremony room.” He stood up and walked down the dome’s backside and disappeared. I walked into his home; it was mostly dirt and sand on the bottom floor. The whole inner structure was black obsidian, including the beautifully carved spirals on the winding staircase that hugged the right side of the wall all the way to the top.

When I climbed it, I found a room of four walls and a circular open ceiling. The skylight was the room’s only source of light and the room had only a bed. Just beyond the bed’s end was another open doorway covered by a thin white sheet, it led to a small room with a smaller circular skylight. Inside the room, the sun shone perfectly on an black obsidian alter in its center. A white cloth was draped over its top and my father was standing behind it in the shadows.

He beckoned me to come in and give him a hug. I walked into the room, around the altar and we embraced one another for several seconds. He was still a very able-bodied, beefy man despite his older age and his strong loving embrace was evidence of that. “Happy Birthday sweetie!” He said, squeezing me tighter. As we broke the hug, he continued speaking, “Now, I have a very special gift I have been waiting to give you for as long as you have been alive. Are you ready to see it?”

“Yes! Of course!” I replied.

“Good, then turn around and remove the white cloth on the altar.” He said.

I turned around and looked at the sun light shining through the thin white sheets directly on top of the altar. As I pulled away the white cloth, it revealed a white silk pillow with a black crystal ball about the size of a tangerine in its center. As I leaned over and stared into the crystal’s depths, I saw decades pass in seconds. Images of places and people lost in the seas of time flashed over and over. Titanic structures would rise and fall with the empires of men and their lineages. Wars, plagues, floods, earthquakes, hurricanes, tsunamis and forest fires flashed again and again and again.

Then my father touched my shoulder and said “Do you like it?” I looked back at the stone but the images were gone. I looked back at him with confusion. He laughed and patted me on the shoulder saying, “I’ll take that as a ‘yes’. And the look of confusion means, ‘what was it I just saw dad?’ Right?” He laughed again and continued “Have a seat against the wall facing the altar. Its time to smoke your ceremonial birthday bowl and I will explain your gift to you. I hope you still like the brown and green smoke blend?”

“Always!” I replied as I sat down against the wall.

He sat across from me on the ground. Pulling a pipe from behind his back, he struck a match on the floor and lit the bowl. The contents burned a smoldering orange and, after taking a few deep in-hales, he passed it to me. While I took the smooth thick grey mint flavored smoke into my lungs, my father spoke:

“That crystal has been in our family for countless generations. It has endless storage space for information and energy, but it’s only able to be wielded by someone of our bloodline. If you saw images inside of it, you were seeing the pasts of the people who once used it. I have stored more information in that crystal than could ever be stored on the sky city’s modern technological devices. This is only possible because, believe it or not, this crystal is alive. Those silicone devices they use in the sky cities are dead; because of this they have great limitations.

I must tell you something Maria. I am very concerned at the direction the sky culture is going. They’ve receded too far into the stars and have forgotten their earthly roots. The only thing I miss about that life up there is seeing you everyday. Those people are so focused on ascension, they have forgotten how wonderful it is to be a human being on earth. They have forgotten the thrill of living where things are wildly unpredictable. Remember: living in the clouds and dreaming your life away in some blissful technological dimension is no way to use your young agile body Maria!”

“I know dad. You tell me that all the time.” I interrupted, as I handed him the glowing orange bowl of the pipe. “What’s your point this time? How does this tie in to the crystal’s story?”

“My point, young lady, is this.” He said, taking a long drag of the pipe with a raised eye brow then blowing out the smoke. “I waited until now to give you that stone and tell you my story for several reasons. If my visions are correct, now that you are twenty–eight and all of the planets are in the exact same positions as they were when you were born, you will begin to grow more powerful than I have in my lifetime. And it is for this reason and many others that I have raised you the way I have. I have tried not to control you, but rather to help you blossom and find your own way in life. However, I also conclude a long time ago that I would offer you the opportunity to learn everything that I know and be the one to follow in my footsteps, if you so choose.”

I screamed with excitement and abruptly hugged him while he still had the pipe in his mouth. He stopped talking and laughed as he hugged me with one arm. “Well I am assuming that is a yes?” He responded.

“Of course Dad! It would be an honor to follow in your footsteps!” I exclaimed.

“Well, let me just say that you may not know the task for which you volunteer, because I mean that literally. I told you when you were young, that I would show you my story in a special way. Well, using that crystal, you are going to see things through my eyes for a short time. You will come here for eight straight full moon nights, from sundown to sunrise. You will record everything that is shown inside of the crystal ball and write it down for other generations to read. In this stone, I have stored only the most important lessons that I've learned in my lifetime and in the exact manner of which I learned them. There will be some gaps in time, but ultimately you will see everything as I saw it. You will hear everything as I heard it. And my narration will serve as a medium for my thoughts throughout the story. Afterward, I will show you how to apply the knowledge and use the crystal's power in your daily life, as well as in the service of others."

"That sounds like fun! Can we start now?" I asked eagerly.

"Well, it does happen to be the first night of the full moon. Do you have a recording device with you?" he asked curiously.

"I do actually; it's in my antigravity pod. My eye lens has a recording function. If I go get it can we start your story tonight?" I asked enthusiastically.

"Go get it and find out." He replied with a grin.

I ran out of his ceremony room, down the stairs to my pod and grabbed the eye lens. When I came back to the ceremony room, he had the long wooden pipe and a bundle of incense sticks in his hands. He sat across from the altar with his back against the wall, and said "Get the crystal ball off the altar and pull the lever next to the door to close the skylight. Then drop the rolled cloth that's hanging above the doorway to the floor. We need to seal the room and make sure its dark, otherwise it wont work."

"What won't work?" I asked, standing still and looking at him curiously.

He smiled and said, "If you want to see, you will have to do as I said, then start your recording device. But wait—before we start, are you sure you are ready? Because once I start the extraction process from the crystal, there is no stopping it. Once I have accessed the information that is stored in that crystal, it is going to pour out like water through a broken dam. I need to know for certain that you will see this story through to its end."

I rolled my eyes and replied, "Dad, if I am going to be your apprentice you need to stop babying me and start having a little more faith in my ability to handle things on my own."

"Okay," he said. "You are right. Just don't forget to turn on your recording device okay?" After a laugh and a shake of my head, I inserted the lens into my eye and turned on the record function with a few blinks and voice commands. I grabbed the crystal from atop the altar, pulled the lever to close the skylight and unrolled the long thick black cloth from above the door to the floor.

When I picked u the crystal it weight much more than I expected. After regaining my grip on its smooth surface, I walked with my hand out in the dark to find my father. A bright flame lit up the room, allowing me to see him use the flame to light several incense sticks and put them into small holes on the obsidian wall, giving me just enough light to find my way back to his location to sit down. With the same match, he lit the pipe, took a few drags from it, and with a wave of his hand, the match was extinguished. My eyes adjusted to the darkness, the lit incense looked like orange stars giving off just enough light for me to see the pipe's bowl as my father handed it to me. I took several inhales of the smooth mint flavored smoke while he chanted aloud in a language I did not understand.

He stopped singing for a moment and took the pipe from my hand as if he could see me in the dark. He smoked it so profusely that his face and focused eyes became visible in the glow of the orange coals. Rivers and streams of smoke poured from the coals, spinning in little spirals just above the glow of the bowl. He passed the pipe back to me and began to chant, his volume rising with each new repetition of the words. As if by magic, when his volume grew, so did the smoke that poured from the pipe as we smoked. After several minutes of smoking this way I heard him stand up and move behind me. When I turned around, I saw above the altar, a small light began to form in the smoky darkness. Its hue was far different from any match flame. It was glowing faintly at first, then more and more intensely until, I saw that the glow was coming from my father's cupped uplifted palms outstretched over the altar's center; his eyes glowing with the same radiant intensity as the ball of light above his palms.

"You are witnessing the power of chi", he said confidently. "It has many names: energy, prana, chi or simply life force. It's all the same thing. Now, put the crystal ball into my palms and step back against the wall."

Astonished, I walked up and put the heavy crystal ball in his palms, stepping back cautiously. His breathing became panicked and shallow as the light was absorbed into the crystal ball. Inside the crystal, a glow began to intensify, eventually it exploded with colorful lightning into the smoke filled room.

The crystal ball lifted from my father's palms and spun around with such speed that it seemed to be sitting still. As it spun, bolts of electricity poured from its center creating a massive holographic sphere above the altar, lighting up the whole room. The lightning's sharp edges began to mingle with the smooth curvaceous swirls of the smoke. Together they both slowly turned into shapes and familiar forms of color inside of the sphere. I watched in total awe at this magnificent display of beauty and power unfolding before my disbelieving eyes. I thought such feats were only possible using lasers, crystals and other machines, yet the smoke and colorful electricity obeyed the vibration of my father's words perfectly, reverberating from inside the spinning crystal ball.

"Throughout my entire life, my dreams have been so vivid, otherworldly, and intense that I thought they were all meaningless abstractions created by my subconscious mind. In many of these dreams, I have telekinetic abilities or I can shape shift into all sorts of animals. In some, I'm so lucid that I accomplish incredible feats of cosmic proportions. However, one dream stood out to me more than the rest; it stood out so much because it was a deeply complex reoccurring dream and it's been a part of my life ever since I can remember."

I looked over at my father. Our eyes met and we smiled. He then sat down with his back against the wall next to me and we watched the hologram continue the story.

02) My Father's Story: The Reoccurring Dream

The dream starts with me observing myself standing shirtless and barefoot on a large red mountain peak in the deserts of Sedona, Arizona. I am bald, with a full black beard, huge muscles, and I'm covered from head to toe in symbols and patterns resembling tribal tattoos. Slightly perplexed, I look at myself standing atop the mountain. When I feel my spirit enter my body, the connection its physical form has to the natural world is overwhelming. The buzzing of bugs flowed in rhythm with the slight hiss of streams flowing in the valley below, and the wind howling around the peaks. After sitting down and crossing my legs, I close my eyes, and start to breathe deeply.

Shortly afterward, a warm sensation of weightlessness moves from the base of my spine, climbs out the top of my head, and eventually moves its way into each of my fingers and toes. The energies run through me, meeting at my heart. My heart beats faster as it warms with each breath, the heat inside my torso plateaus, and I become

distracted by yet another profound but different sensation.

My senses become amplified on a level I'd never dreamed possible. The tap of ants marching feet on the ground becomes audible, along with the crackle of the valley's growing vegetation, all complimented by the titanic drone of Earth spinning in the vastness of space. After feeling particles of moisture being moved around by slight pressure changes in the air, I crack a smile at this new found euphoria. I open my eyes and narrow my gaze to realize I'm capable of seeing for miles in the finest detail, with the ability to zoom in and out. I look down to zoom into the rock's pitted surface below my feet as if I had microscopes for eyes. Inside all sorts of alien looking life forms were crawling, mingling, and fumbling around its core. With my brows lifted, and jaw dropped I was speechless, realizing even rocks were alive in one way or another.

As soon as my vision zooms to normal, a rush of the blowing wind causes millions of dead skin cells to be torn from my body, every one of which I feel individually detach. Then I quite suddenly feel the tug and pull shared by all the planets in our solar system, followed by all the stars in our galaxy. All of this is experienced nearly concurrently and for a few fleeting moments it's all too much. However, the instant the sensations become overwhelmingly intense; the information input returns to a more manageable pace and the euphoria becomes enjoyable once again. Upon realizing my body is a tool for perceiving the entire cosmic ocean, all the way down to the finest quantum wave, I begin to wonder if I can fly.

"Just will it," an intuitive voice says softly.

I try to force the experience using my mind, but it doesn't work. Only when I allow it to come to me does it happens on its own. I feel intense waves of vibration all around my body coalesce into a tangible electric field repelling the Earth's pull. With my palms raised to the sky, my folded legs begin to lift from the warm red rock. I look up into the sun's intense gaze and peacefully float up and above the giant red mountains of Sedona. The cosmic energy pulsing through me is keenly felt over the surface of every cell in my body. However, during my levitation the intensity plateaus; giving me a sense of clarity that makes the use of these new abilities more moldable to my will.

Then an intuitive voice deep within my being speaks to me urgently saying. "They need your help! It is making its way toward the bay now!"

I have a vision of San Francisco in flooded ruins, accompanied by the sound of people screaming for help. A cold rush of terror runs down my spine; still floating in the air, I unfold my legs and turn my body to the west. I move forward through the air by repelling the earth below my torso, shooting energy behind me like a jet engine.

Almost instantly, I'm hovering a few hundred feet over a very dark and stormy San Francisco Bay. Cracks of thunder and flashes of lightning illuminate the surrounding area to show a massive creature rising from the watery depths near the Bay Bridge. An enormous bulbous head, followed by two huge green glowing eyes and endlessly

long smooth tentacles quickly emerge from the dark water causing massive waves to smash into the beach. While I stay still floating above the city in the rain, screams fill the air as countless limbs and torsos move lifelessly with the flooding inner city currents.

The screams are abruptly overpowered by a head-splitting roar that rocks the entire bay area, shattering the windows city wide, causing my ears to ring and bleed. What I had previously witnessed emerging from the water was just the creature's head. A few flashes of lightning, reveal the colossal beast walked with four hard crab-like legs and a massive crustaceous shell that sectioned like armor to cover its protruding body; which included four enormous arms ending in webbed three fingered hands and a monstrous mollusk like head.

Standing tall with its massive skull reaching near the top of the bridge, each slow movement it made caused the whole ground to shake catastrophically, sending wave after wave of water crashing into the mainland. Standing with countless fishing boats caught in its tentacles, the colossal Kraken gave a small toss of its head, releasing the shattered vessels to sink into the water.

Lightening brightened the landscape as I flew in the kraken's direction, I quickly arrived next to the creature's massive smooth head as it walked right through the Golden Gate Bridge completely unfazed, shoving it aside with its gargantuan arms as if it were small twigs. The metal made an ear-ripping screech as it sent the bridge's doomed occupants careening off the side of the mangled structure and into the water.

Then in that moment I hear a distinctly different roar come from above me. I look up, to see a pair of white talons and large white scaly wings. I feel sharp claws dig into both my shoulders. I scream out loud in agony as my mysterious attacker spins me around and throws me into the dark foamy waters of the bay.

I slowly sink unable to swim and eventually inhale the water. There is a burning deep in my lungs; the feeling of hopelessness is unlike anything describable in words. So I surrender to the pain, shut my eyes, and sink for what seems like an eternity. When I finally feel my feet touch what I assume is the bay floor, my eyes open to see I am standing in the dense forest near my grandparents' cabin; soaked in sweat but entirely woundless, with heavy camping gear on my back.

I turn around to look at their cabin from the hilltop I am hiking, and then turn my back and walk into the forest until nightfall. While wandering through the dark woods a pair of red glowing eyes emerge in the thick of the trees. Then everything goes dark, and I wake up.

Every time it is the exact same long and strange dream. And every time it brings feelings of excitement, terror, and wonder. I also noticed this dream often occurs before or after great milestones in my life. Then when I was twenty-five years old I had my heart broken by a woman I loved dearly. A few weeks after this break-up when I came to the end of my emotional rope I had the dream three nights in a row. It was after waking up from this dream on the third morning that everything in my life began to change more radically

than I ever anticipated.

03) Painful Reality

I awoke with a jolt, sat up quickly and rubbed my eyes. Monique immediately came to mind, and like dust in the wind, my dream faded with the memory of her beautiful brown eyes, the sharpness of her straight nose, the curl of her black hair, her hypnotizing smile, and the athletic build of her short body. I tried to go back to sleep but with her memory filling my mind that was no longer an option. I got up to get some water from the cooler in the corner of my small apartment dining room, then went to the bathroom to splash cold water on my face. While looking in the mirror, I began to question my romantic misfortune. How could my athletic build, fierce green eyes, rounded nose, plump lips, well-kept bald head and trimmed beard; not be enough for Monique? Then looking at my phone hoping to see she'd texted me, I realized that it was 8:45 am and I had to be to work by 9 am.

Putting on my clothes and shoes only took me a few short moments. As I walked out the door to my ground floor apartment, I felt glad I was once in the army and trained to be ready within two minutes. I drove to work mentally preparing myself for the day, not that my department store job was strenuous at all. However, this was two short weeks after Monique, and I broke up, and we both worked at the same place. Following the break up, our store got a new manager

named Keith who was a micro-managing tyrant, and very different from our previous manager. At that point, the idea of spending eight hours of my life in that building with either of those two people became exponentially unpleasant.

When I arrived at work, it was 9am exactly. After walking up to one of the cash registers located near the customer service desk to clock in, I made my way to the back of the store to grab my work vest. I walked into the employee lounge to get my vest out of its locker, when the smell Monique's vanilla perfume filled my nostrils. I could tell she had been there a few minutes prior and I was glad in that moment that I had been running a little behind.

The sound of loud dress shoes filled the hallway then the employee lounge and I knew Keith walked into the lounge behind me. His head was shaved bald and the thick glasses he wore made his small blue eyes appear to be enormous. He had a nose like a light bulb, below which sat a thick mustache bordered by cleanly shaven cheeks. He had thin lips complimented by crooked yellow teeth and a weak chin that blended into his neck. His body was the shape of a bowling pin and as if all of this wasn't enough, he had a confrontational attitude. He was very out of place as the manager of a department store because he was, in fact, a failed realtor. Rumor had it, the only reason he got the job was his sister held a high position in the company. Everyone in the store would've felt more compassion for him if he wasn't such a prick. There was an agreement amongst the employees that he might've brought his circumstances on himself based on the way he treated people.

Trying to be pleasant when I turned around, I said "Morning Keith."

Keith looked at his watch "From the looks of my watch, you are five minutes late there Will. What is up with that?"

"Oh, I am sorry." I replied casually, "It won't happen again Keith, I will get to the sales floor now." I walked past him and was about to get to the sales floor when I heard him call for me.

"Hey, Will, hold on a second. I got something for you to do." Keith walked quickly ahead of me saying "Follow me." in an authoritative manner.

We walked to the public restrooms and entered the men's room. Right away it smelled awful, the floor was covered in stains, all of the urinals were filthy, and there were pieces of toilet paper all over the floor some of which were soaked in nasty toilet water.

"Our janitor called in sick today, and this restroom needs to be cleaned." He said in a quick demanding tone, "There's a clog in the last stall's toilet and a plunger inside of it for you. When you get done here, report back to me."

"Keith, cleaning restrooms isn't..." He promptly walked out and didn't leave me any room for debate.

Even though I was furious, and had a real disgust for the nature of the labor, I did as I was told. I cleaned the bathroom spotlessly and even unclogged the nasty shit-filled toilet. When I was done, I washed my hands and went looking for Keith hoping I wouldn't find him.

While walking through the store, I looked around to avoid seeing Monique. I tried to stay on alert, but all of my paranoia came to fruition, as I was turning a corner I bumped right into her. Our eyes locked for a moment, causing several flares of dull, unpleasant warmth to pass up through my torso and exude out of my chest. Ignoring me completely she walked by without even a single facial gesture; which was quite the hurtful blow and the exact thing I was trying to avoid.

This turn of events was very upsetting for me because I had gone to Keith before he made the new schedule and attempted to level with him, man to man about Monique's and my break up. Hoping this would encourage him to separate our schedules. While in that moment of heartache, I remembered I was supposed to leave at 3 pm that day for an appointment to speak with my mom's therapist about my post-break up depression. So, I decided to go back to the lounge and check my schedule before resuming my search for Keith; I just hoped he wasn't in the lounge when I arrived.

When I got to the employee lounge, I tried to be sneaky and peak into the break room from the hallway to see if anyone was in it. Unfortunately, Keith was leaning against the wall next to the door texting on his phone and was positioned out of my view. So, I walked into the room uninhibited, marching straight up to the schedule. First, I noticed that I was working until 5 pm that day. Next, I looked at the rest of my shifts throughout the week to compare them with Monique's schedule, and saw I shared more shifts with her than not.

I was staring at the schedule confused and angry for about a minute when Keith directed his attention away from the screen of his phone to notice me standing there.

"Will! I am not paying you to stand there like a freaking Greek statue! That restroom had better be clean."

I turned around, and I looked him right in the eye. The moment I realized that my life had been boiled down to being ordered around by a walking parasite like Keith, the accumulation of my heartache, anger, and disappointment came to a head. For a brief moment I imagined what would happen if instead of responding to him, I calmly approached to give him a powerful push kick to his fat frail chest. Seeing him in shock and fright would almost be worth the time in jail and losing my job, but instead, I just looked at him, so mad I was unable to speak.

He waited a few seconds then said "Sorry I couldn't schedule you and your ex-girlfriend apart. If you want to date employees, I don't care, but the moment it starts to effect work it's my problem." Seeing that he was enticing me, I tried to stay calm.

Being a veteran I had experience with egomaniacal authority figures, so I retorted in a respectful tone "Ya know Keith, I am not so much mad about sharing a shift or two with Monique because I figured that might happen. What I am a little upset about is that I am scheduled until five today even though I told you I had to leave early because I had a therapist appointment. However, more than anything, what bothers me the most is that it doesn't even seem like

you tried to help or be understanding of my situation at all."

"Well you can't always get what you want in life," he countered in a callused tone. "Sometimes life is hard. Sometimes life craps all over you, and you gotta get over it and get back to work. Now get over to the lawn and garden department, they need you there!"

I knew the best strategy was just to allow him to feel powerful while everyone laughed behind his back. So I simply said in a half serious, sarcastic way "Okay Keith, you got it boss!", then I turned around and walked out of the employee lounge.

I wanted to hit him more than I'd ever wanted to hit anybody in my life, but I knew it was because of the built up emotions that had accumulated to an overwhelming magnitude. So I went to work in the indoor lawn and garden department filled with rage and hating myself for not going off on Keith like I wanted to, like he deserved. I felt so trapped by my circumstances that my attention was not on work at all. While I was stocking garden hoses, I kept losing focus and staring off into space for a minute or two at a time. My heart just wasn't in my work; I honestly felt that my time could be spent so much more constructively. I believed I was meant for more than stocking items and being bossed around by a fat pompous loser. All of this on top of being treated like garbage by the woman I loved.

Amidst my imaginative wandering, an older woman dressed in dirty gardening clothes approached me and asked, "Excuse me sir, where are the gardening tools in this store?"

"Right this way ma'am," I said as I walked with her to an aisle some

distance away. When we arrived at the tools shelf, Keith was in the same aisle helping a man dressed in construction clothes. He looked over at me and said "Will, get over here." as he pointed a few feet in front of him. I apologized to the woman I was helping and walked over, trying to remain calm.

Keith spoke abruptly, "Hurry up and go get a garden hose. This guy needs one." The customer looked at me with compassion and then at Keith with disdain.

I looked to the customer and said: "One-second sir I will be right back with that for you." I ran and got the hose, then brought it back as fast as I could.

Keith ripped the hose out of my hand and said, "Took you long enough," then pointing to some bird houses on the floor near a shelf, he ordered in a sharp, unpleasant tone "Now stock that stuff there ASAP, and when you're done report to me for further instructions."

Once again the man in construction attire and I made eye contact. I could tell Keith was making him uncomfortable and I wanted to tell him so; but for the sake of the customer I didn't say a word and just began stocking the bird houses onto the shelf while they both walked away.

After I had finished stacking the bird houses, a short man dressed as a landscaper asked me where the plant food was, so I took him over to the proper location. Soon after that, I was distracted by a woman in a green dress asking about lawn chairs. After that, a flood of people rushed into the department. Eventually, I helped so many

customers; I had forgotten entirely to tell Keith after I was done with the bird houses. Then I heard Keith's voice interrupt the music playing on the intercom system of the store.

"Will, come to the management office. Will, to the management office." then the intercom shut down, and the music continued playing. *Great*, I thought, this should be interesting. As I walked to the back of the store, a heavy-set man with a beard asked me where he could find a particular kind of water faucet. I was quickly pointing out the faucet's location when I heard Keith get on the intercom again "Will, to the Management office. Will to the management office now please" I looked up to the intercom and shook my head, apologizing to the bearded man, I said, "I'm sorry sir, but I have to leave because that call is for me."

While walking back to Keith's office, I tried to think of what he wanted, and I prepared myself for whatever was to come. When I arrived at his cramped and cluttered office, I saw him sitting in a black leather rolling chair with his fingers interlaced in his lap. "I have been watching you on the cameras. Your work ethic is for crap! Please, tell me why you think I should keep a lazy person on staff?"

"What are you talking about Keith? I'm not lazy" I refuted trying to remain calm. "I was just helping cust..."

He interrupted me in a degrading manner "Oh yes you are! You are extremely lazy! I watch every one of my employees back here on these cameras. You're our worst employee, by far!"

I knew what he said wasn't true; there were far worse and lazy

employees than I in that store. Granted, since my heart break my work level had slowed down, and Keith had only seen that side of me. So, trying to be as understanding as I could, I said "I understand why you feel that way, but you are only half right. Recently my work level has been less than normal and I will admit to that. For that I apologize; I am having a rough time with this heartbreak, and I am just trying to..."

He interrupted me again saying, "And that's another thing. You are causing problems amongst employees. You bring a bunch of drama with you and make people feel uncomfortable. So, you know what? I have made up my mind, you're fired! Give me your vest and get out, you will have your last check mailed to you. I don't want to see you in my store again unless you are here as a customer."

I was shocked, he did not care one bit if losing my job was the final straw for me, and I just couldn't hold back anymore. If I was fired, I was going to at least give him a piece of my mind before I left. Something inside of me snapped, but I surprised even myself with what I said.

"Ok Keith, that's fine,'" I replied nodding my head, "but I would like to tell you something that I am sure is on everyone's mind, just no one has said anything yet." He looked at me somewhat curiously, so I continued. "Your attitude and the way you treat people makes everyone sick. The sad truth that I now see is that it is far worse than everyone expected, your desperate need to be something more than a dumpy pathetic excuse for a human bowling pin has turned you into

a dumb, ugly power-hungry loser of epic proportions. I hope for your sake that you look in the mirror tonight and decide to lose some fuckin weight and get rid of the massive stack of potato chips on both of your fat fuckin shoulders. Otherwise, you are going to die alone, miserable, and having accomplished nothing with your life you pathetic grease ball piece of shit!" Then I turned and walked out while giving him the finger, leaving him no room to speak. He yelled at me to come back, but I ignored him and kept my finger in the air.

When I got to my car, I sat inside with the A/C on feeling stunned. My girlfriend of a year left me a few weeks prior, then I get fired from a job I had for two years, and it was for no good reason at all. I felt the past two years of my life had gone by completely wasted. I was exactly where I was when I got out of the army, alone, unemployed, and confused as to my place in the world.

So, I sent my best friend Isaac a text, venting my feelings. Isaac was a short stalky man of Irish decent. He had curly red hair, large bright blue eyes, a small nose, thin lips and a strong chin, all complimented by the countless freckles that covered his body. His sense of humor was very odd and sometimes off-putting. For example, he often claimed that his curly red hair and endless freckles were because he was a descendent of Gangues Khan. His light-heartedness was always a relief, so I explained the whole situation to him in a text, then made my way home.

After arriving home, I saw a text was from Isaac; he suggested that we both go up to the forest to camp and get away from things for a

while. I liked his idea because we were both the outdoorsy type of guys and had been on several camping trips together throughout the years, but at the time I just wanted to be alone more than anything.

I only vented to him because I had no-one else to vent to, typically I would have vented to Monique, but that was no longer an option. So I told him I would think about it. By this time it was already 2:30 pm and I didn't want to make my mom look bad with her psychiatrist friend who offered to see me pro bono, so I drove to the appointment.

03) Shrunken Head

The moment I opened the door to the psychiatrist's office, a wave of nervousness and shame overcame me. The smell inside was of new carpet and fresh plastic toys. The lobby was lined with black metal chairs along the surrounding white walls, there was a kids section in the corner that was littered with plastic dinosaurs and Barbie dolls. I approached the counter to see the secretary was a pretty brunette woman with brown eyes, a big nose, and a friendly smile. She handed me a clipboard, and I filled out my information while sitting in the lobby's uncomfortable metal chairs.

I was the only one in the lobby until a heavy set woman wearing jeans and a black top walked in. She quickly removed her sunglasses and put them in a black leather purse hanging on her arm. She looked at me for a moment before speaking to the secretary. Afterward she sat down in a chair across from mine, we made eye contact and I got this funny feeling that we both wondered why each other was there, while also feeling slightly embarrassed at being there ourselves. It was an awkward moment, and I avoided eye contact with her again to prevent such a feeling from reoccurring. I turned in the clipboard to the secretary and upon returning to my seat a tall tan man dressed in a light blue shirt, black pants, and a long pink tie opened the door from the hallway into the lobby. He looked at me with his dark brown eyes, stroked his short black hair and then he called my name.

“Will?” I stood up, walked over and shook the man's hand as I approached the doorway, "Hi Will, nice to meet you, I'm Tony." He said with a smile and a firm squeeze to my hand.

We walked back to his office; it was diffusely lit with a small fountain in the corner permeating the room with the soothing sound of running water. He had a nice large cherry-wood desk and a leather office chair with matching wooden arms. I sat down in a black rocking chair across from the desk.

He sat abruptly and spoke as he rolled up to his desk. "So your mom tells me you’re having some trouble with depression due to a breakup?"

"Yeah, but to be honest, it is more than that," I replied.

"Okay, well I helped your mom a lot following your step-dad's suicide, which I give my condolences to you as well, by the way." He said bowing his head slightly.

"Thank you." I said quickly "He wasn't the greatest dad. Actually, he was kind of an asshole, pardon my language, but he was still my dad, and for that I loved him. His suicide was just the beginning of the snowball though."

"I don't care if you cuss," he smirked, "And how was it the beginning?" he asked inquisitively.

"Well it was at the time of his suicide that Monique and I first started having problems. After he died things got worse between us and it wasn't because I was depressed about my dad's death either. She just became a total bore and a never-ending buzz kill. Nothing was good enough for her, ever, and then eventually she just didn't even want to see me. So now I experience a general unhappiness with my life. I have nothing to look forward to at all. I feel stuck. I feel like it's all hopeless. Life seems so dull and boring. There is no zest, no adventure, just the same routine, work, eat, and sleep. I have no source of intrigue or passion in my life and its killing me in every way!"

"Hmmm, okay. What do you think is making life dull and boring for you?" he asked folding his hands on top of his desk.

"Well after I got out of the army I went to school for a while, but with school, work, and paying my bills I had no life. I felt like I was spending all my time in ways that were wasteful of my potential. I hardly ever got to do what I wanted to do, and when I did get to do what I wanted to do, it didn't last very long at all. Then, it was right back to the same old exhausting grind, only with my patience and sanity just a little less resilient than they were before."

"So why don't you take a break from school?" he suggested promptly with a turn of his head.

"I did, and that was a year ago when I met Monique at work," I said rolling my eyes.

"Oh no, it's a working relationship." He sighed. "I've been there myself. Okay. I am guessing you started spending more time with her instead of going to school?"

"Yeah, I did. So what? Is that bad?" I replied in a defensive tone.

"I am just asking," he said as he wrote something down on a notepad. I looked at the pad, then away to gather my thoughts. "Go ahead, please continue, I didn't mean to interrupt." he set down his pen and folding his hands in his lap, ready to listen.

"Well, we were together for a little over a year and then she started growing distant out of no-where. Then she just dropped me and wouldn't tell me why. I tried pressing her for a reason, but she refused to give an answer. So instead of beating my head against a wall, I took her break up as final and walked away with a broken heart."

"She didn't give any indications at all?" he asked slightly confused, "Was there something dramatic that happened to cause her to want to leave? What about your step-dad's suicide?"

"No, I wasn't as badly affected by his death as my mom has been. That's what's so weird. Monique just changed out of nowhere." I responded.

"That is actually more widespread than you may think, I wouldn't take it so personally." he replied with a reassuring tone.

"I thought that might be the case," I said "But still, I can't help but feel inadequate somehow, or invalidated or something. I am the type of person who prefers everything to be neatly arranged and perfectly in order, so to have my whole life turned upside down and all jumbled up in such a short time, is something I just wasn't ready for at all."

"What exactly do you mean? Lots of people go through break ups, did something else happen recently?"

"Oh yeah, I didn't tell you yet, I got fired from my job this morning and for no good reason at all!" I snapped.

"I am sorry to hear that Will. I am sure there was a reason. Would you like to talk about it?"

"Not really, doing that will just piss me off and I want to try to stay level headed and calm during this whole thing."

"That's always a good strategy, just don't run from what you can't change soldier." He said being sure to make brief eye contact.

"I know, you are right, but it's pretty difficult to accept what I can't change and focus my efforts on what I can. Mainly because I don't want to do anything other than feel sorry for myself right now. I mean, everything happened so fast. Life came at me so quickly, and I wasn't prepared at all for the changes that came my way. One minute everything is fine and all is going well, then the next minute I don't have a way to earn a dime, and I'm going through the nine gates of hell."

He giggled, "I like that. You're a funny guy. That's life for ya, but life does have miracles sometimes too Will."

"Yeah," I said in a sarcastic tone "I am a realist Tony, and miracles are bullshit as far as most realists are concerned. However, in all

honesty, I personally would like to believe that the occasional miracle is a part of normality and reality. It would be unrealistic to suggest that unusual things don't ever happen, or events with insurmountable odds of occurring don't ever occur." I paused and collected my thoughts then looked at him in the eye, "I want to believe that Monique wants me back, I want to believe that if I go into work and apologize to my manager, I could get my job back. But I know that isn't the case, in either situation, so I am trying to see this whole cluster of shitty events as a huge victory, temporarily appearing as a massive defeat. I want to believe that this seemingly endless time of chaos and confusion in my life is actually steering me toward something infinitely better, as opposed to sending me toward loneliness and misery. Honestly, maybe that's why I am so depressed right now Tony, because it's happening all at once. I don't know what to do with my life. I feel lost, stuck and forced to move forward all at the same time."

"Well, first let me assure you that you are not the only one in that boat. Next let me just say that maybe by getting away from the environment that has helped create your problems, you might find it easier to heal and grow past the problems themselves. IN that light, maybe losing your job wasn't a bad thing after-all. Besides, if you don't feel like doing anything, staying stagnant is the worst thing you can do. That decision starts you on a cycle of lethargic depression where nothing is accomplished, all for the sake of self-pity and not actual physical inability. If you fall into that mental pattern long

enough, you will stay stuck and eventually the depression will lead to real physical disabilities. Either be humbled or be crumbled Will."

"Hmm...I like that saying." I replied, "I like that a lot."

"Thanks, I read it on a bumper sticker once." He replied, and we both shared a brief laugh.

"My friend Isaac suggested the idea of going camping together in the woods, but I really just want to be alone right now. It's weird; I know having the help and support of others is important, but more than anything I just want to get away from everyone and everything for at least a few months."

"Well I don't know how much I would condone camping alone in the forest for a few months," he replied with a slight turn of his head, "but if you believe that it will help you to heal then maybe think about giving it a shot. Hell, most of the time we psychiatrists simply lead people to their own answers. If we give people the answers and they do what we say, and their situation doesn't go the way they'd hoped, they can blame us for the outcome of their choices. We psychiatrists are simply supposed to lead you to your own answers through questions. Everyone has the ability to help themselves; they just don't have enough faith to try or learn how. So, that's why I went to school for eight years, so I could learn how to ask people questions they already know the answers to," He laughed and shook his head. "Your story is heartbreaking Will, and I don't mean to

laugh, but some of the people I help are so dramatic and childish I feel like a kindergarten teacher sometimes. It's just silly how people don't know how to talk to themselves, so I have to help them do that."

"So that's why you didn't mind seeing me pro bono huh?" I replied in a lighthearted manner.

He laughed, "No, no, it is not like that. This is my lunch break, and your mother is a good friend of mine, so I figured I could take some time for her soldier son, who is in need of a service. By the way, thank you for your service."

He reached out and shook my hand. "Not a problem." I responded, "So you think it would be a good idea to go up to the forest?"

"Well that all depends on your reasons for going Will." he said in a matter of fact tone. "Why are you going up there? What do you hope to accomplish? Always see your situations and motives through to their conclusion. Follow all of your actions to their end; will they create the affect you desire? What affects do you desire this trip to have?"

"Well the reason I am going to the forest I have in mind, I guess, is because ever since I can remember, I had this dream," I then briefly explained the dream to him. "Going to camp alone in that part of the forest is something I've always wanted to do, especially when

spending my adolescent summers at my grandparent's cabin. When playing outside in the open forest out back, I could hear the woods subtly whispering requests for my presence. I always felt a missing piece of my soul was waiting for me amongst those trees. I had always wanted to go searching for it as a small child, but never had the courage, or reason, until now that is."

"A little personal secret of mine," He looked around and leaned forward "In all of my years of psychiatry so far, I've only found two cures for heartache Will. One: Is an intense focus on Self Improvement. Two: Accomplishing childhood dreams, goals or wishes." He leaned back and spoke louder, "Even then, the heartbroken person has to want to get over the pain in order to use these two tools to heal more quickly. These methods are not quick fixes by any means. You have to work on one or both of these things daily following the heartbreaking event. You must also be determined not to attempt to fill the void left by your heartbreaker, with a temporary replacement; whether that is a pill, an alcohol bottle or another person. You wouldn't believe the amount of people that would rather take a pill than have to change their lifestyle or deal with the emotions they are feeling. What they don't understand is, it is only when they feel the pain and move past it, that they will actually be able to heal fully. Anyway, that was a very roundabout way of saying that I admire your courage and I only suggest that you follow your heart and do what you think is best, simple as that solider."

"I appreciate that Tony, I really do," I said as I started standing up. "However, with that little bit of pro bono perspective, I am going to allow you to finish your lunch in peace. Thank you very much for your time." He seemed shocked as he stood up to shake my hand.

He responded with a little concern in his voice, "You don't have to go just yet, you can stay if you'd like. Its really not that much trouble, it's only been like five minutes."

"I appreciate it, I really do, but you helped me to realize that I am the only person who can help me, and for that, I say thanks Tony. You have guided me more than it may seem on the surface, our conversation actually had a hell of an impact on me, and I am gonna make some changes. I think I am gonna to go to the forest alone, to grow past this pain and get all this shit off my mind. Something is telling me that when I get back, I'll know what I want to do with my life. I hope you have fun leading people to answers they already know, with questions they should be asking themselves in the first place."

He threw his head back and laughed out loud. "You are cracking me up! I think you will do just fine up there young man; your army training should keep you safe and you already seem to have the right kind of spirit to beat this thing."

I made my way for the door and said "Thanks Doc, you take care of yourself and I will be sure to thank my mom."

He replied with a smile and a waving gesture of his hand. "Sounds good, take care of yourself and come back to chat anytime if you need to."

I walked out of the office door and through the lobby; which was filled with people who had the same look as the woman I had seen before. Only now my eyes gleamed back into theirs, a look of hope and understanding. For, I actually had a clear idea of what to do to get over the heartache I was enduring.

05) Like A Bewildered Bat Out Of a Helpful Hell

After getting home, I decided to sleep on my decision to go up to the woods of northern Arizona. Upon waking the next morning my feeling had not changed, so I gathered my camping supplies and brought them out to my car. I was standing in the parking lot of my apartment complex while packing supplies into the trunk of my white 92 Buick Regal when I saw Isaac abruptly pop his short stalky Irish frame up from beside my trunk in an attempt to scare me. He realized his failure when I looked at him with one raised eyebrow.

He ceased his smile and looked down suspiciously at how little I was packing. Commenting from behind his smiling thin lips and crooked teeth, "Uh…I am just saying this because I am your friend, but you

don’t look like you’re packing enough supplies. And you of all people know it is better to go camping over prepared than under prepared. Even if that means you can’t stack it all as nicely and neatly into your trunk."

Over the years of our friendship Isaac had observed my need for having things clean, neat, and organized. He would always tease me, suggesting that I had something like obsessive compulsive disorder, but I never took his accusations seriously. I was just a neat, clean guy and have been since I was a kid.

"I know I should be packing more,” I replied in a reassuring voice, “but I have my camel pack, and my grandparents live up there, if I need to, I can always stay there with them. They have plenty of food and water and other stuff for me if I need it."

Isaac handed me a large stainless steel can of bear spray out of his jeans back pocket. "Here, take this just in case your grandparents become possessed by demons. If they start climbing all over the ceilings and foaming at the mouth, this should help you subdue them." I laughed at his ridiculous premise and grabbed the intense pepper spray designed for bears, from his rough, construction worker hands. "You need anything else?" he asked.

“No, I think a can of bear spray should be the final touch.” I replied, “I am sorry I don’t want you to come along on this one Isaac. I just don’t wanna be around anyone right now. That bitch really twisted

my heart into a fuckin knot bro; I just gotta get outta this place for a while!"

"I understand," Isaac said, "But considering you just lost your job, shouldn't you probably be staying down here and looking for work instead of going camping?"

"Yeah? Thanks Mom!" We both laughed a little. "I know you're probably right, but I have plenty of reminders here, reminders of things I just want to forget right now. I'll find a job when I get back in a few days, my rent is paid for the month, so I'm not gonna worry about it for now. Besides I went and saw my mom's shrink today, he said that if going up to the woods is a childhood dream of mine, then I should do it. He said accomplishing childhood dreams is a way of getting over heartache. So I figured I would camp in the thick forest just outside of Munds Park where my grandparents live."

"What? That makes no fuckin sense bro." he said "How is camping in the forest a childhood dream? We do that all the time."

"Well, you remember when we were kids and I told you about that dream I kept having? Well, I have had it three nights in a row now Isaac and you know I have always been drawn to those woods because of that dream. So I figure, it's the universe or something trying to give me a sign to go up there alone to see what the forest has in store for me."

He replied with a skeptical tone, "What, you think just because you go alone you are gonna see some red eyes this time? That makes no fuckin sense bro; it just sounds like a dream to me Will. That's all." Then he changed his tone to a more cheerful manner, "But if you think you will figure out what it means while you are alone in the middle of nowhere, I sure hope you find what you are looking for while you're out there. Are you sure you don't want me to come along? I could see if my wife and mom would watch the baby for a few days while I go with?"

"I appreciate that bro, but please, really, I need this one to be solo. Okay?"

"Okay." he said in a calm defiant tone from behind his crooked smile "Just don't be surprised if I pay you a little visit up there. I will personally ensure you are fucked with and hassled until the latest hours of the night. You will get shit for sleep, and you will wonder what those crazy noises are in the bushes or who collected more firewood for you while you were gone. How does all that sound? I am sure you remember that night when you and your brothers woke me up and had me thinking I was being abducted by aliens. Revenge is a dish best served cold motha fucka." I looked at him with a raised brow, trying not to smile as I remembered the look on his face that hilarious night, "Is that a 'yes please come with me Isaac' I see on your face?", he asked smiling from ear to ear.

Over the years, Isaac liked joking about not giving me alone time when I asked for it; often he'd act as if he planned to continue giving me unwanted bad advice. It was a familiar ruse, I'd gotten used to from childhood, only this time I wasn't sure if he was serious or not. So to ensure my solitude, I replied sternly, "Look, I am confident you're joking, but please, just leave me be while I'm camping. Get me back any other time, just not now. Okay? Otherwise, I might just spray you with your own bear spray."

Isaac laughed out loud and said "I am just playing with you Will" smiling menacingly, he followed his reassurance with "Or am I? Tune in tomorrow to find out on the next exciting episode of, Will Goes Camping!" I was trying not to look amused by his jokes as I was still feeling a little down, so he changed the subject. "So, have you checked your fluids and tire pressure after I cut your hoses and slashed your tires?"

I shook my head and finally smiled, in a reassuring tone I replied, "I took care of all that already, thank you for asking. I will text you when I arrive up there, but before I go I gotta drop off some money to my mom." I shut my trunk and began to work my way toward the driver door.

"What? Money for your mom? Between this trip, getting fired and giving your mom money, you got enough to get by this month?" he asked in confusion.

I shrugged my shoulders and said "I don't know, all I know is I would sooner have less money in my pocket and less stress in my mom's life than more in both categories. Plus, I didn't spend too much on camping supplies."

"Ok," Isaac replied, "Life has just been taking a fat steamy dump in your cereal recently so seeing you like this is new territory for me and I wanna make sure you are doing okay. If you need help with money I got you, and I will ask my boss at the construction site if we need any extra help, maybe I could get you a job working with me."

I smiled and said "Yeah? That would be great bro! Just let me know when I get back in a few days if it worked out." I quickly got into my car and waved goodbye with my middle finger out the window as I sped off smiling; a display of the middle finger was our humorous way of bidding each other goodbye. I looked in the rearview mirror to see he was raising his birdie finger in the air as well as I drove out of the complex.

After arriving at my mother's house, I walked through the front door and into the kitchen shouting for her. She replied from behind her closed bedroom door at the end of the hallway, saying she would be out in a minute. I leaned against the sink; then I heard it drip. My mom's kitchen faucet reliably dripped every few minutes ever since my childhood. Thinking to myself that I should fix its slow trickle, I looked at the clock on the wall by the fridge to my left. It was 11 am, and I wouldn't have time to fix it.

I was feeling guilty for not being of more assistance to my mother when she came out of her room with a beer in hand. Since my step-dad's suicide the previous year she had been drinking early in the day and I could tell by her behavior that she was already inebriated. Her increased alcoholism was a shame for many reasons, the deterioration of her once quick wit and good looks being two of them.

Her face looked far younger than her age. She had smooth skin, brown eyes, a nose just like mine, small pursed lips, and a sharp, strong chin which was usually accented by very long straight black hair. Her face didn't have many wrinkles at all, but she had a beer belly from drinking every day. I felt disappointed to see her intoxicated so early in the morning but I patiently told her what my plans were and where I was going to be for the next few days.

She responded with tears in her eyes saying, "I'm sorry you're going through heartache, hun. No mother wants to see her child in pain. I want you to stay in the city with me but I understand why you want to leave, and if Tony says it's a good idea then I would do it."

"I know mom, it just seems like a never ending tribulation while I am in the city, so I have to get out for a while." I replied quickly.

"Though it may seem like an unending pain," she replied, "heartache finds and leaves us all at some point in our lives."

I knew she was right but I usually ignored her words of advice when she was drinking. I wanted to tell her that I lost my job, but I chose not to for I knew it would just stress her out and she wouldn't accept the money I was going to give her, which she oddly needed more than I did at the time.

I nodded my head in agreement while pulling out some cash from my pocket and putting it in here hand. I closed her fingers around it saying "Here, I know you could use the extra hundred bucks."

She looked at the money in her hand, hugged me tight, then held me away from her to look at me in the eye as she said, "Thank you so much Will, you have no idea how much this is going to help me!" She hugged me again even tighter "I knew the Lord would hear my prayer. I need to pay my electricity bill and I don't have very many clients at the salon anymore."

After a few seconds I broke the hug, but she brought me closer and held me there for what felt like a minute. She always hugged my two younger brothers and I for an extended period before we traveled anywhere. I thought she would never let go the morning I left for the Army at 18 years old. She said it was her way of making sure we knew that she loved us. And I had tried to appreciate hugging my mother after my step-dad's suicide. His death ironically helped me to enjoy everyone that was alive in a different way.

My mom broke our hug, looked at me and said "You are a very special human being Will. I knew it the moment I was pregnant." She always said those particular words to me whenever I was feeling down in life.

I thanked her with a brief smile and said "Thanks, Mom." Hoping that would be the end of it.

"I knew it then." she continued, "Just like I know it now. You are meant to do great things! Great things in your life! God told me so you know..." I nodded my head, smiled and laughed to myself as I walked out of the kitchen and toward the door leading into the garage. "God did tell me Will..." She said in a high pitched affirmative tone.

"I know mom, I know. I believe you." She seemed tense as I made my way toward the exit. Doing my best to console her before opening the door to leave, I said "I love you mom, I will see you in a couple of days or maybe a week or two, I don’t know. If Ed or Jeremy calls, tell them that their big brother loves them. I have plenty of water and food; I am bringing my cell phone, and grandma and grandpa live up there if the weather gets bad. I just really need to get out of town to get my mind off of Monique and on to myself."

She visibly relaxed and replied with strength, "You will bounce back no problem, like always Will! You have a strong heart. You will come

back a more powerful and vigorous spirit; I can see it in my mind's eye!"

My mother was like a melting pot for the world's religions into one person, but I don't think she fully understood each of them to their depths. She had a few medicine men in her bloodline, so she was always very open to the idea of paranormal experiences. However, her spiritual malarkey always seemed like circular logic to me. She would say things like; "God is because God is" and that just never made sense to me, even as a child. However, that didn't keep her from sharing her thoughts after she had a few beers.

I merely replied, "I see it too Mom, I see it too." Intentionally leaving no window for further comment on the previous subject I said, "Oh, I had that dream again. Three nights in a row now."

"The one you have had since you were a baby?" she asked. I nodded affirmatively, her eyes lit up for a moment. I suddenly realized a reoccurring dream was in a spiritual vein of mysticism, so I braced myself for another one of my mother's bizarre drunken spirit based raves.

Only she surprised me by simply saying "That dream means something Will. Dreams are the window to the subconscious and in some cases the past and future. There's a reason you keep having that dream, listen to your heart to find out what it means." She smiled, and I was taken by surprise at the brevity to her words. To

finalize the interaction, I smiled then nodded and walked through the front door. I was closing it to leave when she yelled from inside the kitchen.

"Will? Wait! Just one more thing before you go, wait just one second. I need to give you something!"

I rolled my eyes, stepped back inside the house, and shut the door. I watched as she ran like a giddy school girl down the hallway, into her room and hurry back up to me within a few seconds. Stopping abruptly in front of me with her hands behind her back, swaying in a childish fashion, she smiled and said, "Close your eyes and put your hands out." I sighed and smiled as I put my hands out and closed my eyes. In my hands, I felt the weight an oval shaped piece of glass or smooth stone.

I looked down to see she had placed a polished black crystal the size of a tangerine inside my palm. She commenced closing my fingers around it with her hand as she said "Take this and keep it on you at all times when you are in the forest. It will keep you safe; it is supposed to bring good fortune. It appears black on the surface, but when you hold it up to the light, it's clear." I held the smooth stone up into the kitchen light and saw the light bulb in detail, only through a transparent gray color on the other side of the crystal. "That's how life can sometimes be sometimes," she continued, "Life can appear dark and gloomy, but you just have to shine the light inside to see through the illusion of impenetrable darkness. That

stone has been in our family for generations and brought good fortune and safety to most every man who has had it. It hasn't really worked for me maybe that's because I didn't know how to use it, or because it usually is passed on to the first born, and I am not the first born, I don't know. What I do know is it will do more good in your hands now, than it will sitting inside of a box in my closet. Please take care of it, and try not to lose it. Okay?"

"I wouldn't have it any other way mom! So Grandpa gave this to you?" I asked with curiosity as I explored its smooth polished surface with my fingers.

"Yes, my father had it before me, and his father had it before him, and his father before him, it is given to all of the first born children in my father's family. When my oldest brother died leaving no descendants, my father gave it to me because I was second in line and you are the first born grandchild. He told me that it belonged to several generations of the Medicine men in our bloodline and now something is telling me that I need to give it to you."

I looked at the stone's transparency again in the bright light of the kitchen. Feeling confused, excited, skeptical, and mystified all at once I responded by saying "This is totally awesome Mom! Thank you so much, but why did it take you this long to tell me all of this? Why give this to me now?"

She sighed and looked down, "I was going to wait until you got married." Then she looked me in the eye as if she sobered up and said "I just had this overwhelming feeling, that it would help you now in some way more than it would at any other time in the future. It's weird how strong the feeling is, I mean, as you know, I have always had funny feelings about some stuff, but this one is overbearing. I just had to give in to the urge. These feelings are God pushing our hearts with His will, pushing us to go down a particular path for reasons that may remain invisible to our limited perspective for years. Only later on down the river of time, can we look back to see where the river bent and why."

When she smiled at me, I saw the motherly love in her eyes. At that moment, I somehow understood the real impact of my mother's love and the value she had in my life as a whole. It was then I realized with greater clarity that despite her alcoholism and her occasional childish behavior, she was always an excellent example of how to be a good human being and she was truly a blessing to my life in unparalleled ways. With a genuine grin of surprise, I put the tangerine size crystal like stone in my pocket, gave my mom one last hug, walked out the door as she followed behind, and got into my car. Then waving goodbye to her from my car window with my whole hand instead of a single middle finger, I finally got on the road to go up to the forest.

06) Omen in the Sky

While driving north on the interstate, I'd occasionally steal a look at the surrounding majestic brown mountain ranges covered in green foliage. Their physical presence helped me feel a profound sense that Munds Park was the perfect place to get rid of all my old stagnant feelings and absorb some new ones. I used to spend many adolescent summers at my grandparents cabin and I felt comfortable in that wilderness in particular.

My mother's parents were very sweet, loving people and I always felt comfortable when staying with them. They had a peaceful little north and south facing pinewood cabin equipped with two bedrooms and two bathrooms. Not long after they purchased it, they built another cabin which attached to theirs on the east side. They did this so our whole family could come up and stay with them whenever we wanted.

I began thinking about staying there with them instead of camping when I felt a profound desire to get in tune with nature; and in the process, hopefully find some clue to the mystery of my dream. Then I saw a car that looked a lot like Monique's driving south on the highway and her morose memory once more massacred my happy heart. I only discovered after the breakup that falling in love can become its own mental and emotional quicksand. Never had I felt such deep emotional pain before in all my life; no physical sensation can match its seemingly everlasting grip; its intensity can only be rivaled by the ecstasy of being in love.

I naively asked myself, *"Is this the pain that so many have chosen to commit suicide over?"* **I then gave imaginative thought to driving off of the cliff that was coming up ahead. After mentally seeing my death occur off the mountain side, I got chills and soon realized that that heartache is something countless people have gone through and will continue to go through, forever. It just so happened to be my turn to experience the feeling and no person, or set of circumstances like losing a job, or a lover is ever worth committing suicide. Realizing then that I had every reason to rise to the challenge and move forward as a stronger, wiser human being.**

It was in this time frame that I began to get over Monique. Funny that it took imagining driving over a cliff-side to recognize the depressed world I was creating for myself. However, this phenomenon of heartbreak was new territory for me at the time, and I didn't fully know how to handle it.

As I drove up the winding I-17, I thought as critically as possible about the events that led me to my current predicament; only to recall that my childhood development was a very confusing and testing time. I remembered how at five years old, I had questions about creation that stunned my mother; on one occasion while she drove with me in the back seat of her car, I asked her "What is God?"

To which she replied looking at me in the rearview mirror "God just is, sweetie, that's how God works."

I remember being confused at her answer; I had hoped she could truthfully be able to shed some light on the matter for me. So I said, "That doesn't make sense Mommy. If God is all powerful, didn't he give people a simple explanation for what he is in the Bible?"

She was left speechless as she drove, then she said "I will look into that and get back to you sweetie. Okay?"

"Do you wanna know what I think God is mommy?" I asked

"Sure honey. What do you think?" she said looking at me in the rearview mirror.

"I think God is what we can't see or hear or touch. I think that where God lives, is in the space where there is no space because that is everywhere and nowhere at the same time."

My mother was stunned and did not know what to say other than. "That is really profound honey. I'm very proud of you!"

After this recollection I searched my memory to find where these spiritual inquires were derailed, I realized that they stopped at around age thirteen while my mom worked nights, allowing my drunken step-dad to have full control of the house for hours before

bedtime. Countless nights he insisted that my brothers and I, fall into military ranks to stand at attention for hours upon hours, and listen to him drone on about politics, the military, and religion.

We were forced to stand with our arms and hands at our side, pressing our fingers together tightly, so no daylight could be seen between them; our straight stiff hands were to lay perfectly flat at our sides, with our thumbs touching the seams of our pants. If we had an itch on our nose, we had to wait for an opportunity to ask for permission to scratch it by saying, "Sir. Requesting permission to scratch an itch. Sir". If we moved or interrupted his ramblings without permission, it would result in a punishment of push-ups or abdominal crunches. If we continued to plead our case before completing the exercise, he would raise the number of repetitions until they were completed. Occasionally, I stood up to him by refusing to stand for hours or do unjustified push-ups, however, I found that such rebellions were met with the smart end of a belt, a slap to the face, or a punch to the chest. He knew he could get away with all of his drunken tyranny, as long as my mom was working nights. Coincidentally, I remember the day she quit working nights I had my reoccurring dream the morning before.

My mother always encouraged me to be myself and built up my confidence, while my step-dad tore me down and tried to shape me into something he felt I should be. This strange mix of signals helped shape me into an exceptionally odd preteen and an even stranger

rambunctious teenager, ultimately resulting in a confused 18-year-old with a mind of his own joining the military.

Thinking the Army was a place where my leadership skills would be more appreciated and a place that my desire to take the initiative would be welcomed, I joined. Which it was, at first, but I also asked "Why?" far too often. Asking "why?" is a big "no-no" when given orders. So I experienced much grief for this habit, especially during my short Green Beret tryouts. I completed the two weeks try-out phase of the training with flying colors, or so I thought, but I was dubbed too free of a thinker by the psychologists on staff to move on to special ops training.

I later came to find out this was because I had said that "I refuse to be a mindless kill dog for the government" to one of my fellow candidates during training, eventually this statement made its way to the chain of command. Afterward, I was dismissed from any further special forces training for the rest of my military career. Instead of getting upset that my childhood dream of being a green beret was blown, I concluded the government has no interest in educating or investing in a human being unless they are going to be able to use them as they please. I also concluded that I would have to find a new dream.

Ironically, the Special Forces psychologists were right, because I was later booted out of the Army for not obeying a direct order to shoot all suspected terrorists, which included possible innocent civilians

fleeing the scene. Not so unexpectedly, the military's chain of command, much like my step-dad, strongly opposed my loud and proud perspective on the world, and I was kicked out for disobeying a lawful order. Funny enough, the night before I refused to shoot and the day after I got kicked out of the army, I had my re-occurring dream. Eventually a recognizable pattern emerged, a pattern of trial and perseverance resulting in personal growth. The reoccurring dream seemed to act like glue connecting all the different trials and obstacles I had overcome in my life.

Therefore, amidst the heartache I listened to the only thing that offered me any assistance, the intuitive voice inside and it said to follow my dream. As I listened to that voice, I felt a small amount of stable peace work its way into my heart. I felt as though something significant was happening to me as if some universal force had been waiting for me to make this distinct shift in my life. And for some reason, my heart believed that its broken pieces could only be mended in the bosom of Mother Nature. I began to wonder if moving on entirely from my desire to be with Monique would lead to a much better life. A family life with her sounded so perfect, but it wasn't a reality if all of those feelings were one sided. I wondered out loud to anything or anyone listening.

"Could I have a better life by letting Monique go forever right here and now?" I spoke out loud.

Suddenly above the mountains ahead of me, I saw two ravens emerge, flying side by side. They abruptly split apart and one began flying toward me, while the other was flying away. When the raven passed over my car I thought about how my mother once said that Ravens represented great change on both a spiritual and physical level. I wondered if the raven was a sign of good things to come. *That's the funny thing about these spiritual signs. Good or bad, you can never know how to read them,* I thought to myself. Shortly afterward I was among the pines of northern Arizona.

I got off of the interstate and going down the narrow two-way street that wove through the heart of the small town, I made my way into the pine covered community of Munds Park. I gazed at the surrounding forest which was sporadically littered with cabins and little homes. Everybody living there was pretty much retired or wanted to be. During the spring and summer seasons, the tiny town would come to life and get as busy as a retirement community can possibly get. Eventually, however, the wood cabins are once again left cold and abandoned in favor of warmer weather during fall and winter's snow.

As I drove my way through the small community, memory after memory began to flash in my imagination. Passing the local pond, I remembered fishing with my grandfather. Driving by the golf course, I remembered hitting golf balls at the driving range with my grandmother. I saw the small restaurant at which I remembered getting the most awful food poisoning one year. After passing my

grandparent's car sitting in their gravel driveway, I recalled hiding behind it as a child when playing in the snow with my brothers. Even then the surrounding forest felt like a place of solace and it would prove to be once again. While I wanted to drop by and say hello to them, I chose not to for the sake of my broken hearted state.

After making it to the dirt road which led out to the heart of the vast, nearly endless forest of pine that made the Mogollon Rim, I continued cautiously. My 92 Buick was not built for the dirt road terrain, but I went slowly and it wasn't an issue. About two and a half to three miles in, I saw a cleared spot on the side of the road, across from a foliage covered hill. It looked like it was the perfect place to park, so I fit the vehicle snuggly in the patch of dirt, and got out to have a look around. The air smelled incredibly fresh and seemed to fill my lungs with peace. The semi-large hill across from my car had some rocks and bushes nearer the road but beyond them was deep forest, so thick; it was hard to see into its depths.

This was the place to camp I thought. I pulled out the supplies from my trunk, put on my backpack, and prepared for my hike. I touched the bulging polished black crystal stones in my pocket and tried to absorb its power while walking toward the foliage covered hill. Looking up, I noticed that the massive clouds in the sky had morphed into the shape of a mother holding her infant in her arms. I knew then that I was in the perfect spot and I had done the right thing by going to Mother Nature for healing. I knew that she would

hold me in her arms like an infant, then I heard a raven call again and again and again.

07) The Inverted Tree

Once atop the hill, I took a deep breath and began the descent into the next tree laden valley. After a few minutes of walking, I noticed the forest got so thick I had to work around living and dead trees, through bushes and climb over boulders just to move forward a short distance. The hike was initially exhausting and tedious, but eventually it got easier as I either became more aware of simpler routes or the forest became more navigable.

Three to four miles into my hike, I came upon a large peculiar tree located on a slight plateau near the top of a hill. The tree was unlike any other that I had ever seen, prompting me to say "Whoa! What a weird fuckin tree! How the hell did this shit happen?"

The trunk was covered in patches of rough dark gray bark with light gray, porous wood below, which was normal, but the entire tree itself had been uprooted and thrust back into the ground upside-down. Its long curvy roots towered high in the air; they looked as if they were ripped from their soil long ago and had been bleached by the sun. This initial assessment of the tree being deliberately inverted seemed impossible. The trunk was so thick I could barely reach both my arms all the way around it. Upon examining the anomalous tree

further, it appeared to have been deliberately shoved into the ground several feet deep at least, while its inverted bottom towered at least eight to ten feet in the air. The branches were either torn off or shoved underground and it had been there for a long time!

After looking for evidence of its origins, I convinced myself that the tree could not have been placed there by machines, because there was no road or trail so far out in that dense, remote forest. Nor could it have been done by a group of humans without several days worth of effort and danger. And if so towards what purpose? Despite its mysterious origins, I decided that the tree would be a novel and memorable place to meditate.

I looked at my phone to see it was 4:20 pm and remembered the sun would be setting around 7 pm. I deduced that I had time to clear my mind of everything that was stressing me out. I did not believe in prayer, but meditation I did believe in, even if it only worked for me sporadically. So, I set my backpack on the ground, cleared a spot for myself in the soil and sat under the shade of the gray inverted tree.

I decided to do a mental exercise I had learned in a college meditation class. The exercise is intended to aid with the healing process. To begin the exercise one must attempt to recall, retrace and relive through memory all of one's years back to infancy. Working backward from the present moment, one goes through one's memory bank and attempts to retrospect their location a week prior, then a month, then six months, then a year, and so on. Each time, picking and choosing only vivid memories as the common thread. These vivid

recollections can then be used as a launching point to branch to other less retentive memories which are not frequently accessed. After seeing, feeling and retracing one's life through memory, the person doing the exercise is supposed to have a greater sense of self, and their role in the world.

Within a short time I had centered myself entirely, which was extraordinary for me considering my emotional state. Monique's memory was not easy to get through with suspended judgment, but overall it was quite a profound journey, and it put many things into perspective for me. For example, my lack of past romantic partners was because of my unwillingness to compromise as a teen, and my desperate need for neat and organized cleanliness was ingrained into me by my step-dad at a very early age. The inverted tree's location seemed to have a vibe that helped me to center myself in a way I had not experienced during meditation before. Meditation had not worked for me except for a handful of times, however, this time it worked flawlessly. I sat and cleared my mind to a peaceful state without effort or distraction.

After meditating while standing up to stretch, the looming inverted tree felt mostly powerful but slightly ominous for a moment. Its unknown origins intrigued me, allowing my imagination to wander as I walked back to the hill by the road to make my campsite. It made me feel more in control of my situation being close to my car; the road seemed like a small extension of civilization out there in the wilderness. Even though my campsite would be secluded in the forest just beyond the hill's crest, my need for order and safety wanted me

close enough to the road and civilization to not fear getting lost.

I spent the rest of the dwindling daylight collecting firewood and setting up my tent in the woods near the road. Monique occasionally came to mind while I collected wood. We spent more than once night laying by the fireplace in her house watching the embers glow and feeling the heat of the fire and the warmth of each other's naked bodies. However, her memory began to fade with the sunlight. Strange sounds made my hair stand on end, filling the night air with mystery and replacing her memory with terrified wonder. So for mental comfort I made a rock circle and built a small fire to light the dark.

While I sat alone outside my tent poking the fire with a stick, the unpredictable dangers that existed in the darkness around me became a bone-chilling reality. The unexplained noises of the nocturnal forest filled me with streaks of fear and excitement. Feeling uneasy, I found adding my own sounds to the strange range of nightly audible communication was an occasional necessity to keep calm.

"This is what living is all about," I said looking around in the surrounding darkness. "I am glad I did this." I sat and looked at my fire for a few more minutes while all sorts of flying nocturnal insects of all kinds flew around my face, causing me to slap my own cheeks every so often before I made my way inside the tent. Despite the surrounding bizarre echoing tones, and strange bird calls, I surprisingly fell asleep. When I awoke the next morning, I felt

drained and exhausted. After eating some jerky and drinking some water and coffee, I decided to make my way to the inverted tree to meditate.

Once again, after only a short period under the inverted tree, I felt energetically recharged, entirely aware of my surroundings, and quite grateful to be alive. However, after I arrived back at my campsite near the road, the feeling of exhaustion plagued me, and I dreaded the idea of being alone in the wild. Large horse flies, mosquitoes and every other forest dwelling insect relentlessly tormented my campsite all day long, giving me no peace for lunch or dinner. After some internal deliberation, I decided I would make camp at the inverted tree, as no bugs were bothering me there, even when I meditated. Something about that location seemed to do for me whatever it was that I felt I needed to heal. It seemed much more logical to recharge in a place that gave me energy than a place that sapped it.

I hastily packed up my food, water and camping supplies and moved everything to underneath the inverted tree just before dark. After erecting my tent next to the tree's gray trunk and inspecting it for holes or tears, I made a rock circle to build a fire farther away from my tent and the tree. I got comfortable for the magnificent sunset which the tree's location captured perfectly. The slight plateau was positioned half way up an enormous hill, overlooking the vast pine tree populated mountains. As the glittering, golden sun fell below the mountain laden horizon, the sky still full of clouds was colored every shade of pink, purple, orange, and yellow. The whole scene once

again brought me a sense of peace, and for a short time I felt strangely at home. Unfortunately, as the forest grew darker, I began to get an uneasy feeling in the pit of my stomach. My gut somehow sensed that my presence there was a disruption to the forest's nightly routine. Nevertheless, my rational television-soaked mind brushed this peculiar suspicion off as mere paranoia.

It wasn't until later that night after looking into the fire for several minutes, I got the same uneasy feeling again and could sense a pair of eyes locked onto me from a distance. When I looked in the direction I felt the gaze coming from; I swear I saw two red eyes focused on me with intensity from behind some trees. I couldn't tell if it was light residue in my vision from staring into the fire or not, but my heart leapt out of my chest, and adrenaline filled my veins. I felt frozen in a staring contest, with what I could not say, oddly enough, as quickly as they appeared the two red glows faded in the darkness. I was confused, scared, excited, and nervous all in the same moment. I didn't know if it was a projection or a clear perception of reality. Only after not seeing the red eyes again, did my rational mind chose to conclude it was just my imagination.

08) Prankster or Predator?

I awoke to a cool, crisp morning; I had slept so deep that I'd forgotten I was camping. The sound of the wind moving through the swaying trees complimented the chirping birds and the scent of pine perfectly. Looking around I saw my backpack was exactly where I left it, but unexplainably over the course of the night a piece of lava rock about the size of baseball ended up inside of my tent. I knew it was not there when I fell asleep, and there was no hole in the base of my tent for a stone to slip through. I had inspected the tent for such imperfection when I put it up because I didn't want any insects or spiders deciding to visit my nether regions during the night. The undeniable fact of the matter was that there was no purpose or reason for the lava rock being there at all. Despite my confusion and mental dissection of the events, Monique randomly came to mind, and any curiosity as to the origin of the stone was lost completely.

I had grown so tired of her angelic face repeatedly disrupting my internal peace. The whole reason I went out to the forest was to get her and the pain that came with her memory, off my mind for good. Even still, love is a powerful force, and I checked my phone hoping to see a text from her or anyone. Only to see I had no texts or calls at all.

I tried to call Isaac because I forgot to text him the day before, only my location had no service. To get my mind off of things I gathered firewood from around the perimeter of my campsite. As I walked through the woods, I heard what sounded like another set of footsteps moving in the forest as well. I stopped to listen more

carefully, but the sounds seemed to stop along with my movements. I couldn't determine if I was hearing my footsteps echoes or the footsteps of something else. So I convinced myself that I was just hearing my own footsteps and the noises of the forest around me, nothing more.

Yet, I could not shake the feeling that I was being watched. I tried to rationalize my experience by remembering how in a psychology class I heard that some people feel a mysterious presence when they are alone in an unfamiliar environment. I naturally assumed this was the origin of my strange feelings and tried to focus on gathering firewood. I thought that if I felt abnormal, then focusing on doing something normal might help to change that.

On one of my trips back to camp with arms full of wood, I smelled a foul stench that reeked like a mix of bad body odor and skunk. The scent was so strong that I could taste its sour, salty flavor stick to the roof of my mouth. I held my breath the last 100 feet back to my camp and gasped for air as I neared the inverted tree's trunk and dropped the wood.

I stood panting and hunched over with my hands on my knees. The smell was gone, but I suddenly heard a loud, unfamiliar howl echoing in the distant forest. I perked my head up, stopped breathing, and attempted to listen more precisely. I heard the howl a second time but still couldn't tell how far away it was, let alone the origins of its permeating bellow. When I didn't hear it a third time, I opted to keep my ears open while picking up the wood and piling it neatly next to the small stone fire circle. As this process continued for several minutes, I once again smelled the same foul odor fill my campsite. Thinking a skunk must be in the area, I held my breath for a minute or two hoping it would pass. After several minutes the smell didn't subside and only grew worse. Given the circumstances, I figured it would be a good idea to leave the area and walk to the road to ensure my car was still there. This activity gave me something to do, and it was my hope that the smell would be gone when I got back; otherwise, I would have to move my campsite.

When I got to my vehicle, I saw that there was a significant amount of dirt that had accumulated on my car windows. Apparently, the result of passing vehicles throwing dust into the air. However, in the dirt on the driver side window, I saw a large hand print that was more than double the size of my outstretched fingers. And for the first time, I began to believe that Isaac was playing a prank on me just as he had promised.

The rock in my tent could have been placed there while I slept, and the stinky smell in the woods could easily be a stink bomb (which Isaac was fond of using in our old high school's bathrooms). I also reasoned that the sound of footsteps around me while I collected firewood was him following me around. The big hand streak on my windows was the final piece of proof I needed to believe that he was teasing me in a playful, but provocative way. So, I yelled out loud as I looked around.

"Whatever you are doing, I get it! You can stop playing your silly games now Isaac, cuz I have figured you out!" I looked around to see if Isaac was going to come out of the bushes.

"Touche'! You got me!" I yelled. "You can come out now!"

"Isaac?"

"Where you at bro? Quit playing games." there were no smells, or feelings of being watched, no one was coming out of the bushes nearby, nor were there any strange howling noises, there was nothing. I tried to call Isaac on my phone again, hoping his ring tone would give him away, but I still didn't have any cell service in those remote mountains. Suddenly all the hair on my body stood on end, and I felt like I was being watched again. The feeling felt intensely invasive and in an anxious rush, I pulled out my keys from my pocket, jumped in my car, and for some reason, I decided to go to my grandparent's cabin down the road. I sped far quicker than the residents of Munds Park would have, going 45mph on a dirt road is not advisable, but I was kinda freaked out. The familiar sound of tires rolling across my grandparents gravel driveway came as a brief comfort.

I got out of my car and walked in haste up the five or six wooden steps to the door. I knocked and heard the sound of their little dachshund barking inside. It did not matter how many times I had

stayed there that old dog always barked at me ever since I was a child. My grandfather peeked his green eyes through the blinds then answered the door with excitement.

"Well hey, Will!" he said with excitement, "What a wonderful surprise it is to see you, grandson! Come on in!"

I stepped in and greeted him in return, then I gave him a hug, and afterward we shook hands. He had quite a grip to his handshake and was a burly man for 80. He moved around like he was 50 and joked around like he was 25. His face looked younger than his age, which was funny because we both looked so much alike. It was like I was interacting at an older version of myself. I only hoped I could be as fit, fun, and filled with love as he was when I was his age.

He took me to his bedroom where my grandmother was sitting on the bed knitting a Christmas stocking while watching the news. She smiled, stood her small five foot frame up, walked over with active steps and gave me a hug saying.

"Well, all right! Nice to see you Will! Didn't expect to run into you today!"

I immediately apologized saying "Yeah, I know sorry for not calling first. I would have but..."

My grandfather interrupted me "No, it's fine! I'm just glad we are here."

From behind her reading glasses, while running her fingers through her long gray curly hair, my grandmother asked "Are you hungry? Are you thirsty? Can we get you anything?"

"No, no, thank you." I replied. Realizing I didn't want to admit to my own fear, I gave the first reason I could think of for dropping by without notice. "Actually, I'm here to ask you both something kind of funny."

"What is it?" my grandfather replied as his brow looked concerned.

I asked if we could sit down, and we each walked a few feet and pulled up a chair at the table for four near the northern facing window. After sitting down, I took a deep breath and explained further "I am camping in the woods a few miles north of here and I think my friend Isaac is playing a prank on me."

"What do you mean? What is he doing?" my grandfather asked curiously.

"Well, when I was in the forest I encountered this awful skunk smell around my camp during the day, and I swear two red eyes watching me last night in the dark. I also heard this strange howling sound once while I was getting firewood, and this morning I saw a large

hand print streaked on my driver side window." My grandparents looked at each other for a moment and back at me, "Like I said, my theory is that Isaac is messing with me, it being a small town, have either of you seen him around?"

My grandmother replied first and spoke with slight skepticism as she said, "Well, that's some story Will. I can't say we have seen 'em. It is probably just other campers or a group of your friends. I wouldn't worry too much about it."

I couldn't blame my grandmother for being skeptical, as I was known among the family to be a prankster; however, my grandfather looked slightly intrigued and almost sure when he said: "It sounds like it's a Sasquatch encounter to me." My grandmother and I both shared a glance and a laugh, as neither she nor I believed in any of that stuff, while my grandfather most definitely did.

"I don't think that's what it is Grandpa. I don't believe in Bigfoot. I'm far more confident it is Isaac or even other immature campers stink bombing my camp, and wearing intense looking luminescent glasses, as opposed to a nine-foot tall beast of folklore." I replied with a laugh.

My grandmother complimented me with a chuckle saying "Right! Where is the evidence for the Sasquatch? Ha, there is none! It's all just a bunch of people with stories and footprints, which can easily be faked! If a real one existed, science would have found one by now."

She and I shared another skeptical grin and laugh; afterward, I elaborated.

"I am pretty sure it's Isaac Grandpa, what I didn't tell you yet is that he said he wanted to come with me, and when I said no, he said he would come up here anyway and mess with me from a distance. I wouldn't put it past him to venture up here just to mess with me for a night, then go back home either. I have played enough elaborate pranks on him throughout our friendship to merit something like this. A few months ago during Christmas vacation, before my brothers went back to college, we all worked it out with Isaac's wife, and in the middle of the night, we woke him up using high-voltage tasers while wearing intense looking alien masks, and speaking through demonic voice modulators. To say the least he freaked out and we had to take off the masks to calm him down." They both laughed shaking their heads because they knew it was true.

"I would have to get you back if you did that to me too." my grandfather said laughing to himself, then shortly afterward he rebutted my logical deduction by saying "But, you know we have something in Arizona called the Mollogon Monster, right?"

"No, I have never heard of that at all Grandpa. What's that?" I asked inquisitively.

"It's a Sasquatch that lives in these forests, and in the White Mountains on the Apache reservation." He replied seriously, "I have not seen it myself, but I know others who have."

"And you just believe them?" I said skeptically "How do you know they aren't just trying to..."

"They are all credible and would have no reason to lie Will," he said in a calm, stern tone. "That being said, would you like to stay here tonight instead of camping?"

A large part of me did want to stay there but at that moment, I figured it was Isaac and I didn't want to give him the satisfaction of running me out of the woods, so I decided to turn down their offer.

"No, I appreciate it," I said looking at the ground scratching my neck. "I kind of want to stay in the woods. I am getting quite the thrill out there despite everything that has happened. I only wanted to make sure to tell someone what was going on, just in case it isn't Isaac and instead it's a bunch of weird toothless inbred hillbillies that wanna make me squeal like a pig before they eat me alive." My grandmother looked disturbed and slightly upset at the thought.

My grandfather pierced me with narrowed eyes, then reprimanded me with a firm voice and the use of my full name. "William Patrick Sage! Don't say stuff like that while your grandmother is around; besides what we speak we reap. If you don't want inbred toothless

hillbillies taking you away, then don't joke about it happening! We WILL see you again grandson! You will be just fine out there."

"Sorry Grandma, sorry Grandpa, it was just a joke," I replied with a little reluctance.

"It's okay." My grandmother replied.

"Just give us a call if you need us." they both said at the same time.

They looked at each other, smiled and gave each other a little peck on the lips; their bond seemed unbreakable. They had both slaved away most of their lives, saved a lot of money, eventually investing in real estate and stocks. Their personalities blended so well together, often complementing what each other had to say with equal wisdom and love, even if they didn't always share the same opinion.

I got a refill on water and decided to leave after giving both my grandparents a hug. I thanked them for their hospitality then departed for my campsite and its intriguing mysteries. When I arrived back to the rectangular dirt spot where I previously parked my car, I did so with a stronger spirit than I had before. Despite my very real uncertainty and my well-managed terror at the idea that is wasn't Isaac, I got out of my car and stretched. As I brought my legs together and bent over, I began to wonder if I was wrong about Sasquatch. I didn't want to admit it to my grandparents, but the thought that one may be watching or following close behind my every

step, both terrified and excited me equally. I had always wanted to believe in that kind of stuff but had far too rational of a view on reality for any of that malarkey.

None the less, I began searching my mind for any reasonable scientific explanation for the existence of Sasquatch. The only theory I could remember was that the Sasquatch were gigantopithecus or a Neanderthal that outlived the ice age and now lived in the forests. After hiking the few miles back to my camp at the inverted tree in the afternoon sun, I was once again awestruck by the inverted tree's enormity and mysterious origins. I had been so carried away in my thoughts that I had forgotten to tell my grandparents about the inverted tree. *Why didn't I tell them about the tree?* **I wondered. It had completely slipped my mind for some strange reason.**

I looked around and surveyed my campsite to discover that I had far more firewood than I remembered collecting and it was not stacked neatly at all. At this point I was certain that Isaac was messing with me, who else would gather wood for me? How else did a stone get inside my tent? He had definitely stepped our little game of prank tag up to a new level, I thought.

This time, I wasn't going to let him know I was on to him, so I pretended not to notice the firewood and instead, I decided to go on a hike, purposefully leaving my backpack and camping supplies at the campsite for better agility and stealth. However, I still chose to carry the bear spray with me for self defense. I filled my back pockets with

white plastic bags and glow sticks, filled my camel pack with water, then made my way through the forest; smiling and hoping with every step that I would run into Isaac along the way. To find my way back, I tied a single white plastic bag and glow stick to an elevated tree branch every one-hundred yards, and continued to advance through the trees and bushes of the seemingly endless forest.

09) Getting Lost To Find Myself

The crunchy sound of the earth beneath my feet was soothing, and the smell of the wilderness filled me with the serenity that only it can offer. With a grin and a deep inhale I continued my hike north, occasionally pulling out a white grocery bag and a glow stick from my back pocket to mark a nearby tree. Figuring that if I got lost, the glow sticks would help me find my way back if night fell. After a mile or so, as I tied them both to a branch, I suddenly heard movement somewhere in the distance, and my body became covered in goosebumps. There was stillness in the air, the surrounding silence seemed to have an echo. The sense that someone or something was present was overbearing. I listened carefully but heard nothing. I was sure it was Isaac, for this type of prank was just like him.

I smiled at the thought and I decided if he were going to follow me, then I would give him a good long hike. So I started walking for miles

deeper into the forest, marking trees as I traversed the endless hills and valleys; all the while I could hear pursuant movement in the distance behind me. Eventually, I ran out of plastic bags and glow sticks. Still, I continued to hike for a long time, assuring myself that all I needed to do was turn around and go back the way I came to hike back to camp.

However, among the endless amounts of identical trees that surrounded me, and without any clear trail markers I unwittingly got myself very lost. It was then that I decided if Isaac was in fact following me, I could very well turn around and run in his direction causing our paths to cross. After turning around and quickly hiking for a short distance, I heard the sound of several heavy footsteps rapidly moving behind me. The footsteps didn't sound human and felt rather large based on the vibration being pounded into the ground as it ran. Despite having the bear spray in hand, I ran as fast as I could.

As I sprinted, I could hear the footsteps getting closer and closer, so I turned my head to see what was chasing me and found that it was a group of beautiful deer running through the forest. I immediately moved out of their way and felt so relieved that I began to laugh out loud at my panic. Shaking my head and laughing, I thought about how I was going to get back to my camp. I concluded that it must have either been the pack of deer I was hearing behind me, or it was Isaac. Either way, the anticlimactic scenario relieved some tension in me, and I assured myself more and more that I was not in the presence of an immediate threat.

After a long while of trying to navigate my way back to camp I began to get antsy; thinking that just over the next hill I would see something familiar, or one of my plastic bags and glow sticks. Only as I traversed the forest, hill after hill and valley after valley, I saw nothing. *"Fuck! How could I have gotten myself so lost?"* **I thought. Sometimes the trees grew increasingly dense making the forest less navigable, other times the trees were very sporadically distributed, leaving my options near endless.**

As I climbed each new hill, my heart would float on the hopes that I would see a recognizable valley once I reached the top; only to reach its apex and peer into yet another unrecognizable slope of shadowy trees, causing my heart to sink once again as I descended into yet another unrecognizable valley. *"This can't be happening to me!"* **I thought to myself,** *"Just keep moving forward, you will find your way out of here."*

Time went by so much slower when I was lost, but it got much more stressful when I began to fill with shame. I started to talk to myself out loud, *"How could I have gotten this turned around? How could I have been so dumb to be lost without my supplies? What is the matter with me? Don't I know better than to put myself in this kind of position?"*

While lost, I thought about all of the people who had gotten lost in the forest never to be seen again. I worried that I too would be among that group of unfortunate souls. In my anxious state, I remembered a story my grandfather once told me about a woman who got lost in the Coconino Forest, only 20 years prior. He said she

was never seen nor heard from again, all that was found by search parties was one of her shoes and a tattered little blue dress. I even remembered her name amidst all of that worry; it was Christine Wellington.

As the sun started descending below the horizon I heard a wolf howl in the distance and I wondered if Christine was eaten alive by wolves. Then I wondered if I would share in a similar fate as night fell around me. Despite my military training I began to worry, as I walked, I began to feel as though something or someone was watching me from a distance again. I felt their eyes move over my body as I walked through the forest. I felt the gazing presence to my right but tried to convince myself that there was nothing there and it was only my mind playing tricks on me.

As I wandered the woods, my camp's location seemed more elusive and obscure than ever before, night deepened and the ground became far less visible. Still marching south, I assured myself with each careful step that soon I'd see some familiar terrain or one of my trail markers. Except, with the sun’s disappearance I started to panic. My hands began to shake, my breaths started getting shallow, and my legs tried to outrace my heart as I marched frantic and frustrated.

Eventually, the starry night made the forest floor turn black, and I stopped my quickened pace after nearly spraining my ankle in a hole. I stood catching my breath on a hillside, feeling more frightened than I'd been in my whole life. I had been through a similar situation

during my special forces tryouts, but I was equipped with a map of the night fallen terrain plus a flashlight, and landmark identifiers. I also had a GPS on my jacket during my training, so getting lost in the backwoods of the Carolinas was not possible. However getting lost in the forest, at night, without any supplies, scared me as much as it would have any other city dweller.

After I arrived at total despondency, I sat on a large rock to breathe and calm myself down. It suddenly dawned on me how alone I was out there in the wild. I had no friends to tell me that I was a good guy, nor a woman to look at me with want in her eyes, I didn't have a family to care for me, or a modern appliance to get me out of my situation. It was only then as I sat desolate in the dark that I realized the largest part of my identity, was my socialized sense of self. Until that moment, I had not realized how much I had looked into the eyes of others for my self-image.

There in the night fallen forest, I instantly felt the full impact of this social handicap and my personality's adaptation to it. My humor was determined by sit-com laugh tracks and my desire for a woman's love drove me to change my clothing style. My need to be accepted caused me to drink alcohol and smoke cigarettes while at the club, even if I felt sick afterward. What I ate was often dictated by what was advertised to me on TV.

As I began dissecting my personality, I saw it was built around wanting to be liked by others, not wanting to be liked by myself. I wanted the approval of strangers more than I wanted my own it

seemed. Feeling disappointed in this truth about myself, I made a very empowering choice there alone in the dark. I decided in that moment to live without fear and simply be myself in every way that I knew how, whatever that meant. I felt less lost in those fleeting moments, despite the fact that my being lost had not changed.

Then out of the corner of my eye, I saw bright white head lights far off in the distance. It drew my eyes immediately. Looking up into the tree covered sky, I exclaimed *"Oh my God a car! Thank you God! Thank you! Thank you! Thank YOU!"* **The relief I felt was tantamount to taking a diesel engine off of my shoulders. I was so elated that I began to laugh uncontrollably as I moved toward the headlights.**

After some careful maneuvering, I made my way to the road trembling and relieved. I never thought I would be as happy to see another human being until being lost for miles in the dark. I got to the road in time to see the truck drive-by; I was so happy I waved at the people in it, even though I couldn't see whether or not they waved back. Then I started walking southwest on the road towards my car.

After a few hours and miles of walking on the dirt road, I got to my vehicle. Luckily I still had my keys in my pocket, so I unlocked my trunk, pulled out a flashlight and gave serious thought to going to my grandparent's cabin for the night instead of back to my campsite. Then I thought *"Grow a pair and go back to camp!"* **Even though I may have been terrified of getting lost again, the panic and the thrill of having such a real experience excited me beyond anything I could**

find in the city. I felt a sense of novelty like never before; I may have been half mortified by going back to my camp in the dark, but there was another half of me that was thrilled beyond measure. My seemingly fragile, cultured mind may have been overwhelmed, but the primal man in of me thirsted for more.

It was very strange walking with a flashlight in the forest that night, everything around me except for where I shined the flashlight was pitch black and morphing into strange shadowy figures. When I got close enough to my camp to see the inverted tree a few yards in the distance, I heard a twig snap on my left. I turned the flashlight to the source of the noise, but the light was only bright enough to illuminate a few feet in front of me. I heard another sound of movement to my right, but still I couldn't see anything with the limited power of my light. Then I heard something moving in the bush behind me. I was already too far to go back to my car for shelter. So I ran with my flashlight and bear spray to my campsite. I quickly unzipped the tent and climbed inside. After grabbing the machete that was clipped to my backpack I waited; staring outside the tents entrance with my hand on the bear spray's trigger and the machete's blade at the ready.

After a long silence I attributed all of my actions to a foolish state of panic and emerged from my tent to make a fire. As I got the fire started, I kept my ears open, my eyes peeled, and my head on a swivel. Once fully lit, the fire light gave the inverted tree quite an intense presence. It was then that the peculiarity of the whole camping experience began to dawn on me in an entirely different

way. While I could easily write off everything I had experienced up to that point as paranoia and or an elaborate prank on Isaac's part, everything suddenly began to take on a more eerie tone. Feeling slightly vulnerable, I decided to go inside my tent and contemplate my scenario. After a while of staring into the fire from inside my tent I realized that I had to take a piss. I didn't want to go outside, but I didn't have much of a choice seeing as how I didn't have a bucket inside of my tent.

I decided to brave it with the bear spray in hand, convincing myself that I was just being paranoid and acting a fool. I mentally did my best to write off the strange occurrences on my trip as Isaac's revenge and made the trek out of my tent pointing the bear spray in front of me with an extended arm and finger on the trigger. I continued assuring myself that it was only the impenetrable darkness that awakened the fear that it may be something or someone other than Isaac was responsible. But I eventually believed that my fear and paranoia were unjustified.

Laughing nervously, I walked approximately ten paces into the dark to take a piss. As I finished, I smelled the same skunk ridden body odor as I had before. I looked up and saw two glowing red eyes belonging to an enormous dark figure approximately ten feet away from where I stood. My heart racing, I let out a primal scream of fear and successfully covered the shadowy beast with the bear spray, afterward I ran in the opposite direction. Scrambling past my tent I scurried past the fire and into the night toward my car.

My shoes shielded my feet from the dark forest floor but my arms and legs, however, were battered, scratched, and whipped as I ran past trees, through bushes, and jumped over rocks. My flashlight, and army training sure came in handy while I ran to my car that night. I was scuffed up and bruised a good bit because I tripped and fell several times along the way, but all I cared about was putting distance between me and the red eyed monster in the dark.

When I got to the hill bordering the road, I lost my footing half way down my decent and I rolled the rest of the way to the gravel covered base. With my tires kicking up gravel behind me I began to drive toward the small town. As I raced down the dirt road, I looked in my rearview mirror to see if anything was following me, only to find nothing was pursuing me at all.

I drove through the dark along the winding bumpy dirt road at high speeds, jostling my dash and rattling the coins in my cup holder. After a few short miles, I abruptly arrived at the end of the dirt road and suddenly decided to stop when a voice said "Turn around. Return."

I began to doubt what my own eyes had seen. *"Did I really see anything? Could it have been residue from the fire? Could I just be acting paranoid? Oh shit! I forgot to put out that fuckin fire! I can't be responsible for a forest fire! I gotta go back."* **I thought to myself. Even though I was terrified and horrified at going back, I knew I had to return to put out the fire at least. Otherwise, the whole forest would be put in jeopardy.**

While sitting in my car on the edge of the dirt road, my heart was torn by unparalleled terror and pure excitement, by a desire to live adventurously, versus living a life totally free from danger. Ultimately my curiosity and sense of responsibility outweighed my fear. I concluded that I would return to assess the situation and if I needed to put out the fire I would do so. And if all seemed well then it would be clear I overreacted and I would stay the night.

Inspecting my face in my rearview mirror, I saw I had a large scrape on my right cheek and my nose was bleeding. I cleaned myself up a bit and drove back. After parking, I grabbed the flashlight and a small knife from my glove box then made the heart-pounding trek back to camp. Upon my arrival, I saw everything was just as I had left it. The fire was still burning, but it needed more wood, my tent was still open, and my backpack was still inside. The only thing that seemed out of place was there was more firewood on the ground which had been tossed sloppily near the fire circle. *Did I knock the wood over when I ran away?* **I wondered.**

Thoroughly unsettled I changed my dirty shirt, grabbed my machete in case I needed to defend myself and sat staring at the fire with my back resting against a large bolder. I will admit, I was frightened and wanted to leave, but after getting lost in the dark, I was done allowing fear to direct my life. Despite my initial instinctual retreat, I was determined to face this fear head on.

Whether or not I was going to get killed or abducted by a Sasquatch or become the butt of an incredibly legendary prank on Isaac's part,

it didn't matter. I was just glad that at last something interesting was happening to me in my life. Something told me to stay just a little bit longer, and I would experience something extraordinary. Then it occurred to me; the excitement and chaos of the day kept Monique off my mind almost entirely.

10) A Broken Leg to Break the Ice

I didn't remember falling asleep against the bolder, but I woke up with a jolt and immediately looked around the perimeter. The fire was only ash and smoke, the sun was up, and it was a beautiful warm day. I felt assured that I had only spooked myself the previous night. I reasoned that it was dark and my mind being stressed simply projected the rest. However, the scrapes and bruises I had on my face and body were clear evidence that something did, in fact, scare the shit out of me.

In an attempt to knowingly cause an encounter with either Isaac or a cryptid, I grabbed my supplies and decided to walk down the same path I'd taken when I thought I was being followed the previous day. Only this time I would keep my phone's video camera at the ready. If something strange was following me, I wanted a video or something to validate my story. Only after I had some proof would I leave the forest willingly.

As I approached the several trees where I put white grocery bags and

glow sticks I found that they had been moved to different branches on the same tree. *What the fuck is going on?* **I wondered. Oddly enough, I was intrigued and excited by the strangeness of it all. It created an uncertainty that made me feel alive in a new way. This entirely sober rush was unlike any buzz or kick I had ever felt before. I was having an authentic experience of enigmatic euphoria.**

I had been silently shouting for a mysterious experience ever since childhood, mostly because I never really believed my mother when she spoke of all of the psychic phenomena that she experienced. I always assumed she just had a few too many beers. Now I was having a brief seemingly trivial interaction within an unexplainable phenomenon that was driving me to the brink of my own sanity while alone and sober in the forest.

Nevertheless, I still could not assimilate the magnitude of what was happening. So I tried to rationalize it all somehow and find a logical explanation for the bizarre chain of events. I concluded that it must be Isaac, it wasn't that hard to put red LED's in sunglasses and stand on a tree stump after letting off a stink bomb. Everything I had experienced up to that point was easily explained away as a prank, and considering the one I pulled on him I had something elaborate coming my way for sure. The extra firewood was the final piece of proof that led me to believe that it was, in fact, Isaac at work.

I stopped my day lit exploration in a similar place where I was the day before when I felt the eyes watching me. After a short time of standing there feeling a similar way, I decided to communicate.

"Isaac I know it's you! You can come out now, and we will call things even! Okay?"

As I stood there facing North, I felt a rush of air go past my back accompanied by the smell of skunky body odor. I didn't have any time to react or get a video; I was fumbling with my phone when I heard a very prolonged and loud "Hooooot" from almost 10 yards away. Then, I heard a similar internal voice to the one that I heard when I was on the dirt road the night before.

Then the same voice said, "Northeast. There is white stone circle." I got Goosebumps, accompanied a sudden rush of being out of my body, followed by a profound bouncing plummet back into my body.

Am I going crazy? **I wondered.** *Has everything in my life finally reached a peak with me entirely losing my mind? Is this how its starts? With hearing strange voices? How would I know the difference? What the fuck is happening to me?*

These questions kept me paralyzed for a short time while I internally debated my sanity and safety. Unexplainably, I could feel that whatever was there, it wasn't dangerous, so I decided to trust my intuition, and I made my way northeast. When I reached the top of a nearby hill I looked down to a valley which had a treeless flatland at its base. It was crowned by a large circle made of approximately a dozen huge white stones. The internal voice wasn't just a hallucination, as I thought it must have been, it was something real. Astonished I ran toward the white stones in the distance.

As I approached the 100-foot diameter circle, I noticed it had an X

pattern made of white stones in its center, dividing the circle into four equal quadrants. The moment I stepped over the large white bordering rocks and inside the circle a calm but profound peace permeated my being. An overwhelming sense of gratitude and humbleness engulfed me. A stream of childhood memories spiraled through my consciousness and out of the top of my head. Then I felt a warm energy rising from my feet, around my legs, through my torso, and out of my head's crown. This spiraling metaphysical wind took all of my inhibiting concerns about Monique, where my career was going, and my confusion about who I was as a human being with it, as it ascended out of my body and into the blue sky.

Upon realizing the holiness of the circle, I dropped to my knees and leaned my head forward toward the dirt as tears of reverence came to my eyes. For the first time in my life, I perceived some form of profound purpose to all of the coincidences that led me to that place. At that moment my whole life and the pains I'd suffered made perfect sense. I realized whatever I experienced, good or bad, it had led me to that location; which was ultimately a real blessing.

Amongst the blue and purple static that swarmed vision behind my closed eye lids, I had the most intense déjà vu of my life. In that moment, I saw and felt exactly where I was on the earth, followed by exactly where I was in my journey of life as a whole.

I felt very thankful for my life. As my awareness settled back into my body more and more, there was a unique euphoria to this experience that felt relieving and exhausting at the same time. After I had

decided to sit up from my moments in grace, I smelled the skunk again and I opened my eyes to see near the edge of the circle a few feet in front of me, stood a nine-foot tall black hairy primate creature. It did not move, it only stood there and stared with its dark eyes from under its protruding brow, into my soul. At that moment, every legend I had ever heard about a Bigfoot or Sasquatch instantly became begrudgingly validated. *"Holy Fuckin Shit!"* **I thought to myself,** *"This cant be real! This can't be happening right now!!"* **My brain found the prospect of seeing a Sasquatch near incomprehensible, and I felt hit by several blinding flashes of light.**

Despite my euphoric state, this was the last thing I expected to see when I opened my eyes. I immediately jumped up from my knees to my feet, screamed like a child and tried to run my ass outta there. However, in a panic I wedged my foot in-between two rocks just outside the circle. The twisting fall of my botched get away broke my right shin bone clean in half; the sharp snapping echo it made inside my body filled me with dread. Even though I could not see the damage through my jeans, I knew it was broken badly. I felt the excruciating pain of my bone ripping through the skin of my leg as I fell face first into a large tree in front of me, knocking me out cold. I awoke a short time later dangling over the stinky creatures shoulder as it was carrying me somewhere. Attempting to get away hurt so excruciatingly bad I came close to passing out again. Whether I liked it or not, I was at the mercy of the sizeable sour smelling creature that carried me on its shoulder.

I woke up to the stinky, hair-covered giant laying me down gently

onto a large flat rock slab inside the sun illuminated entrance of a cave. My leg was throbbing all around the break site, and the exposed marrow of the bone seemed to give a cold burn down to its bare core. I couldn't move without it hurting to the point of almost passing out, so I tried to lay as still as possible. I had never broken a bone before, the pain was so intense it didn't seem like it was real, and it felt like I was watching the whole thing from a third party perspective half of the time.

I was in a daze, when the creature lifted my head and started pouring some sweet, earthy tasting liquid from a stone bowl into my mouth. I resisted drinking at first and after some of the liquid went down the wrong tube I coughed uncontrollably for a few minutes. I was thirsty though and I didn't fight it the next time the creature tried to give me the flavored fluid. It tasted kinda earthy, but good. So I drank more after the hairy creature returned from the depths of the cave with another bowl full. No matter how much I tried, I couldn't make out any details as to the primate's appearance in the dim light of the cave.

After a few minutes the creature lumbered into the darkness, and a short time later emerged with a stick about the size of my shin in its hand. For a short time I felt cold and shaky, then suddenly I felt slightly woozy, warm, fatigued and totally unconcerned about my leg. My bone was no longer in as much pain and I figured this must have been because of the liquid the creature gave me. Oddly, I started to feel good. After observing this change, the creature decided it was a good time to investigate the damage, and possibly reset the bone.

It sliced my bloody jeans with its sharp thumbnail from around my knee down, then moved the cloth out of the way. The protruding bone was plainly visible, but also indicated that it was a clean break. I sat up to see this painful stomach-turning sight and I screamed out loud as the smell and site of all the blood filled me with nausea; causing me to throw up uncontrollably all over the floor, then pass out.

While I was passed out, the giant being pulled my foot out straight, and the bone receded inside of my skin, then it used the stick and some makeshift rope to tie a splint for my bone. What was once two broken pieces was now set into one; this process was enough to wake me from my fainted state as one would imagine. I sat up almost instantly, screamed with ferocity, threw up on the creature arm, and then passed out again. Only this time it was as if I was half conscious and able to watch everything as I floated disembodied a few feet away in the darkness of the cave. For some reason this didn't concern me at all at the time, and I oddly felt calm and interested in what was happening from my distant state of consciousness.

The helpful hairy humanoid wiped my vomit from its arm, and then it placed its palms together in front of its chest and closed its eyes. It commenced a very deep humming vibration from inside its chest; the sound moved up to its throat and out of its pursed open lips. By funneling the frequency with its lips into bursts of bright vibrating waves of light and sound, its hum turned into a very deep low pitched tone, and the ripples of luminescent frequency shook the cave walls and gravel with their echo.

The creature grabbed my ankles with one of its massive hands and held down my knees with its elbow, then it leaned its face toward my set shin bone, directing its vibratory waves at the torn flesh and the broken bone. This process was painful enough to wake me up, and I was shot back into my body. I awoke with a shrill yell and began chaotically reaching for my shin. My bone began to mend the instant the ringing light waves hit the bone fibers.

"Fuck! Stop! Please Stop!! That really fuckin hurts!! FUCK!! AHHH!" I screamed aloud in agony.

As if my bone was metal and the creature's hum was a welding torch, the fibers melted and mended together giving off a bright yellow glow. The powerful creature used its elbow to keep my knees pinned while it continued the high-frequency vibratory tone over my broken shin bone. I could feel the pieces painfully mending from two into one as I screamed obscenities in pain. The vibration shook my shin all the way to its core, eventually reverberating throughout my entire skeleton. Ultimately, it felt like a stream of lightening and fire coursing throughout the marrow of all of my bones, and into the tendons and cartilage of every one of my joints. Then the pain and noise ceased, and I passed out for the final time.

I woke up in the dark of the cave feeling delirious, my equilibrium was off, and my head felt like it was full of water. I tried to look around, but couldn't make out in the darkness of the cave where I was located. I had temporarily forgotten the trauma that I had experienced earlier, and as my fingers touched the torn fabric of my

jeans, the rope and the stick still tied to my lower leg, I remembered bits and pieces. I tried to stand and did so successfully without putting too much pressure on my right shin, but when I tried to walk my leg was weak and painfully tender. I could tell it wasn't broken anymore because I could put weight on it and obviously, it was no longer in two pieces either. It felt more like a really bad bruise instead of a break, but the location was still painfully tender and a little swollen. I limped slowly to my right, navigating the dark with my hands out in front of me. I didn't know where I was going, and I didn't know if there was a wall or a drop off in front of me. So I yelled.

"Hello?" and heard nothing in return. I decided to try again, only louder.

"HELLO?"

The distant echo of my voice was evidence to me that wherever I was, it was enclosed and seemed to stretch for miles. My shin was still extremely tender, so I carefully crawled on the floor and slowly felt my way around with my hands until my fingers touched the roughness of the cave wall. The porous texture of the wall and the floor felt like the whole cave was made of lava rock. I was not comfortable in any position; even still, I decided to lean against the wall to sort out my possibly vulnerable position there in the echoing darkness.

I was sweating profusely, the pain in my leg and moving around blindly in the dark had not created an environment that was

conducive for healing. I started to freak out a little inside; my heart began pounding so hard I could feel it pumping from underneath my sternum. The culmination of all of these crazy coincidences led me to believe for a moment, that I had in fact gone, entirely off my rocker. In a moment of sheer panic, I was going to stand up and do my best to run and desperately find a way out.

Then I heard the same very calm internal voice again. "Do not walk. Remain still to heal."

Strangely enough, the voice calmed my nerves, it gave me a strange sense of peace, just as it had each and every time it echoed in my psyche. The tension inside my body faded as I leaned my head against the rough cave wall, even though I had been knocked out all day, I was still exhausted. The mental and physical stresses I had endured were manageable, but entirely unlike anything I'd ever experienced in the military, and sleep seemed to be the only respite from my wild, seemingly impossible, bizarre scenario.

11) An Offer I Couldn't Refuse

I awoke a few hours later to the sound of birds chirping. I noticed as I stood that my shin wasn't hurting at all so, I took off the stick tied around the lower portion of my leg. In the shine of morning light, I saw why my voice had echoed in the dark during the night. I was facing away from the entrance to the cave which was only 10 feet

behind me. I began to wonder why the cryptid creature had healed me there; I didn't understand why it would help me, let alone how it healed my leg. Then from inside the darkness of the cave I felt eyes move over me once again, goosebumps covered my entire body; I stood up in fear that the creature was watching me and left quite quickly.

I had to climb over some large lava rocks to make my way out of the cave. When I emerged to scan my surroundings, I saw that I was in a very dense part of the forest. I started walking away from the cave in hopes that I was near civilization or more people.

Then I heard the internal voice again. "From whom do you run in such a hurry? You are no prisoner of mine. Go if you must, but you will not remember me beyond the trees ahead."

This stopped me dead in my tracks, "Who are you? What the fuck is happening to me?" I said out loud.

I waited and listened; then the voice said "Return to face the answers. No harm will come to you, I am your healer. You are hungry, your food is here in your bag. Come eat and sit a while."

I looked back at the large lava rock hole I had just escaped from and cautiously walked back toward its opening. The darkness inside of its depths seemed as enlightening as it did intimidating. I knew that after entering the cave, my life would never be the same. Even though I was trembling, I decided to climb over the large lava rocks and back inside. There in the light of day, I stood at the entrance and waited for the creature to emerge.

I saw two red eyes slowly approaching me in the darkness. I felt the creature slowly lumber toward me and I stood frozen as my whole body became numb. It was at this point that I strung all of the incidents together. I realized no matter how much my rational mind wanted it to be Isaac that was about to emerge from the darkness; I knew the truth, the voice belonged to the same red-eyed being that had been toying with me ever since I camped outside of the inverted tree. The massive hair-covered humanoid slowly stepped into the light and its image crowned the entire bizarre string of events perfectly.

The benign beast took a deep breath then exhaled slowly. When I reassured myself it meant me no harm, its nine-foot-tall, tree trunk like size, was no longer intimidating. The only thing offensive about its presence was its pungent odor. I could barely handle its wretched stench in the confines of the cave, but its appearance was not dirty or filthy in the slightest.

2-3 inches of black or dark gray hair covered its entire body except for its face. The creature's hair shimmered and sparkled in the sunlight; it had large arms reaching around the lower middle half of its thigh, it had huge black hands with long black woodchip like fingernails and opposable thumbs. Its legs were over 4 feet in length and as round as my torso, they lead down to gigantic dry dark gray feet which were accented by long black toe nails. It wore a single large, tan loincloth around its waist, decorated with some strange red symbols.

Upon first look, the skin on its face was a brindle of black, gray and dark brown colors. Its kind looking eyes were the size of half-dollars and spaced 6 inches apart below a slightly protruded brow which ran across the top of its eyes. In the sunlight, I could see the amber color to its deep dark brown irises. Its nose did not have much of a bridge and protruded slightly from its face as two big nostrils which nicely blended down to plump black lips, proportionate to the size of its face. Its cheekbones protruded boldly from its face, and it had a set of straight white teeth with two pairs of small sharp canines on its top and bottom jaw.

There was a white crescent moon tattoo, running across the top of its forehead with the crescent points touching its protruded brow. The symbol sat nicely below its bald coned head, it had a large set of approximately two dozen dreadlocks hanging like a beard around its jaw bone each getting proportionally smaller up the sides of its face; each dreadlock was equipped with either a dull red or turquoise stone bead at its base. Its ape-like ears stuck out around the middle of its head and were covered in small hairs. The only places that were not covered in hair were its palms, its feet and some portions of its face. Around its entire body seemed to be an inner glow of light.

For a creature that lives in the wild, it certainly looked well groomed, **I thought to myself. Then I heard, "Thank You", as the creature handed me my backpack.**

I responded with "Thank you for what?" verbally as I unzipped the bag. I pulled out a couple granola bars and a water bottle, opened

them furiously and began to chug the water and eat the bar. The creature waited then looked at me for a moment, smiled, and tilted its head in inquiry. As I chewed my food, I realized it was a 'thank you' for what I was thinking and feeling. The being was able to know my thoughts and feelings without my verbal expression. It was communicating with me telepathically even when I wasn't trying to communicate with it. Then it made some strange noises with its mouth that sounded something like mindless monkey grunts, followed by a smile and tilt of its head.

The creature looked deep into my eyes then said telepathically, "Don't talk with your breath, talk with your spirit."

This direct intense form of telepathic communication felt like two open, and unexplored tunnels of communication had manifested a few feet above my head. One tunnel was devoted to sending messages, the other devoted to receiving messages. I was able to send and revive whole paragraphs of thought and feeling simultaneously. I was also able to affirm and respond to each message far more quickly than I ever could have with words. However, given the nature of the nonverbal communication which is telepathy, our conversations would have been seen by all neutral observers as a hairy creature and a human locked in a staring contest.

I laughed out loud and replied telepathically, "Ok, I will try to keep that in mind. But how is it that I can understand you, and you can understand me telepathically, but when we speak out loud we are speaking different languages?"

The being smiled, "I have read your mind, and I know the way it speaks to itself. So that is how I shall speak with you." He smiled for a moment and tilted his head slightly to one side, "You are wondering when and how I read your mind, so, I shall tell you. When you felt eyes on your back or your hair stand tall, I was reading your mind through the language of energy, of feelings, of Spirit. We call it 'En'aa Taasha'ka', it means "heart talk". Touch also makes telepathy possible but beginners tend to start with eye contact. Eventually, there is no need for either, and the Spirit can communicate freely through reading minds. If exercised enough, telepathy can be used to communicate over large spaces."

"Wow! Can I do that right now too?" I telepathically asked excited.

"No, you telepathic strength is not strong enough yet and I must open my spirit enough for you to see inside my mind." it moved it head up and down in an affirmative gesture.

I smiled and asked "So, what is your name? Do you have a name?"

It touched its heart with an open palm, then stretched its open palm out toward me speaking its name out loud "E-Su."

I repeated its name out loud then curled my hand into a fist and touched my heart then said "Will."

He closed his eyes and bowed his head, saying my name out loud. I then bowed in return out of respect, and upon rising from my bow, I touched my heart with a fist then said "Human" out loud, then I motioned to E-Su and telepathically said "We call our species

humans. What is your species called?"

Touching his chest with a fist, "Ularu." It said out loud, "It means 'Spirit'." he replied telepathically.

I looked at E-Su and asked, "Does your species have genders?"

E-Su laughed and said, "Yes, I am a male like you."

"Do you always wear a loin cloth?" I asked pointing at his attire.

He looked down and looked back at me, smiled, then replied "Oh, I did that for you. We Ularu don't wear clothes; we only wear decorative cloth during ceremonies. I will get rid of it; I prefer that anyway..."

As he reached for his loin cloth, I spoke quickly saying "No, no, no! Don't do that. Please, keep that on! I very much appreciate it; that is very thoughtful of you, we humans prefer that our friends not be nude. Please just keep that on." Trying to politely change the subject I asked: "Why do you have a white moon on your forehead?"

After taking his hand away from his loin cloth, he sat on the floor and pointed to the symbol above his brow and said, "I was given that mark by my teacher when I was no longer his student and I became a teacher myself. All Ularu are given a symbol on their face once they reach a certain stage, mine looks like a moon, no one symbol is the same. Also, each hair lock and every crowning bead I have represents an accomplishment or a sacrifice of mine."

"Wow, that's cool." I replied, "So, I have got to ask, why were you

messing with me at my campsite and following me around?"

His gut protruded in and out and he snorted a little, it took me a moment to understand that he was actually laughing then he replied "At first, I saw you from a great distance, and decided to scare you off. Inverted trees are the Ularu way of marking our territory and the tree you camped at marks sacred ground. I was going there to pray one night when I saw you and I was enraged. I wanted you gone. I tried to confuse you without giving myself away. When you didn't leave, I was planning to scare you off. It's a good thing I decided to read your thoughts beforehand."

"Why is that?" I asked quickly

"I saw your dream, and I began to see you differently than other humans. Then the night you sprayed me with that bear spray, I saw that hook birthmark on your chest intrigued me even more."

"Why?" I asked

"It was an omen, our paths were supposed to cross. I looked deep into your spirit that night and it made sense why you found my prayer tree; you were drawn to it for a reason. To be friendly I brought you firewood and tried meet you that night, but you sprayed me with that burning spray and ran off."

"Yeah, sorry about that," I said with a laugh and smile.

"I am sorry I frightened you. I thought I had scared you away forever. So I tried telepathy and was shocked when it worked and you came back. I knew then, you were a special human." E-Su said

narrowing his eyes.

I stood silent for a few moments, considering everything I had just absorbed; already E-Su had introduced some far out spiritual concepts that I was familiar with thanks to my mom. I had always assumed that things like telepathic spiritual communication over vast distances, message bringing omens, and reading people's energies was nothing more than a money-making scheme. Only this Ularu creature knew and spoke of them as if they were real. As if he firmly believed in them as an existential fact of life.

"So is that why you healed my leg?" I inquired.

"If I had left you, you would have died. The wolves of the woods have been howling these past few nights, they smell the stranger in their home. They would've happily made you their meal had I left you alone. The moment they caught the scent of your blood in the air, it would have been over."

After a brief internal silence, I said, "Wow! Well, thank you for saving my life! But, HOW did you heal my leg? That was pretty unbelievable."

"You may not fully understand but I will tell you. I healed you using a form of vibration healing. By showering the body with certain frequencies, I am able to mend flesh and bone with ease as well as kill all sorts of mental illness, cancer, and disease." His telepathic answers seemed so matter of fact I couldn't help but remain skeptical, leading me to wonder what his motives were.

"So, why bring me here? Do you just want someone to hang out with or something? Am I free to go? What exactly do you want from me E-Su?"

E-Su narrowed his vision as he looked at me with a clear focus. "All of creation is midst radical transformation. My kind does not interact with yours anymore, it was once another way, our species used to frequently interact with your medicine men. But, we have stopped for our own safety. Your kind has become more hostile for reasons that I will keep to myself for now. Trust me, it is as strange for me to see and meet you, as it is for you to see and meet me! I am shocked, yet, very pleased you are here." He smiled and bowed his coned head ever so slightly.

His confession seemed to calm me, knowing that he too was a little bit freaked out, became a strange comfort while he continued. "This is a time for omens of great change, and spiritual growth among my kind. I saw a Spirit as strong as yours finding its way to that tree, as an omen of positive change for the humans and the Ularu. So I must ask you, are you interested in staying here and seeing where the flow of nature takes us?"

I replied quickly "I am strangely comfortable with it. But do I have to stay here the whole time? I mean can I go back to spend time at my grandparent's cabin, and then come out to visit instead of staying in a cave?"

He answered very quickly, "No, you can not leave, you must either choose to stay or choose to leave forever. I would like it if you stayed

to eat, and heal, so we can communicate. What do you say?" he seemed calm but also eager to hear my answer.

"So, what? You want me just to stay here with you and hang out all day?" I asked him skeptically.

"That depends on how long you would like to stay. It could be for a day, a half moon cycle, a full moon cycle, its up to you; but this offer does expire. If you choose to leave now, I will wipe your memory, and no matter how many times you return, the opportunity will be lost. This is for your safety and mine. It may seem strange or unfair, but I have good reasons."

I took a few minutes in silent deliberation to eventually say "It is a lot to think about."

E-Su replied graciously "Yes it is, that's why I'm going to give you time to think about it at your camp site. But if you go beyond the dirt road, if both of your feet touch the black asphalt, your memory will be wiped. Walk south for four or five hours and you will find the road, your leg is healed enough by now for the journey. From there you can find your campsite. If you want to stay here with me, go back to the white stone circle and telepathically call my name."

Then, just like that, before my disbelieving eyes, E-Su dematerialized and disappeared in a flash of light. I was in so much astonishment that I reached my hand out to touch the air where E-Su was sitting. "E-Su?" I said out loud; there was no response.

"E-Su?" I said with telepathy and still got no reply.

Then I got a sudden headache in the center of my brain, and it quickly spread behind my eyes. So, I picked up my things and climbed out of the cave trying to figure out what had just happened. I began the headache filled five-hour trek back to the road and from there to my camp site.

Over the course of the remaining daylight, any and all experiences of the strange were nil, and I had not seen, nor heard from E-Su at all. I tried contacting him via telepathy from my campsite to no avail, occasionally hoping to smell his wretched stench or feel his powerful stare. However, he was right to leave me be, as I thought a lot about the life I would be going back to in that time as well.

What life to go back to? **I remember thinking, I didn't have a job or career, I wasn't loved by the woman I wanted, and most of my friends either had kids on the way or were already married with children. Then I realized, that I had not once thought of Monique or my problems at home in the time I spent with E-Su, and thus concluded that getting the opportunity to stay with him for a brief period was the reason I kept having my reoccurring dream. For some strange reason, this was why I had been called to the forest for most of my life.**

Despite the bizarre nature of the things I was experiencing, there seemed to be a strange energetic order of cosmic proportions at work. An order that was only visible to me when I was in the places that existed beyond my comfort zone. Ultimately, I concluded that the extraordinary did not arrive in the laps of the stagnant and

mundane people of the world, and I suddenly had a proclivity to obey this chaotic cosmic order of unbridled energetic design. I decided to stay with E-Su for as long as I felt necessary. I felt an overwhelming desire to let go of my previous sense of self and throw all of my prior worldviews to the wind.

However first, being a tester of limits, I wanted to know what it would feel like to go near the asphalt at the start of the dirt road. So, I drove the few miles back to where the pavement met the earth. I got out and walked over to where the asphalt touched the dirt. I stepped a single foot onto the pavement, being sure to keep one on the dirt road. That was when I felt what could only be described as a tear in the fabric of reality.

It felt as though I was living in two worlds at once. On one side was a gray dying world, full of pollution and death; I felt as if it had a piece of my heart that it wouldn't let go like it was a bad addiction that I couldn't shake off. On the other side, however, was a beautiful colorful world, full of life and purity. I did not feel slavishly bound to it at all, which gave me a much more liberating feeling and a much stronger desire to stay there with E-Su, instead of going back to the gray dead world of bondage on the other side of the black asphalt. Undoubtedly, the bright life filled world seemed to be where my heart belonged. So I put both feet back on the dirt road and felt entirely free and clean again.

I replicated the experiment several times before concluding that on one side of the dirt road was the living free world, where my mind

knew that I made contact and communicated with what our species call a Sasquatch. And on the other side of the road was the cold world of cultured industrial consumerism, where cryptids like the "Sasquatch" were a legend of the fringe or the focus of naive thrill seekers, and nothing more.

I put a single foot on the black asphalt once again and thought about the consequences to putting both my feet onto its black surface. Suddenly, I felt a very sharp chilling sensation crawl from the pavement, through my foot, into my spine and up to my head. It felt like a force field was being penetrated by my foot to touch the asphalt, a force field that if I dared to cross, would wipe my memory of E-Su's presence. I immediately withdrew my foot and backed away. I got in my car and drove back to the place I had previously parked. I didn't really want to go back to my old life, but I had to know what it was like to go to the edge of the road. I had to prove to myself, if no one else, that if I wanted to cross that line, I could.

I did not know where I would get food or water, but I did not care. If E-Su lived in the forest, that meant he knew where to get food and water, and the idea of spending more time with E-Su sounded much better than going back to unemployment, an ex-lover, absent friends, and a grief-stricken mother. While I would miss my friends (Isaac in particular) I would not miss anyone as much as I would miss the opportunity of a lifetime. For the first time in my life, I felt full of equal amounts of excitement, wonder, and anticipation for the future. I finally had something to look forward to in my life. The monotony and dullness were gone and had been replaced with vigor

and passion.

I pondered this whole array of concepts as I ate some dried fruit, drank some water and sat under the massive uprooted tree while the sun set. I could hardly sleep that night; I kept laying awake thinking about what I should do, even though it was quite clear. To live in the forest with a Sasquatch was quite a bold move to take. *Was I ready for such a move*? I wondered. *Could this really be where my reoccurring dream was leading me? Why would it lead me to such a bizarre conclusion?*

At the end of the night, I concluded that if I wanted to go back to my old life, I could always do that, but I would not always have the opportunity to live with E-Su for an extended period. So, I decided to stay and my mind briefly rested, allowing me to fall asleep in my tent for a few hours. I woke up in time to watch the sun's rays break the black sky, then I packed up my supplies, put on my backpack, and I made my way toward the white stone circle a few miles north of the inverted tree.

Soon walking there became too slow and in my excitement, I began to run. When I finally arrived at the stone circle, I stepped inside, and with closed eyes, I yelled "E-Su!" at the top of my luungs. I followed my beckoning call with some hoots and howls of excitement and exhilaration. When I opened my eyes, I saw E-Su standing with a gracious grin a few feet in front of me.

"Will," E-Su said out loud, and then telepathically he replied, "Your excitement is good, but I said to call me telepathically, not scream."

He laughed then smiled as he motioned for me to walk with him, "Let's go to my cave, we have many things to discuss."

13) Conversations with E-Su

As we walked several miles back to E-Su's cave, I spoke of the severe headache I had the day prior after I left. E-Su explained this was a symptom of my mind being new to telepathy and that it would go away as I continued to use my telepathic abilities more and more frequently. Upon our arrival to the lava rock cave, I set my backpack on the ground and immediately sat down.

We both stayed near the entrance of the cave to converse telepathically. Even though E- Su was able to see in the dark, for my sake alone, he hung out near the entrance. Having already read my mind, he saw everything that had happened between Monique and me, and he boldly asked:

"So, what do you think went wrong between you and your mate Monique?"

I was shocked by his question and slightly put off, "Wow, that's really personal and came out of nowhere. Why would you even ask me that?" His sudden turn to such a sensitive topic made me feel vulnerable and slightly confused as to his intentions.

"I am sorry," E-Su replied "We Ularu are very open and see no

reason to be shy about our feelings. I forgot humans are sensitive about expressing how they feel inside."

I felt slightly childish for acting so uptight about the truth of my inner feelings and replied; "No, I am the one who is sorry, I didn't mean to snap at you, I am obviously still a little sensitive about that topic and was also confused as to how you know so much so quickly just by reading my mind. To be honest, I don't know what happened between us. It was like one day she was in love with me, and then the next day she wasn't. One day she wanted to be physically close, the next day she didn't want to be close at all, she sent countless mixed signals over the course of the year we were together. Eventually, I got tired of it and called her out on it, saying she was playing games with my heart, and that I didn't want to stay in an unstable relationship. So she refused to talk to me after that, I tried going to her place several times, once, even bringing flowers, but she still refused to see me. I texted her, and I called her, but she refused to answer. So, through a text, I told her I still loved her, but I had to let her go. I hoped to get a reply, but I never did. So I stopped texting or calling, and she hasn't spoken to me since."

He laughed a little and said, "That's not what I asked, I asked what you thought went wrong."

I replied sharply, "I already said that I don't know. Maybe she wasn't in love, maybe she was just using me, maybe she cheated on me, I really don't know E-Su. Why are you asking me this? Do you have a theory you would like to share? Why do you even care to ask?

How would you like it if I asked you about you and your wife?"

"Relax your nerves," He replied casually. "Almost every being goes through heartache, humans and Ularu alike. I think she was afraid of being in love because of past abusive relationships. Shame her negative past affected you, I know that you loved her and treated her well. Sometimes after abuse, the spirit doesn't know how to act when they are treated with love, respect, and kindness. And I know you may not have expected an answer to your last question, but we Ularu don't get married or commit to one another for a lifetime even if we mate and have children, so I don't have a wife. I had a son, but I do not speak of him or his passing."

"Oh, I'm sorry about your son, I didn't mean to bring up a painful topic. I am just a little confused as to how the hell do you know all of this? And why the hell you even have an opinion on the matter?" I replied in confusion.

He laughed for a moment, "I have insight because it was very difficult for females in my culture when it was ruled by a dominator mentality, the way yours is now. Humans do not have a partnership based culture at all, for it is dominated by one gender and this ends up changing the view of what males and females should look like, act like, sound like, smell like and so on. Ularu culture once shared many of the same problems, only this was thousands and thousands of winters ago."

"So which gender is the one who are supposed to be in control then?" I asked quickly.

"One gender being in full control is never a good strategy." He replied with a patient sigh as he folded his hands in his lap, "A cooperation of the genders is what's needed. If humans are going to do the tribal-family structure, than you're the structure must have a balance of both gender's energies. Dominance on either side creates more problems than it solves."

I didn't have much to say on the topic; I was honestly a little upset that he brought it up. After some inner silence, E-Su shut his eyes and began to breathe deeply for a few minutes. Then he opened his eyes, stood up quickly and said: "Eat something from your bag. After you are done, I want to show you how I find peace when I am feeling bothered about things that I can not control. I am going to take you to the tree that you decided to stay under when you were feeling frustrated and depressed."

"You mean the inverted tree?" I asked.

"That's correct, now eat, then we will get going." He said motioning for me to go get something from my back pack. I only took me a few short minutes to eat, afterward I followed behind his large powerful steps.

We hiked the several miles to the tree rather quickly, E-Su moved very nimbly and quietly for such an enormous creature. His head didn't bob up and down with each step like it does with humans, its just stayed level and steady with each large step forward. When we arrived to the inverted tree E-Su sat on the ground next to the patchy gray trunk under the tree's overhanging roots and patted the soil

across from him. As I sat down, I curiously noticed his smell was no longer bothering me, I was wondering how this was possible when he spoke to me telepathically and broke up my thoughts.

"To get over the things I can not control I begin by inhaling deeply and feeling thankful for being alive. Remembering what a blessing it is to lift my eyes to the infinite skies and see eternity before me; I close my eyes and bring my first finger to my thumb. When my hand is in this position, I find peace at my core. I let go of all the desires that I cling to and I am thankful for simply having a living body.

When I achieve a deep enough state of self-realization, I switch my thumb to contact my middle finger. Then, I use my mind to see a root grow from the peace inside my body, down my spine and into the soil, connecting me to the earth. Then my Spirit becomes one with the Earth and all of the living beings in nature as a whole.

After becoming one with the earth I change fingers and put my thumb on my third finger. Then I identify my Spirit with the Sun, and the planets around it. After that, I touch my pinky to my thumb, and focus on identifying my Spirit with the core of our entire galaxy along with all of the countless stars and the life filling each planet. Once oneness has been fully embodied, I release my thumb and leave my palms open while I say this prayer out loud, and send this message to all beings that I connected with during my meditation:

I create the feeling and embrace the reality of all beings choosing here and now to imbibe peaceful prosperity, loving understanding, humble reverence, gratitude, honesty, integrity, and intuitive

wisdom. May all spirits do this while full of joyful independence, compassionate symbiosis, unified oneness, harmonious balance, careful creation, and eternal love for all, forever and ever.

Then I focus on giving all of the positive energy of my prayer away in equal portion to all the life that I became one with during my meditation. This releases my peace into the cosmos, and in the process, I end up getting the energy right back, especially if I am at my prayer tree or in the stone circle.

Through-out this prayer, something called the creative process is performed; the "creative process" is simply the use of thought, speech, and action to consciously make choices and create our life path through those choices. Visualizing these images is the thoughts, being followed with speaking the prayer's words, combining them both with the movement of my thumb to each different finger is the action. In this way, the being creating the prayer completes the creative process while sitting and remaining mostly unmoved.

A Spirit who conquers their inner demons is far more powerful than one who has conquered a thousand men in battle. If you ever get into a rough spot you can use this technique to draw in energy from all things around you, and you will be able to increase your strength and power by double. I used this technique several times during very rough portions of my life; now I give it to you."

"WOW! Thanks, E-Su, that's a cool prayer. I will have to try it sometime." I replied somewhat sheepishly.

"Why not now?" he asked.

“I guess I could do it right now,” I replied reluctantly. I sat down and performed the meditation as E-Su instructed, then I repeated his prayer out loud as he spoke it to me telepathically, and ironically I felt a million times better than I did after talking about Monique.

Eventually, we walked back to his cave, after stepping inside E-Su pointed down at a large pile of forest foliage stacked approximately 2 feet high on the cave floor and said "That's your bed. Try laying on it." This thought really rubbed me the wrong way, as I had no idea what could be living in foliage while I slept, and it was after this unpleasant surprise that I actually began to wonder how much I wanted to be there.

I could sense he knew this, so I smiled and nodded, even though the piles of branches did not look comfortable or clean, at all. I laid down some spare cloths on top of the foliage, and I wrapped myself in my sleeping bag as I slept. The" bed" was actually very comfortable to my surprise; it felt like I was floating on a soft cushy cloud. I came to find later that this was because of a bed blessing spell E-Su had put on the debris before I even arrived there.

Later on, I woke up in the middle of the night with a desperate need to take a leak, but I couldn't see anything in the dark, so I grabbed a flashlight from my backpack, put my shoes on and walked out the cave’s entrance. It was so dark outside that my tiny flashlight looked like a little spark adrift on a giant black ocean. As I was in the middle of reliving myself I heard something move in the distance. I shined my light where the sound came from, but I saw nothing.

I got a terrible feeling in the pit of my stomach, so I zipped up my jeans and started to walk backward. I heard a wolf howl ahead of me, followed by a bark to my left, then another on my right; I was about to turn and run when I heard a deep rumbling growl come from behind me. E-Su was right, the wolves knew I was in their territory, and in those bone chilling moments I was clueless on what to do.

As all the blood drained from my face, I turned around and shone the flashlight into the hungry eyes of a large gray wolf. It showed its teeth and licked its jowls as if it could already taste my flesh. I was frozen in the moment, petrified like scared prey. Everything had happened so quickly and I was lost in thought as to how or why this happened to me in the first place.

The wolf pounced and made a leap for my throat, but a stone suddenly struck it, causing it to yelp as it rolled onto the ground. Suddenly, I heard a deafening primal roar that was so loud; I felt the pressure wave hit my body before I heard the sound. When I turned around to see its source, I saw two angry glowing red eyes moving in the darkness of night. It was E- Su; he came out of the cave just in time to stop the pack of wolves from tearing me apart.

"Get inside the cave!" E-Su said urgently as he challenged the pack of wolves who had turned their focus his direction. After E-Su threw them around like rag dolls, they departed whimpering and injured as suddenly as they arrived. They fled into the night as I hastily made my way into the cave using my flashlight.

Afterward, E-Su walked into the cave and calmly said "Sleep. Tomorrow will be a full day.", Then he rubbed my head and walked into the darkness. Maybe the universe put those wolves there so I would finally feel safe with E- Su, I still don't know, but I understood then, what my intuition knew all along. E- Su meant me no harm, and I was safer there with him than I was inside the walls of my grandparent's cabin. Oddly, I got the strangest feeling of being at home as I lay on the bed of foliage, and E-Su felt for a brief moment as if he were a father figure. Then I rolled over and fell asleep.

Over the course of several weeks, E-Su and I had endless amounts of communication. I ate the food I brought with me or the food he gave me, I got water from local streams that E-Su showed me and my leg was so well healed that I forgot it was once broken. During this time, E-Su shared many of his personal views on life with me, as well as information about his species, its history, and the planet Earth's history as well. These conversations, more than anything, opened my mind in an almost frightening way, to the peculiar lens through which I and all humans perceived the world we lived in. He also spoke briefly about the history of humankind and possible futures for humanity given certain directions taken from that point forward. However, not all of these conversations will be included; this is for similar reasons to why E-Su would not share all of his secrets with me. His reason was that too much information at once can make the truth seem incomprehensible and all of my previous understandings would crumble under the weight of the full truth.

12) Ularu History

We sat near the entrance of the cave for another riveting conversation one morning when I asked:

"So do you have a community of Ularu that gather together in one spot? If so, how does your society work? What is your culture like? You do have a culture, right?"

He replied by taking a deep breath and saying "In order to tell you of my species way of life, I must first tell you about my species' history and how we ended up in this planetary realm."

"You are not from this planet?" I asked quickly.

"No, our race is from a planet called Ularu, which is where we get our species name from."

"So how did your race get here?"

He laughed out loud and said, "I will tell you, just let me say everything before you ask questions."

"Okay," I said and by the light shining through the cave's entrance, we began communicating telepathically.

"My race started off having a symbiotic relationship with the life on our home world." He said, "Our home planet was very much like this one, as planets like this are relatively common in the universe. Our species had a harmonic partnership between the two sexes, and we all acted like sacred gardeners and veterinarians for the plants and

animals. There was a beautifully balanced relationship existing between all of the species within the web of life that was our home world of Ularu. We had massive falls of clean water, oxygen-rich air, endless amounts of food bearing vegetation, even predators and prey lived in balance with one another; we also had natural cures for all forms of disease and illness. Our calendar was based off of the cycles of our sun and two moons, and allowed us to know with incredible accuracy the weather, and times of celestial events on which we would plan our ceremonies. These ceremonies allowed us to consciously connect with the spirit of our planet and all the life that existed on it.

As a species, we were on the verge of a breakthrough in the uses of the think, say and do aspects of the creative process; nearing the point of being able to create miraculous events. It was during this time in our evolution that we attained the ability to see into the spiritual, non-physical realms of life as well as the physical; it was also during this period that a group of the thirteen most powerful and cunning disembodied dark spirits in the universe, paid our planet a visit. Each dark predatory spirit, picked a very influential and strong leader in a different location of our world; then while the leader was alone, they each appeared before their prey disguised as a spirit of light, with a message and a proposition.

Each spirit said it had been sent from a distant planet, and had been instructed to aid our species in its evolution. But, their proposition was much more sinister, as it also said that the only way to impart the esoteric knowledge was to allow the spirit to fully possess their

body for a brief time. Which the spirits also explained could easily be accomplished through a very specific, but simple possession ritual performed inside a circle of fire. A process which they also promised would be entirely painless. The predatory spirits convinced each of the clan leaders that the new knowledge promised would make our whole species more powerful than they'd ever imagined.

All of the clan leaders agreed and in secret they each performed the possession ritual inside the circle of fire. It was only after the ritual was completed, that all the clan leaders discovered the truth. When each of their rituals was finalized, the spirit already inside the fiery possession circle with them, changed from its disguised form of light, into its true dark form. To the clan leader's horror the ritual was never meant to relay cosmic knowledge, it was designed to trick a spirit that housed a powerful physical body, into opening itself for absorption by a dark spirit. The fire turned black and blue as the circle became filled with a thick grey smoke pulsing with electricity, eventually surrounding each confused leader's body.

As the smoke enveloped their bodies, it seized them with electricity, wrapping their nervous system in a painful electric web which rendered the Ularu leaders incapable of resisting the dark spirit's possession. It was then they all realized they had unknowingly sacrificed themselves to the deceptive dark spirit who had approached them; then their body, mind and spirit's were fully absorbed and they were entirely possessed. This ritual allowed the dark spirit's full control of the Ularu leader's body, enabling them to use the possessed body to absorb the life energy from our planet into

themselves, through their continuous rituals of sacrifice. From then on each of the Ularu leader's bodies had a very dark field of sharp ghastly shadows always surrounding them.

At first, the dark spirits chose to masquerade as the charismatic leader, and displayed extraordinary powers to the local clans. After they convinced everyone that they too could reach this next stage in evolution, the possessed leader gathered everyone in the village together to stand inside of a magical circle. Little did they know the circle was designed to wipe their memories. In a flood of mental darkness everyone inside the circle had their memory erased by a single spell, and just like that our species lost all memory of its history and its relationship to the world we lived in. Afterward, our species did not know a time when we were not ruled over by the possessed leaders who we were to call Dark Lords.

After the dark spirits possessed our leaders and wiped our species' memories, they changed every aspect of our society. They gave us a new culture and a new history, making them our infallible Gods. The dark lords then became our highest authority, and once the authority of a culture is corrupted, there is no real law or order, there is only the illusion of law and order. We were to abandon all previous tasks and serve them in every way, including: performing all manner of sensual pleasure for them, tending to their every desire, destroying our environment for resource accumulation; in particular, mining metals and gold from our mountains for their personal adornment, consumption, accumulation and use in construction. Our species also had to perform all manner of ceremony, and ritual sacrifice in praise

of these dark lords. In some cases, those who served the dark lords were forced to give up their loved ones as a part of the ritual sacrifice to show their devotion. The first really significant change the dark lords made was they insisted only the males of our species be the decision makers in the clans; which effectively ruined our partnership between the sexes. After that both sexes argued and fought with one another instead of communicating and working together.

Then the dark lords gave us a different calendar totally erasing our sun and moons calendar. Through controlling our perception of time they erased all our sacred ceremonies. This was the second step to putting my ancestor's hearts and minds into a false reality. Once our populations grew in number, the dark lords continued their control through the use of monetary systems which were rooted in debt. Through this technique, our populations were controlled until their near extinction. The dark lords created systems to keep everyone busy by giving everyone meaningless jobs to acquire the money they had created. By removing spirits from the natural systems of their planet, and putting them into a false system constructed to serve the dark lord's agenda, the connection that my ancestors Spirit's had to the spirit of our planet was lost.

Then the dark lords began penning my ancestors together in communities of millions of Ularu. Each community was stacked next to one another in a line of tall buildings. Once everyone was packed tightly together, the dark lords created the illusion that food was scarce. The illusion of scarcity caused us to fight amongst one

another over the chemical products that the dark lords designed to look, smell, and taste like food but were, in fact, designed to keep our spirits from breaking their spells. They kept us alive to be their slaves, for their amusement, for their sensual pleasure, and for ritual sacrifice, nothing more.

My ancestors lived in those filthy, poverty filled skyscrapers for countless decades, while the dark lords enjoyed luxury inside the beautiful palaces and gardens they had us build for them. They kept almost every Ularu either diseased or depressed by keeping food scarce and filling everyone's mind with chemicals and terrifying lies. When an Ularu would discover a plant in the environment that cured a disease or broke their spell over our minds, the dark lords would kill that Ularu then forbid anyone from owning that plant.

Under the dark lord's rule, we had turned our beautiful planet into a toxic wasteland. The use of our world's natural resources as well as the dark lord's excessive metal mining polluted our pure waters and filled our clean air with poisonous fumes. By putting spell bound Ularu into large community buildings, everyone became much more easily conditioned from birth. After they had most everyone living in buildings, they used the invention of electricity to create music and entertainment that degraded our species' self-image, promoted territorial violence, and glorified debilitating substance abuse or embraced the dark lord's destructive culture. In this way, every Ularu young and old was given a worldview that embraced the destruction of the planet for the sake of our great Ularu civilization and its progression. In the end, this mentality lead to global war,

famine, slavery, poverty, and ruin.

Even if they had us under their spell, the dark lords knew eventually an overthrow would come. So, whenever they saw that the masses were ready to revolt, they would start wars between the clans that they commanded on our planet, which forced the Ularu men to kill one another instead of turning on the dark lords. While the Ularu men slaughtered one another, the dark lords used cultural programming to keep future rebellions suppressed. By keeping the women and children frightened of intense physical pain and the torture of their loved ones, the rest of the masses within our species were kept in mental cages without the need for a spell. The dark lords came to find they could use my ancestors primal instinct to live and see their loved ones live, as a very efficiently tool for manipulation. Their mindless culture kept my ancestors distracted and fighting each other, while the whole planet was destroyed all around them.

Once this destructive process became more and more unpredictable on the surface of the planet, the dark lords feared discovery and revolt with much suspicion. This led them to live underground and stop being worshiped as Gods; but they still continued their rituals of sacrifice. To ensure everyone forgot the Dark Lords even existence, incredible technologies of all sorts began to be dispensed to our species; making everyone more comfortable and distracted while this process got worse and worse all around them. The technologies acted like a coercive spell. It entertained everyone, while also keeping their intelligence low, thus stopping their spirit from waking to their

spellbound nature.

The dark lords made our slavery much more comfortable in this way, and we accepted it happily at that point. For countless millennia more, our culture continued this perverse and morally distorted view of ourselves and our planet. Which eventually caused the death of all planetary life, as well as our near extinction as a species leaving only six thousand Ularu left over from two billion.

After the dark lords had absorbed all they could, they opened a portal of darkness in a nearby mountain side, and shipped endless amounts of gold filled crates through the dark portal. After the few days it took to complete this process, the dark lords left the bodies of the thirteen leaders behind as dead useless meat. They had the energy they wanted within their spirits, and the gold was shipped back to their home world; there was no reason to stay on a dying planet. So, they left our world in a line of thirteen levitating dark distant orbs going through the black portal on the mountain side. The dark lords only choose life filled planets like Earth and Ularu for their parasitic desires. They go from one world to another, always taking over through the exact same methods. Then they leave the once life filled planet as a wasteland of death and destruction.

My species later came to find this whole process of planetary vampirism is so that the dark spirit's physical bodies may live eternally in another realm. By absorbing the life of entire ecosystems and eventually whole planets, these spirit's physical bodies act like immortal cosmic parasites. They know exactly how to use sacrificial

ritual as a tool of energy transmission and absorption. They somehow discovered a method of using the creative process to pull the life out of other physical bodies and absorb it into their disembodied spirit.

However, the absorption of an entire planet of energy was not as easy as absorbing a single spirit that invited the dark spirit into their body. So, to maintain their stable form of vampirism on our planet, they needed strong physical bodies, adapted to our world specifically, in order to complete the intense rituals. They also needed continuous sacrifices of any and all forms of life to fill their endless spiritual thirst. This is why they needed the powerful bodies of the clan leaders that were adapted to our particular planetary physics; they used these bodies to siphon the massive amounts of energy from our planet as well as wield their dark powers.

When this group of dark spirits arrives on a planet, over enough time all its life will eventually be sacrificed. Like a plague of spiritual locusts, this group continues absorbing all the worlds they find. After absorption, like clockwork, they create a black portal going back to their home planet inside the wasteland of each newly consumed world. Then each dark disembodied spirit returns to its physical body for a short time; which absorbs the life energy from the living spirits consumed on the foreign planet, keeping its physical body's life prolonged with each new refuel.

The dark lords left my ancestors there to die on what was left of our nearly dead world. None of those Ularu knew who they were, where they were from, or where they were going, one thing everyone did

know was, they were doomed. That was until a small, bright light shown through our planet's dirty gray skies. Suddenly this luminous object landed at my ancestor's feet, revealing itself to be a small humanoid being made of light. Without saying a word, the being lifted one of its hands, and everyone in the group of six thousand Ularu was healed of their diseases and flesh wounds. Afterward, the being pointed to the same nearby mountainside that the dark lords used for their black portal and a large opening of light appeared. Then, the being telepathically communicated to all six thousand Ularu and said to walk through to the other side if they want to live a better life, then it went through the light portal itself.

The eldest Ularu stepped through first, then everyone else followed; on the other side of the portal was this world we are living in now. The light being introduced us to this world and taught us the way that it works. It taught us what to eat and what not to eat, what animals to watch out for and the best ways to use the plants and the environment around us. It showed us the primary uses of the think, say and do portions of the creative process; then it said it must go. However, before it left it telepathically spoke a message to everyone saying:

'It is imperative that you and your children do not worship or idolize me as a God like you did with the dark lords. I have imparted to you, enough knowledge to gain similar abilities to the ones you have seen me perform. You are extraordinarily powerful spirits, and you must act as such. Work with the plants of this planet; they will help you to remember the history that was stolen from you. If you develop a symbiotic relationship with all nature in every way possible, you will survive far longer. With enough faith in yourselves, your Spirits will eventually be able to accomplish anything. There are other intelligent beings here, work with their leaders if you can, help them to evolve if you can, love one another as you love yourselves, and you will suffer far less as individuals and as a species. All of what has happened and is happening will make far more sense in the future, allow your confusion about things to inspire curiosity in your hearts, not frustration. All will be made clear in its time.' A light portal opened in the middle of the air, and the being stepped through and vanished as the portal quickly closed.

14) Ularu Culture

E-Su elaborated further on his culture.

"After my ancestors watched the light being leave this world, they talked for weeks as to what we should do in this new world. In the end it was determined that due to the destructive nature of the dark lord's culture, which was all we knew; we must first dissect its remains and find out what was wrong with it at its core and do the opposite.

After several years of staying in a close group and exploring the memory of their spirits, the group of six thousand became certain of a few things: first, every culture's cornerstone is the relationship it

has to its environment. Second, through the use of the environment as well as a healthy interaction and communication with other life forms in that environment, cultures are born; third, it is on this foundation that cultures grow and take different shapes. They take different shapes as they each explain, understand, and perform -- what we Ularu call—'the unstoppable processes of life' in unique ways.

These unstoppable processes are, sleeping, dreaming, mating, birthing, and dying. And from these fundamental processes working themselves out in our day to day lives, other complexities develop. For example, the need for food, water, shelter, friendship, love, tool building, child raising, ethics, and spiritual growth. How each of these things are managed and imparted to the next generation is through methods used by our ancestors.

The methods of our ancestors have always played a role in all species behavior. Only, we Ularu lost the memory of our ancestor's true ways due to millennia of generations of our species being under the spell of dark lords. Only through an intense examining of the truth, massive amounts of dream exploration, and asking for the help of Earth's plants, did my ancestors find the evolutionary origins of our species was accessible in the code of their DNA. From there they spiritually observed our whole species enslavement unfold and that is how we know the story of our past.

After watching their entire history play out in front of them, my ancestors concluded that cultures which denied fixed views of reality

were the only social structures flexible enough to allow for growth of the individual's Spirit as well as the collective whole. So, my ancestors changed our culture to factor in the mistakes of the dark lords and the intuitive wisdom of our culture prior to their meddling; shaping a new culture entirely from a mutual understanding between Spiritual freedom and personal responsibility. They called this new form of transcended culture, Shama.

Ultimately, Shama is the use of one's abilities as a conscious spirit with a physical body, to know one's self as a Spirit instead of a body; combined with the use of this spiritual awareness to perceive reality as it is for itself. Shama allows for total social freedom, if you want to have a family life, you could do that, if you wish to be left alone you may do that, if you wish to have multiple mates you can do that too. If you wish to gather a clan in large numbers you may do that also, though very few of us gather in large numbers like you humans. Some of us move with the seasons, but many of us stay in one place for several winters. It does not matter which path is chosen, we Ularu are taught to view each and every one of our kind as family.

As said before the shape a culture takes is based on the unstoppable processes of life (and their emergent properties), being explained and performed in different ways. These explanations and performances are expressed through various forms of what you humans call Art. We Ularu believe Art is the expression or application of creativity and imagination. Which includes all kinds of activities such as music, cooking, shelter creation, hunting and gathering, fire building, animal raising, love making, architecture and the list goes on. While

you are staying here with me I am going to show you many forms of art that I personally have mastered.

Everything in life is a form of Art to the Ularu, and because Art can change based on the individual, the shape a culture takes is moldable as well. Given this information, it is easy to see how it is possible to mold a culture in the most harmonic modality possible or in the most destructive modality that only profits a small few.

For this reason, the first change we Ularu made to ensure our species survival was to make all our individual decisions while bearing in mind the children living six generations ahead of ourselves. We Ularu do not take any action if it is believed it will negatively effect the generations ahead of our own; which is the exact opposite of the dark lord's policy of consuming for greed, only to waste for comfort.

The ancestors realized that if a change in our culture was desired, the best way to create that change would be to change their own personal bad habits which affected the generations to come in a negative way. Acting as if their individual actions made a difference, was the first step. We, therefore, believe in order for the future generations to be ensured, we Ularu must always reject any cultural model if it runs counter to the interests of the those generations best interest. This is the reason why it is so vital that everyone discover the truth of their spiritual being for themselves. They must see for themselves the truth about their connection to that future generation. That is the only way they may know the real power which they wield on the future of our children and choose to use it wisely. The guide may show us the path,

but we must always walk the path on our own.

Once Shama was our new model for living, everyone's primary focus was their own relationship to their Spirit and all creation as a whole. As opposed to focusing on converting others to their personal view of the world, they instead focused on making their own view as clear as possible. This created a loving blend of understanding connection and boundary abandonment; everyone embraced themselves as their own Shama while respecting one another as a Shama as well, learning from one another, and loving each other with the same acceptance as they have for themselves and all life. This created more symbiosis and abundance for an infinitely longer period than ever before, one that is still lasting to this day. Doing what is best for the individual and the group by thinking of future generations has taken us much farther for far longer, then competing for independent abundance ever allowed.

When we rebuilt our society, we thought it would be best and most productive, if everyone practiced their own Art of Shama. My ancestors believed that if everyone practiced their own form, we would have little need for experts. Because we openly share knowledge and discoveries, the best ideas would spread like fire. Everyone would be empowered with the same tools and would have the same power to transform their lives in the best ways known. Growth and evolution are the keys to survival, though ruthless in some ways, this new culture required every Ularu young and old to accept responsibility for themselves and their impact on the world around them.

This is the reason Shama is so effective in deterring spiritual derailment, it takes on many different forms which most individuals can make their own in one way or another. There are five different categories of Shama specialty: The Healer, the Adventurer, the Visionary, the Warrior and the Artist; each category has a different specialty. The healer knows how to heal themselves and others; the adventurer explores their own spiritual being, including the other spiritual realms and the natural world itself. The visionary receives visions of the future or the past; they can see spirit fields and are given grand epiphanies about the truth of reality. The warrior path involves a lot of pain and suffering to still one's mind to new levels of peace which transcend the flesh, creating an intense spiritual awareness, most Ularu don't have what it takes to walk this path. The Artists Shama is the master of all of these roles into one extremely powerful Spirit. The Artist Shama often combine all of these techniques, giving them the added ability to use the creative process in specific miraculous ways only known to the few who have achieved that level of awareness and understanding. But that understanding can not be taught, it has to be learned on ones own or not at all. In one or all of these roles, every Ularu acts as their own Shama after their initiation.

While every aspect of daily life varies from individual to individual, all Ularu are told what happened in our history and why things are the way they are now; all are taught the same basic survival skills in the wild, plus basics self-defense techniques. It is also during this time that culture is explained and thus how to interact as an integral

part of nature. We ensure each and every Ularu reaches its maximum potential.

A fully mastered Artist Shama acts as its own healer, protective warrior, moral authority, spiritual adviser and loving friend wrapped into one package. I am an Artist Shama and have been for many, many winters, hence the tattoo on my forehead; there are several different levels after achieving the first basic level of Shama. The first basic level is an initiation ceremony that all Ularu must go through after twenty-eight winters, this ceremony is called the spiritual rebirth. This is because in the Ularu belief the planets are in the same spots at age twenty-eight as they were when you were born. For this ceremony, the initiate consumes a plant that allows them to leave their body and explore the cosmos as well as their entire personal history up to that point in time.

The lack of an intensely profound coming of age ceremony in which the maturing human's Spirit travels outside of the body is one of the many reasons your materialist culture is so distorted in its views of reality. Having no out of body initiation ceremony to guide your youth to its own sacred spirit creates for a lack of self-awareness and thus no honor or self respect.

Once the Ularu has completed their spiritual rebirth ceremony, the individual can explore their own consciousness at will and choose a path of Shama for themselves. We believe that if a spirit is not free to explore its own consciousness, then it will inevitably become a slave to some form of lifeless law and thus the will of others. This is why

we believe this ceremony is so important, because it gives a perspective that will change the course of the rest of one's life.

If an Ularu feels it is near the end of its life, we use vision plants for those who wish to facilitate facing their death. Afterward, if an Ularu is ready to die, then we have a ceremony for that as well. Unless through terrible misfortune, all Ularu die at a very old age and by choice. We have a very particular kind of ceremony involving the consumption of a fatal plant and the cremation of the Ularu's body after forty-nine days. We believe this is the only way a being can be reincarnated consciously. This is why we Ularu do not mourn our dead for long, as we believe all spirits reincarnate as different life forms determined by their spirit's post mortem desires. Many Ularu children have remembered their past lives and have spoken of events or objects that they could not possibly have known about. This is why we believe so strongly in this truth, the reason I believe it so strongly is, I am one of these children." Then the telepathy stopped abruptly. I assumed this was my opportunity to communicate in return.

"Wow!" I said while still fully absorbing the load of information I just received. My mind was completely distracted from my original question and entirely focused on the notion of the Dark Lords being here on earth, so I brought it up, "Forgive me for backtracking, but I didn't want to interrupt you when you talked about the dark lords. A lot of the things you said the dark lords did on your planet seem to be exactly the same as the things that are happening here on earth."

"I know." he said, "Most of the Ularu live in the wilderness for this

reason alone, this is also the reason we do not gather in high numbers like you humans and we do our best to remain hidden. We do not wish to get entangled with the dark lords again, for we fear they will wipe us out. Their presence here on earth is the reason your species has become so hostile. We have already seen a large drop in our population since their arrival. Many Ularu suspect they may already know we are here, so we avoid humans and their cities as much as we can, but the dark lords culture keeps on expanding the size of human cities and this expansion keeps them reaching further and further into the lands where we hide. We fear that if the dark lords are not stopped soon, the Ularu will have nowhere else to run or hide, and we will become extinct."

"But how in the hell would we stop them E-Su? If they have done this to a bunch of other planets, how can we just stop them all of a sudden? That seems pretty fucking improbable to me." I responded in a worried telepathic jolt.

"They can be stopped." He replied smoothly and confidently. "Right now your species is early enough in the parasitic absorption process to expel them from this planet forever. If the people of this world incorporate the ways of Shama into their lives and learn how to consciously use the creative process, your species will be able to recognize the truth about the Dark Lords and the fact that they have hijacked your planet. I would like you to try to imagine what a different world you would live in if half of this world practiced a form of Shama. When you consider such a possibility, it's easy to see how your kind has become as domesticated as house pets; your

refrigerators are your feeding bowls, your massive cities and tall buildings are your pens, and your phones are your leashes. Your kind is just the way we Ularu used to be on our home world.

Only now the entire Ularu species lives a free, non-domesticated life thanks to Shama being a part of our culture. Food is abundant and free among our species, and no Ularu goes hungry. There is no parasitic government or monetary system to regulate goods or tax us. Yet, everyone is taken care of with equal care, because all Ularu works off of a selfless service mentality. We have cures for all diseases and illnesses in the environment using the resources made available to us by the planet. There is no pollution created by our way of life, nor is there any illusions of scarcity and thus no crime. Shama has shown us the course to a mutually beneficial way of living. Only through the loving, compassionate exploration of our spirit and the world around us, can we live fully as a Spirit. Does that make sense?" He turned his head inquisitively.

I agreed and said, "It all makes perfect sense to me E-Su."

He smiled and replied "Good, it is for these reasons and many others, that it is so important that your species adopt the Shama way of life. It is the only way to empower your spirits and free your minds from the clutches of the dark lords. If not your entire planet will die. We Ularu shared many of the same social problems as your species does now; the dark lords arrived on this planet at the same point in your evolution as they did with us on Ularu. Your medicine men were beginning to discover the truths about reality and their immense

power as physical conscious beings. This is why the time is now, you humans must change your ways, or it will soon be too late!"

I scoffed in a defensive manner then said, "You act like all of the problems the world has are because of the humans. I mean if we are being manipulated by some group of cosmic parasitic assholes, then it's not fully our fault, is it? Why are you so critical of humans if your species use to be just like us?"

"Most of the destruction that is currently in the world is due to destructive human behavior on behalf of the dark lords, yes." He replied, "I am not being critical of humans. Humans have the power just as we Ularu did, to stop the planet's destruction and their extinction. If your species wakes up from the spell it's been put under, and starts using the creative process to create things to solve the world's problems; then the planet can be saved and your spirits will no longer be enslaved. Once the dark lord's spell has been lifted, then symbiotic harmony can be seen in your species future and pursued by everyone with eyes to see it.

The catastrophic problems can only be corrected by humans embracing the truth about their own conditioned behaviors and consciously behaving differently. If the people performing the destruction change from being a blind fool to a conscious, connected part of the planet, then the destruction can be ceased and repaired. This will cause the dark lord's cultural programming to be dissolved. Then they will be seen for what they are and all the spirits of the world—human and Ularu alike—can unite in banishing them from

this planet forever. If they do not get the energy they need, then they will starve and die."

With skepticism and doubt, I said "So do you really think that Shama can save our whole species E-Su? I mean how can it be that simple? I don't understand? Just because people eat fresh veggies and fruits, or eat some magic mushroom doesn't mean the problems of the world will get solved, even if everyone started doing that right now. I mean, I am convinced that the way of Shama is a better path for long term living, but I just don't see how the world will ever be able to see it without being out here with you and me experiencing the bliss of this perspective for themselves."

"I had similar doubts and I said many of the same things to my teacher about you humans. But these are his lessons I am giving you and it was by his advice that I decided to make contact with you at your campsite. It was he that predicted you would be under the inverted tree nearly 100 years ago. And it is he that declared the Ularu way of Shama will liberate your species from the dark lord's clutches, and thus bring this entire planet into the realms of light and love.

Even with my teacher's hopeful words considered, I still understand and acknowledge many of your doubts are valid. What you don't understand is that your species was on the right path for thousands of years before the Dark Lords took over. The memory of your true history is much easier to recall than our own because it is far more recent. This puts your species in a very unique position. For it was

not too long ago that tasks which used to be handled by the most compassionate and wise men—the medicine men—were handed over to the ruthless and selfish businessmen of the world. The dark lords disempowered the medicine men and thus your entire species.

When your people used to get sick, they would go to the medicine man. Now, they go to a salesman in a white coat called a doctor. It uses to be the tribe's majority that decided who their leaders were going to be. Now, you have a selection process made to look like an election, with puppet candidates acting as false leaders. They are henchmen for the dark lords and continue to keep everyone enslaved in exchange for their own personal luxury and power. These business men have no interest in leading your people to freedom or exposing the truth.

In many cases in your history, the medicine men use to help with and in some cases cure, the mentally ill. Now your culture sticks these people in padded rooms and gives them pills, or cut out parts of their brain until they act calm enough to be considered sane. The current system does not try to cure the self-destructive mental patterns of a spirit in pain; they only perpetuate its cycle for the sake of the massive amount of profit it produces. Granted there is so much chaos in your world right now that locking some people up is the only alternative, next to death that is. It is so terrible that such a blessed place as this planet and such a magnificent species as yours has been subjected to such terrible atrocities.

Countless medicine men use to help and counsel the people who were

considered "criminals" in human society. Now, your prisons are filled with people in small confined cages. In many cases, people live in these cages for decades, just because they possessed a mind-altering plant that lifts the spells of the dark lords.

Your military leaders are paid men of business, not real warriors full of Spirit. They do not lead their forces from the front the way the warriors of old did, they are wealthy businessmen who treat people like numbers and speak orders from behind a safe desk as if...."

I interrupted him and said "Hold on a second E-Su, I am really sorry to interrupt, but now I really feel like I am going fuckin crazy. How the hell could you possibly know all of this stuff about our human world and culture? I mean you live in the bush, out in the middle of the fuckin wilderness. That makes absolutely no sense to me, so please explain. Am I really going crazy or do you know way more about us humans and our culture than you should?" He took a deep breath and sighed. Then he closed his eye and grinned as he shook his head back and forth slowly causing the dreadlocks on his chin to bounce around at their base. He looked at me then replied in a very matter of fact, but gentle tone.

"Your interruption is considered rude amongst the Ularu. But, I will answer your questions. It is true, yes; we Ularu live in the forests, swamps, jungles and endlessly vast wildernesses all over the planet. But, we also know all about the way the creative process works, even to miraculous proportions.

We communicate worldwide and we can do so without the use of

small silicone and metal devices sending radioactive signals to one another. We use our bodies and their connection to the earth as our tools for communication. We use the wireless electronic web of the earth's magnetic field to communicate with one another on a global scale. We also use it for electric-power whenever we need electricity, which is rare, but easily accomplished. We use this net of energy that connects all species on this planet for many things, in fact, we use it so often that we developed a term for it. We call it the Life-Net, and it allows me to know many things that you will not understand right now even if I told you.

To answer your other question, yours isn't the only human mind I have read in my long lifetime. Throughout my life, I have telepathically siphoned many things from the minds of campers, military employees, and top secret government officials; plus, I am several hundred winters old. During the last hand full of centuries, I have telepathically conversed with some of the greatest minds of your species. I am sure they would have been amazed to find out the voice they heard was coming from an Ularu.

If an Ularu sees your species' mining operations dumping countless gallons of deadly toxic waste and chemicals into a river that everyone in the area drinks from, we must leave that area and tell others to avoid it; we do this by using the Life-Net. If your species tests terribly destructive, highly top secret weapons in the wilderness. Or the government flies its anti-gravity black project vehicles where they think no-one is watching, at least one Ularu sees it and tells everyone where to avoid. If your species destroys countless acres of

sacred jungle in the Amazon rainforest to create a farm where cattle are maliciously abused, slaughtered and processed for consumption, we Ularu all know about it because we see it, we smell it, we feel the pain and we are hurt deeply by it. We live in those jungles and we communicate with the trees and the wildlife that dwell within it; you have no idea the suffering caused by the destruction of that holy jungle. We always know what your species is doing and to ensure our continued survival we use the Life-Net to make sure that everyone else in the species knows as well.

If your species is digging up rock and dirt to create massive deep underground military bases and enormous tunnels connecting each one; its construction is always known about, and their connecting caves are intentionally avoided. If there are top secret wireless frequencies used to relay messages, codes or signals, you had better believe we are enlightened enough to perceive them and are smart enough to decode them.

We are spirits with bodies, not bodies with spirits; we are able to do these things which you humans would call magic, only because we have evolved far beyond the limited perspective given to you by the dark lords. We know more about your species actual history than you do because we must know to survive and not be captured, killed, or experimented on." I was shocked and appalled at how horribly we humans had affected the Ularu and the planet as a whole. "Don't look so shocked Will, you ask me how and why I know these things, I know because my whole species must know these things, for our lives depend on it."

I felt an equal mix of morose, irate, invigorated and disgusted after he stopped his communication. Then I suddenly had an epiphany, I was supposed to be the first human to learn and walk the Ularu path of Shama, and this was why I kept having my reoccurring dream. I'd been lead to the forest to discover the way of this lost way of life, so I could free the human race from the powerful spells of the dark lords. This rush of understanding prompted me to ask, "E-Su, I think learning the Ularu ways of Shama is the reason I was led to the forest and that inverted tree of yours. Would you be willing to teach me the ways of Shama?"

E-Su remained silent with his eyes closed for several minutes; then he smiled a massive grin, and a single tear rolled down his cheek. "It would be an honor to teach you the ways of the Shama. But you must first do the Ularu cleansing to get rid of the dark lord's cultural conditioning and the four walls of personal inhibition. Don't bother asking what that is; you will find out in time. After that you will be given a tour of the cosmos, then after that, you will be ready for your spiritual rebirth. Only after this process will you be able to learn the ways of the Shama, but not from me, for your potential should be fostered by my teacher if he will accept you."

"Do you think he will accept me?" I inquired.

"I don't know; It depends on how you do with the first three ceremonies. If you want to do this, nothing would make me happier than to be the one to prepare you for this path, but I must warn you there is a very real danger of losing your mind or physically harming

yourself if you cling to tightly to the dark lord's spells of confinement. So, you must be absolutely sure before you embark down this path. Just be sure to think about what I have told you and reflect on the path you desire to take. For this is not a fleeting interest or a hobby, it will change everything in your life!" He got up and walked out of the cave, and I was left to contemplate his radical notion of insanity or self-harm as a possibility on the path I thought was supposed to be peaceful and liberating. I remained sitting, we had been communicating all day and he certainly left the cave at an opportune time. I don't know if it was my fear of radical change or the last of my ego fighting to stay alive but later on that night after I fell asleep, I woke up and had a panic attack which rocked me to my core.

15) Piercing My Cocoon

I awoke in the cave, confused and disorientated, causing me to wander around in a clueless daze for some time. All the while wondering *Am I dreaming? Why can't I see? And what exactly is happening to me?* **A cycling rush of profound confusion and fear kept a slew of new unanswered questions surfacing in my mind, never giving my brain enough time to respond to its own inquiry. As I wandered around in the darkness, I heard loud, heavy breathing in the distance and began to panic. Then after a while I finally remembered that I was living in a cave out in the wilderness with an**

Ularu. However, it was upon this reflection of circumstance that the full implications of those facts hit me; E-Su being real meant that the world was not only far stranger than I had supposed, it was far stranger than I possibly could have ever imagined. After wandering in the dark for a short while longer my feet hit the foliage of the bed E-Su had made for me, so I laid down and tried to sleep.

Only my mind wouldn't stop racing as I continued to wonder: *Was E-Su real? Were these telepathic experiences scientifically possible? Was the realness of the experience the driving force that led me to believe it was an illusion? Or was the total collapse of my mental world urging me to believe that the "science-based worldview" was the only real world there was? What if rational materialism, was using the conveniences and technologies it provided, as illusionary proof of accurately discovering the truth about reality? How would I know which was the case? Was it crazy to want to stay in the remote forest with E-Su and learn the ways of the Shama? Was it insane to want to see where this odd path led? Real or illusion? Magic or Madness? Was it lunacy to live in a world where the mythical Bigfoot existed as a very real and intelligent race called the Ularu from another planet? Was it crazy to believe their race communicated via telepathy and had profound wisdom about the secrets of the Earth and Cosmos? Was this the remote and less traveled path to enlightenment? Or a giant step toward total self-destruction and insanity? What if someone was aware of their mental illness, would that make them saner*? **These thoughts raced like cars for first place inside my head until dawn, and I got no sleep after my panic attack.**

When the light of the sun started to enter the cave, I got off my bed

of foliage and walked outside to look around and collect my composure. It was only another minute when I heard E-Su lumber up from behind me. He stood near my side and put his arm around my shoulder.

As we both looked into the forest he said, "You've been taught to fear, mistrust, and expect pain from the unknown in almost every way. This is the dark lord's prison for your mind, the Truth about reality is much more empowering than that! You will inevitably have to purge that perspective to move forward on the path of Shama. You can't expand awareness that wishes to stay confined, nor can you fill a cup that's already full; it's the same thing with your mind."

My intuition sensed some mysterious force was guiding my every move, and to turn back at that point would surely mean a life of mediocrity and meaningless repetition. If I did turn my back on this opportunity, I would unarguably live a life based on a lie and die full of regret for having passed up on this once in a lifetime opportunity. I looked up at E-Su and said out loud in English: "I am sure I want to be a Shama E-Su, in fact, I have no doubt in my mind."

My head felt better, it didn't hurt at all anymore when we spoke telepathically, but I wanted to say it out loud. There was something about saying those words that felt completely human to me. I wanted to learn the ways of the Shama, but I also wanted to retain my humanity as well, which I was determined to do from that moment forward, even if it meant the death of my ego.

"Good," E-Su said "Now begins your training. I meditate every

morning after I stretch. If you start your day off on the right foot in this way than it is easier to stay walking the right path. Many of your human yogis use this same formula when they wake up."

I felt a sudden rush of weightlessness come over my body as I realized, E-Su was showing me how to get on the path of daily growth. My intuition rang like a bell, and so after doing some stretching I sat next to E-Su, closed my eyes and tried to meditate. I found it very difficult to clear my mind at first, as I was still processing all of the experiences I had gone through in the weeks of communication prior. So I telepathically asked for help from E-Su but got nothing in return. I didn't understand why he wasn't responding; little did I know E-Su did not reply because I had to learn to overcome the struggle of quieting my mind on my own. I tried for an hour to no avail and felt disheartened. When the hour was over, E-Su patted me on the back and said, "Let's go to the circle. You may have better luck there."

We made our way to the circle in silence, E-Su seemed distant, and I didn't understand why. Once we stepped in the circle of white stones, he spoke.

"Did you know that if you help a butterfly out of its cocoon, it will not be strong enough to live?"

"No. I didn't know that, is that true?"

"Yes, for a butterfly to get all the blood into its wings it must first crawl through the hole that it made in its cocoon. As the butterfly crawls its way out of that tiny little hole in its cocoon it gains the

strength that it needs to survive outside its cocoon. Through the process of escaping its cocoon, the butterfly may gain the strength to overcome obstacles that it will face outside of the cocoon including its first flight. If I help you in the ways that you want help, you will be the butterfly that was aided out of its cocoon, and your potential will die with you. You can do too much good for the world for me to allow my compassion to override my logic. I made that mistake once already, and I won't again. I helped one apprentice, one time and that was all it took."

"Why? Why did you help?" I asked

"Because it was early on in her training and I didn't really know better at the time." he replied, "I felt sorry for her, so I helped a little. I did not know, I created instability in her spiritual foundation and when things got really heavy, she crumbled. That's why I can't give you any of the answers Will. I can only show you the door; I can only lend you the technique. You must find your own way of meditating; you must find your own way of discerning what is real and what is not, you must make your mind up about everything in reality on your own, based off of your experiences, not just the words or experiences of others. If you build yourself in your own way, when things get heavy in life, you will not crumble under the pressure."

"What you mean when you say 'when things get heavy'? that doesn't make sense to me?" I asked.

"When you stack profound spiritual understandings atop of one another, either the spirit's foundation breaks or it remains solid. If it

remains solid, it causes the vibration that particular spirit emits to increase exponentially with each new cycle of understanding. But, if the understandings accumulate on top of a compromised spiritual foundation, the immensity becomes too much to process and the mind collapses. By giving you the answers, I give you a compromised foundation to build on. By finding the answer yourself, you base your entire internal spiritual understanding on your heart's intuition, not logical conclusions made in your brain. The heart at the core of the body is the only thing strong enough to handle the immensity of endless spiritual awareness without collapse. The reason for this I will not explain just yet but will be explained later in your training." His eyes pierced mine with intensity then we both heard something that broke our telepathic connection.

While we stood in the white circle of stones, we heard the sound of somebody shouting. There was another yell; it was someone calling my name. I listened carefully and once again I heard my name being yelled by a new but familiar voice. It sounded like my mother, and then I heard Isaac's voice, followed by a third voice that sounded like Monique's. Then I heard other voices that I didn't recognize; I concluded then that it was my search party. My heart began to race, and my palms began to sweat. I didn't know what to do.

I looked to E-Su, and he said, "Tell me now. Do you want to stay or not?" My mind raced, I did want to stay, but going back to my old life sounded way easier at that moment.

This was my opportunity to go back to the familiar, I thought,

Monique was there, so she obviously did care about me, and I am sure I had everyone worried sick. My mind raced while my heart pounded. I looked at E-Su, and he could see the doubt in my eyes, mixed with fear and pain. Then a butterfly fluttered by above my head and I thought about the butterfly analogy that E-Su had given me. I knew then that I wanted to walk the path of the Mystical for myself and I was sure I wanted to stay. E- Su read my mind, and put his hands on both my shoulders then said: "This may be a little disorienting."

Suddenly I felt all of my surroundings accelerate upward, everything had turned into varying shades of a color I had never seen before, there was a loud high pitched white noise that surrounded us and the pressure I felt all around my body was dense but easily broken. Our bodies were in standard color, but the bushes and trees around me were vibrating with a varying foreign color that had a static charge to it. I heard people yelling my name as they got closer and closer, then I heard Monique in particular as she was making her way toward us. Everyone else seemed to be making their way through the forest nearby while she, in particular, ironically walked right through the stone circle.

I could see the worry on her face as she yelled my name. I could feel the concern she had for me emanating from her body as she walked through the circle. Coincidentally, she stopped right next to where we were standing and looked around; she apparently could not see E-Su and I standing right in front of her. I saw a single tear rolled down her cheek as she yelled my name, then she held her nose in

disgust. I guess E-Su could not hide his smell, even if we were invisible to her eyes. I wanted to say something to her, but I knew I shouldn't, my heart was so torn at the time, and it was physically painful. I reached my trembling hand out, bringing it inches from her face. With my eyes overflowing with tears, I pulled my hand back, and she moved forward continuing to call out my name as she covered her nose with her shirt.

Holding back the desire to touch her was one of the most difficult things I had ever experienced. More than anything I wanted to tell her that I still loved her and I still wanted her. However, the knowledge and understanding I had received thus far from E-Su seemed to be the strange and mystical path I had always desired to walk in my life; only I never believed it would be a possibility for me. I figured if Monique's decision to leave me led me to live my dreams, then she was my angel like I always said she was.

That was when I heard E-Su say "Congratulations, you poked a hole in your cocoon, now we must go, don't worry no-one can see us."

Despite his praise, I was rather despondent on the quiet, careful walk back to the cave. It wasn't about Monique however, I was morose because I finally fully understood in those fleeting moments, that I could never return to my old life like I imagined I could before I decided to stay with E-Su; which was saddening to me on several levels at the time. I was going to be forever changed by the decisions I had made in those brief few seconds. In front of me was an entirely unknown ocean of possibilities, an ocean on which, despite E-Su's

interesting company, I was lonely and adrift. I felt alone for the first time since I started my journey with E-Su, for only then did I realize that I had no other human I could relate to in the whole world. If the dark lord's spell over my spirit was going to be broken, I would be among the smallest minority of humans on the planet.

Once we got back to the cave I collapsed onto my bed. My heart was broken for a short time, but it was also stronger than it had ever been. I suddenly stopped being depressed and despite my less than hygienic state I began feeling happy and refreshed. I was renewed and very sure of the path I had chosen, I could almost hear the sound of empowering music emanating from the cosmos as I got up and started to laugh hysterically. As the echoes of my laugh filled the cave, the metaphorical emotional storm passed, and the enlightening sun of my inner spirit shone on my chosen magical path, I knew I made the right choice. E-Su walked into the cave "Happy you let your old perspective go?" he asked in a playful tone.

"Yes, I have and I am ready to walk the path of Shama E- Su," I said confidently, "Bring on the next step!"

"Good." He said, "Now that you have a hole in your cocoon, next you begin the climb out. What we Ularu call the Om Hee Wha Ha. It means something like spiritual cleansing in your language. We were going to the stone circle today to start that process, but it seems you were supposed to let your old life go today and start your new life tomorrow."

"Okay that makes sense," I said, I hesitated for a moment then spoke

quickly "Forgive me for asking, but how did you turn us invisible? And why was everything in a color I had never seen before?"

His big dark lips smiled revealing the white of his teeth in the dark of the cave before he replied "Remember what I said about being given the answers? You are a growing butterfly, if I tell you I would be giving you an answer. I did what I had to do to get us out of the circle without being seen, invisibility was not on my agenda today."

Putting two and two together I asked: "Is that same trick how you disappeared right in front of me that one time after we first met?"

"Yes." He replied, "Had you decided to leave today, I would have wiped your memory and allowed you to believe you have been lost in the forest for almost a month. Because you chose to stay I turned you and I both invisible, I did this by tuning both our spirits to be just outside of the human eye's visible frequency range; that's why everything was a color you had never seen before. But, to answer as to how it was done would risk your sanity."

"Try me." I said confidently, "I have been able to handle things so far."

"No." He replied firmly, "It is a complex understanding and you must first comprehend many another truths before you will understand that power. You just focus on taking one balanced step at a time, and you will gain the most progress, okay?" I could sense the severity and the seriousness of the situation. E-Su was not upset, but I could tell he would get upset if I pressed the issue any further. Unfortunately, my desire to test the limits combined with my

curiosity and I chose to press the issue once again a short time later.

"What harm can it do to me E-Su? I am just curious. I mean, can't you just tell me or show me somehow through telepathy?"

He narrowed his eyes and shook his head then said, "If you really want to know what will happen if you are given answers that you aren't ready for, I will show you tomorrow. I am going to take you to meet the apprentice that I helped and thus handicapped for life. However, I am going to warn you; it may prove to be dangerous."

"Well, here I am in the middle of the wild talking to an Ularu, how much more dangerous can it get?"

He laughed hysterically, his nose snorted, his belly popped in and out and his hand slapped the ground as he rocked back and forth before saying, "You will see for yourself tomorrow! You just wait!"

15) The Witch

The next morning I walked out of the cave to see E-Su was outside stretching, I tried to make conversation with him, but his vibe seemed to be closed off. His telepathy on this morning was very matter of fact, and my vibe was definitely more excited than his was for this meeting. I wondered to myself what had happened to the warm, gentle character I had spoken with the weeks before. I thought that maybe I had offended him by questioning his judgment the

previous night.

E-Su unexpectedly replied to my personal quandary telepathically "I am being serious with you because this is a deadly serious matter. If you want to know why I can't give you answers, I will show you why."

"Okay," I said, "but still, why so serious? Did I offend you?" I asked intrigued.

"No, you did not offend me. I am serious because learning the ways of Shama is a serious matter, especially if the apprentice tries to rush the process. Now that you have chosen to learn the Shama way I will take you to see the witch, who is a result of rushing the process. If you want to take this life path, you must know the risks and see what the dangers are for yourself." he tilted his head slightly to one side and said "So cheer up, I am not mad, but I know when to be serious, as all mature beings do."

I had an incredibly deep fear of witches growing up, and I replied with worry by just saying, "The witch?"

"I only use that word because that is the only word in your head that comes close to what she is."

I was confused so I asked for more details, "What is she E-Su?"

"We call her kind, 'Poloota Shan' which means 'Demon's Tool,' her body is an empty spiritual vessel which demonic earthbound spirits have possessed in mass numbers, thus combining their strength making them all more powerful. They use her body to suck the life

out of lost hikers and children, or the trees of the forest itself to keep their dark spiritual thirst quenched."

I laughed nervously because while growing up I had heard endless creepy stories from my Hispanic babysitter about the witches in the forests and deserts of Mexico. She said they keep themselves young by stealing the souls of children and weak adults. After eating an infant's heart, bathing in children's blood or sucking the life out of people's mouths, they are able to use their energy to cast all sorts of spells, including a convincing illusion of youthful beauty. My babysitter said if you upset Witches, they cast spells of misfortune, and curses of disease or madness on you, most lasting a lifetime. Over the few years that she babysat my brothers and me we had heard all of the stories she had been told by her babysitter while growing up in Mexico City. Her spooky tales of supposedly true encounters with witches, kept me lying awake in terrible wonder countless nights as a child.

"We must be sneaky," E-Su continued, "she has heightened senses of perception, so we must keep our quiet distance until we are ready for her to detect you are near. Otherwise, my presence will scare her away." he said, "She will try to put you under her spell then suck your spirit dry."

I looked at him concerned and with hesitation said, "So, why do we want her to detect that I am near?"

He ignored my question and said, "I am going to do a protection and concealment spell on us right now. It won't shield us entirely, but it

will at least allow us to get closer and remain undetected. Hold still."

He said some words out loud in his native tongue and waved his hands around himself and me. Then he looked up, put his palms toward the sky, then placed them together in front of his chest and bowed. This whole display was not enough to distract me from being concerned about confronting the witch, however.

E-Su read my mind of course and said "Don't worry about your safety when I am near. I know we are still getting to know one another, but I promise you, my species is far different from yours. I will never lead you into harms way. I will be watching you the whole time, so don't worry. If it gets too intense, I will rescue you." His words were exactly what I needed to hear to calm my apprehensive nerves, it made E-Su seem more in control of the situation somehow, like he wasn't afraid like I was; after this we began our walk to see the witch.

After hiking for several hours, we climbed to the top of the tallest peak in the area to see below us, a vast valley of nothing except dense forest. A few miles off in the distance, there was a faint trail of smoke amongst the thick trees. He pointed at it saying "There she is, you must be very careful when you see her, she will try to put you under a hypnotizing spell. She won't be able to fully read your presence because of the spell I did earlier, but just in case, keep this protection stone in your hand, and use it if you must."

He gave me a long, slender sharp piece of smoky quartz about the size of a penny roll. "The demons that possess her body are masters

of illusion; you mustn't let them get into your head. Don't believe what you see to be real, the witch knows how to mix pleasant lies with ugly truths. I will do my best to help you, but in the end it's your willpower that is tested here. When you come upon the witch, you must walk by as if you were a lost hiker asking for help, do you understand?"

"Yes," I replied.

E-Su pointed at his ears with his index finger and looked at me saying "Make sure she cant hear you. Just to be safe, not even mental conversation can be had when we get close enough."

We walked silently for a few more miles in the direction of the smoke trail. Once again, I was shocked at how nimble and quiet E-Su could be, despite his size and weight. I walked with my eyes on the ground most of the way, periodically looking at E-Su's enormous gray feet and trying to step inside of his massive cryptid tracks. I eventually lost myself deep in thought and I did not realize E-Su had stopped moving and was standing in front of a large group of trees. I bumped into his back and almost said sorry out loud. He turned around, his eyes wide giving a seriously intense glare.

He crouched down near the base of the compact group of trees. Then he moved a small branch enough for me to see the witch a short distance away. Her bare chest was covered in dirt, and her matted gray, frizzy hair hung from her head all the way down to her butt. She was wearing what looked like a skirt made from animal fur and her whole body was creased with deep wrinkles after being beaten by

the harsh sun and age. Looking closer, I saw that the forest around her was populated by dead trees with a few random living ones scattered among them. She was dancing and singing wildly around a small fire flailing her hands in the air madly.

From the distant foliage, we both silently watched as her madness proceeded. She was screaming incoherent nonsense, and then wailing wildly into the air, kicking dirt up with her feet as she danced and raved around the smoking embers on the ground. After a few minutes, E-Su motioned for me to speak with her as we had discussed.

Not knowing what to expect, I moved with slight hesitation at first, but momentarily welled up my curiosity and courage enough to walk through the dense trees in her direction. As I was walking quietly, my eyes were focused entirely on the witch and her bizarre ritual causing me to crush some forest foliage, creating a loud crunching noise. The sound was enough to give away my position, and I panicked inside for a moment, knowing I was now visible and thus vulnerable to the witch.

I was about to pretend I was lost as E-Su had instructed, but the moment her cold dead blue eyes met mine, everything around me dissolved. She was no longer an ugly half naked old witch, suddenly she became a beautiful young woman in a wondrous green enchanted forest. Her body was very curvaceous, she had sparkling blue eyes, her lips were thick, and her skin was flush and smooth. She wore a necklace of daisy chains and approached me with a pretty white

smile. She walked up slowly with a sensual swagger and put her arms around my neck looking deep into my eyes. "Well hello there. Are you lost sweetie?" she leaned over and whispered in my ear "I've been waiting for you."

I was hypnotized, I couldn't think or speak. I was pulled into her presence more than any woman I had ever known. Even Monique could not touch the love trance the witch put me under. Putting her hands on my shoulders and slowly sliding them down my arms, she wrapped her fingers around my hands which remained in fists, one of which still contained the smoky quartz wrapped in its grip.

As she stared into my eyes, my intuition screamed *"You know she wants to devour you, get out of here before it's too late!"*

She instantly squeezed my fists tighter; as she felt her spell slipping, she made sure to keep eye contact with me, maintaining her illusion of youthful beauty. As I remembered the crystal in my hand her illusion weakened more and more by the second, revealing what the cursed witch actually looked like.

We were both again surrounded by dead trees, and she'd transformed back into a dirty, old, half naked hag with no teeth, stank breath, wart covered skin, and incredible strength. I was about to run away when she forcefully threw me to the ground with a trip and a shove, knocking the wind out of me as my back hit the earth.

She jumped on top of my torso, put hands firmly on my arms and tried to suck the air out of my mouth. Lucky for me, because the air was knocked out of my lungs, this was impossible for her to

accomplish. I began to fight back as I tried to regain my breath and eventually I worked my arms out of her grip. Afterward shoving her against a dead tree, the attack seemed to cease as I caught my breath.

With the smoky quartz still in my hand, I tried to stand up, but she somehow went back on the offensive and jumped on my back. We began to wrestle on the forest floor, when I heard a woman's innocent voice say, "Please stop! Don't hurt me! Why are you hitting me? I didn't do anything! Please, Stop!"

In a very confused state, I attempted to stop the wrestling match and jumped up to run, which only half worked, as she grabbed my foot causing me to trip and fall, knocking the crystal from my hand. Her speed was inhuman and her strength supernatural, she was definitely not behaving like an old woman, she was acting like a crazed rabid animal!

We rolled and fought on the ground for another minute as she groaned and growled like a beast. After we rolled toward the place I dropped the crystal, I got really pissed off and screamed as I used my elbow to uppercut her chin. The blow was debilitating and allowed me to break free for a moment. I crawled over and grabbed the crystal with my fingers. I pulled its long slender shape into my palm with over half of its' sharp base sticking out of my closed fist, suddenly she jumped on my back again, wrapping her arms around my neck, she placed her head next to my ear. Thinking quickly, I jabbed the sharp end of the crystal right into the witch's eye with full force. Even though I couldn't see it, I knew the blow was effective

because I felt her eyeball burst its warm gooey fluids and blood all over my hand, followed by a horrible soulless scream in my ear. When I let go of the crystal, she let go of my neck, and I decided to leave the quartz shard in her bloody socket as I fled.

Suddenly, I felt her iron grip on my forearm, and I heard the demons roar. I turned around and kicked her in the chest. The force of the kick, plus the momentum of my weight peeled me from her clutches, however, in the process, her long dirty fingernails scratched my arm rather deeply, and dark red blood began to pour from the wounds instantly, dripping all over the dirt and rocks surrounding us. Worried she would use her speed to assault me again, I jumped up and ran away as fast as I could.

When I looked behind me, I once again saw the same young attractive woman as before in a beautiful enchanted forest, only she was crying with a trembling hand extended, while holding her bleeding eye socket. She began begging and pleading on her knees for my help, as I stared in confusion.

I felt a very deep desire to help her in the pit of my stomach, it felt like an itch that could only be scratched through guilt-ridden action. Little did I know I had just fallen under her spell again, I was mesmerized once more by her beauty and her desperate need of rescue. When I was about to go back to help her, I felt a large hand grab my ankle and pull me up into the air. It moved me with great speed in the opposite direction of the witch's crying illusion.

I began to freak out, yelling "Stop! Take me back! That poor woman

needs my help!"

As I tried to pry the iron grip from my ankle, I saw the enormous firm black-hand belonged to E-Su. He was running very swiftly while holding me upside-down as if I were a sack of potatoes. I watched his feet move across the ground so quickly they became a blur. I looked back and saw the witch was left far behind, laughing hysterically. The demonic inhumane wails of laughter echoed throughout the forest for miles as we ran back to the top of the peak we had previously traversed.

After we had reached the top, E- Su finally set me down. I was in so much disbelief I couldn't stop my hands from shaking as I gazed at my blood covered arm in shock. In those fleeting moments after meeting the witch, I remember briefly regretting being in the middle of the forest experiencing things I had only heard about in bizarre childhood stories. As I looked into E-Su's eyes the intensity of what I just experienced combined with the oddity of simply being in the presence of an Ularu, hit me like a tidal wave and I got nauseous, then threw up everywhere.

At that moment I did not know what was real and what was an illusion. *If the witch could fool me into believing she was an attractive young woman, what other illusions might I be under?* **I wondered.** *Was any of this real? Was E-Su real? What was "real" anyway?* **At that point nausea and fatigue had inarguably won me over, and I sat down against a tree entirely spent.**

17) Explaining Who and Why

When we got back to the cave, I cleaned the scratches on my arm as best I could with the limited supplies in my back pack. Then I laid down inside of the cave to sleep for a short while. I awoke in the middle of the night, stepped outside, and saw E- Su sitting by a fire he had built. His eyes closed in a meditative position.

I walked a few feet in the darkness to find a tree to pee on and as I walked back I noticed that E- Su had his eyes open and had changed positions. He had both of his legs crossed in front of him, with his arms wrapped around his knees and his back slightly arched. He was rocking back and forth, his eyes were staring right into mine when he began to communicate

"That witch was once a woman named Christine Wellington." the moment he communicated that familiar name, my attention was completely focused on his informative telepathy. "She got lost in the forest 20 years ago. When I came upon her, she was only a young, scared girl; ironically she was not afraid of me at all. She did not know it, but she was being hunted by a pack of hungry wolves when I found her and I did not want her to die like that. Through reading her mind, I saw she came from a very abusive home. She was an orphan who was beaten and raped by her drunk uncles on a regular basis. I felt endless amounts of compassion for her and I wanted to help her heal, so I took her in and gave her shelter. Much the way I did for you.

I showed her the cleansing ways of the Ularu, despite the warnings of danger from my teacher. He said only humans of the greatest spiritual strength would complete the training without dying or going crazy. He said that very few humans have the will power to complete even a portion of an Ularu cleansing, let alone an Ularu initiation ceremony. He claimed we as a species have stronger spirits because our bodies are conditioned from birth to not fear the unknown but to embrace it. The Ularu's intoxicating brews and special stews are far stronger than any human booze. The sequence of the metaphysical vibrations that are physically experienced is quite a lot for the human mind and body to handle. Some humans can't handle it at all and they spiritually break away from their body; leaving the body open to possession by dark spirits.

This is what happened to Christine; her body is now the vessel for several earth bound demonic spirits that use her body to absorb energy from the physical world into their spirits, much the same as the dark lords, only the dark lords are a hundred times more powerful than the witch. The demons that inhabit the witch's body are evil earth spirit's that have chosen to not to move on after death, but instead they opted to possess a body. They do this to keep their spirit in this realm; which can be accomplished by absorbing life force through that body. That's why all of the trees in that area were dead, because, through her body, the tree's life force was absorbed. Her body is a walking parasite for life energy, and the demons absorb that energy in many different ways.

I have tried to exorcise those demons out of her body for almost two

decades, but they are always too shielded when I approach. We both have had several near fatal encounters with one another over the years. I have found that the trick is to catch them when they are heavily distracted while absorbing another being's life force. That's when they fully come out of the body to feed, that's when they are all most vulnerable. The feeding process leaves all the demonic spirits open to exorcism. If they see me coming, the demons always withdraw into Christine's body like a turtle does into its shell, and I can not expel them."

"Okay," I said expecting more, "so explain why the hell it is I had to meet her and almost get killed? Because I am still a bit confused as to why you didn't just exorcise her there and then when she was trying to kill me?" I replied skeptically.

"I didn't exorcise them there because, without my staff, you too would have been affected by my powers. The staff makes the process far easier and more direct-able. If the demons saw me, they would have used her body to flee at high speed. Don't worry though, I have plans for her and this time she wont get away. The reason you had to meet her was because the same thing that happened to Christine's body will happen to yours if you try to rush the process or if you give up at any point during your cleansing or your Shama training. Only she could show you how real the dangers are, and how powerful the dark forces can be if they possess your body. Your encounter with her, alone, was the only way you could see these forces at work and how deceptive they can be. If you choose to go down this path, you will encounter far more intense enemies than her." He stared

intensely into my eyes, and the reality of what E-Su was telling me was conveyed distinctly.

I could tell he was speaking the truth; there was a very real risk of losing life and sanity just by being there with him. My knowledge of E-Su's existence, combined with the ignorance of the masses as to the dark lord's presence on earth, made me one of the smallest minorities of people on the planet. Even if I didn't go crazy, I would never see the world the same way again, and in the process, I would only continue to grow more distant from the mental worlds of the people that I loved. Until eventually, we would be oceans of mind apart from one another.

It's an entirely different thing to make yourself esoteric to most of your peers by going to college. For you have other peers there with whom you can be enigmatic with, other specialists in your field, that also know and understand the arcane jargon. It is quite another to have an understanding so impenetrable, that you are the only one in your species that understands it. Such a unique comprehension of the world would make that individual's perspective so novel, it would be incomprehensible to all of the mainstreams of society, and thereby labeled fraudulent or insane.

"I'm going to allow you to go into town without wiping your memory," E-Su said abruptly "You need to get your scratches cleaned far better. I would heal it for you, but as I am reading your thoughts, I think it is important for you to go back amongst your species for some time. Make sure to clean your wounds with really

hot water and soap, the witch's sharp nails are covered in feces as a defense measure. You will get an infection if you don't tend to it soon."

"I could just use the first aid supplies in my bag like I did earlier E-Su. There is no reason to leave." I rebutted.

He replied with a slight grin "I could do the same thing for your wounds with some herbs, or use of my healing powers, but I think it's good that you go back to your species right now, I can feel you need that. You need to see what your human world has to offer compared to the world of the Ularu. Say nothing of me to anyone, and you can come back here with your memory intact; you can also come back with fresh water and your preferred human food if you wish. But if you try to tell anybody about me, your memory will slip and you'll forget all of this as soon as you think to mention it. Search your spirit Will, if you choose to cleanse yourself like an Ularu and walk the path of Shama there is no going back."

"Well, I hope we can still have a little bit of fun too E-Su? I don't want it to be all work and no play." I replied.

"Just because you will be forever changed, doesn't mean we will not have any fun. But there will be discomfort, stress, pain, and bizarre experiences in your future. So, when you return, do so ready to dive into the deep end of your own mind." And as those words echoed in my mind, I watched as E- Su dematerialized in a glimmering ball of light once again.

17) Bitter Sweets

I hiked back to my car's location to find it was gone; evidentially it was taken away when the search party didn't find me. After walking the few miles of the dirt road to the pavement, I began to feel slightly strange. As I passed the local cabins I sensed an unmistakable weirdness in the air. I didn't know why, but for some reason the forest had become more comfortable for me than the little town where I found so much comfort as a child.

Something had happened to me during my few weeks of freedom in the wild, something that I could not put my finger on. It was like there was a crisp newness to the air that followed me everywhere. It felt as though a completely unknown profound clarity of rising culmination and endless significance was forging its way deeper into my life in every moment.

I remember not wanting to go back to normal society at all. Then I realized Monique's face had not plagued my thoughts—or emotions—in the weeks I had been with E-Su and my obsessive need for order and neatness had also reduced to nothing more than an afterthought. I knew I couldn't pass up the opportunity of my lifetime; I wanted to learn the ways of the Shama, no matter what the risks. I believed my life had far more to offer than simply working as a gear in a corporate machine; for it was a machine that only saw me as an expendable and replaceable commodity. I wanted my life to matter far more than that, even if it meant leaving my home town and social circle behind. Of course, industrial society did have its amenities—and its perks—but after spending so much time in the forest I realized that the industrial world was as artificial and as temporary as the notion that it could be sustained against the elements long term.

As I made my way down the road to the only convenience store that the town had, I saw more clearly in the sharp angular structures of the building how the industrial, consumerism culture absorbed the life around it, only to convert it to its own processed way of lifeless living. The withered facade of the convenience store was made of sheet metal, plastic, and brick, its windows, and square corners had been beaten and weathered by the elements. The metal was rusted, the plastic was breaking, and the bricks were cracking. Were it not for human maintenance, the structure itself would not have lasted more than a few hundred years before being swallowed whole by the forest. The buildings and structures of the industrial world with their hard, square edges were evidently abrasive and offensive to all of the natural curves that existed in Mother Nature's weathering repertoire.

Upon entering the small convenience store, I made eye contact with the cashier, who was a tall, thin woman with blonde hair, a face full of wrinkles, and large blue eyes. As I walked by she looked at me funny and put her hand to her nose. I hadn't showered in weeks and I had been hanging out with the forest dwelling Mollogon Monster. I must've smelled bad and just gone scent deaf to it, so I smiled and

nodded as I made my way to the restroom to wash the scratches with hot water and soap.

Upon entering the restroom, I looked at myself in the mirror and saw my beard had grown large and frizzy, as did the hair on the sides and back of my scalp, leaving approximately 50 long hairs on top of my balding head. *I didn't look like the clean and organized person I used to be at all,* **I thought to myself as I washed my wounds with vigor. I wanted to stop scrubbing under the hot water but my need for cleanliness briefly resurfaced, and I scrubbed even harder. I powered through the pain by grunting loudly to release the painful energy. I am sure the woman at the cash register, which was only a few feet away from the restroom, was alarmed at my loud grunts and moans of pain; I would have been too if I heard that kind of painful moaning coming from a smelly frizzy-haired man inside a public restroom.**

After scrubbing and putting some antibiotic ointment on my wounds, I dressed them neatly and walked out of the restroom. The look on the cashier's face was one of suspicion and disgust as her hand hovered above the store's telephone. When I made my way to the register with some produce and a few gallons water, she didn't look happy to be ringing me up at all. Trying to be polite, I asked her how her day was going.

Intentionally not making eye contact with me she replied, "It will be better when it's quiet in here again."

I smiled and said, "I am so sorry about the noise; I have just been

camping for a while and scratched my arm, scrubbing it wasn't very fun." She ignored my apology completely and I decided that my horrible odor not to mention my less than pleasant appearance was a fair exchange for her rudeness and I left as quickly as possible. While walking out, I looked back through the window to see the cashier spraying air freshener all around the store in frustration. I laughed for a moment, until out of the corner of my eye I saw a picture of myself in the store's window, causing me to do a double take as I looked back at the window in shock. I saw that it was a missing sign with a reward for any information leading to my safe return.

I looked at my reflection in the window as I approached, looking like a frizzy haired wild man, I resembled nothing close to the neat and clean gentleman in the photograph. That was when I realized the full impact of my choosing to spend time with E-Su, but I felt as if I'd already gone too far to turn back at that point, and I continued forward on my path. I could not afford to allow my compassion for others to override the passion I had for living a life of freedom and understanding. My appearance and less than hygienic condition normally would have bothered me, but instead I laughed that all the things use to offend my uptight nature and I figured it was better to go to the forest where all these things seemed more acceptable.

Along the way back to the woods, I passed my grandparents cabin. I wanted to drop by to say hello, but I remembered the missing sign and decided it was far better not to at that juncture, if I wanted to stay with E-Su and learn the ways of Shama. When I got to the white stone circle, E-Su was waiting there with a grin. Then I heard the

sound of his telepathic voice say "It's good to see you!"

"Good to be seen," I replied back.

"Are you ready to begin your cleansing?" He asked.

"Very much so!" I replied.

E-Su took a deep breath and said "Good! Two lessons for today; the first lesson is that this stone circle we are standing in, is sacred. It expands your awareness and magnifies your perspective whenever you are in it. There are many other places like this on earth, some are stronger than others. This one is of average strength; it is through the energy of this circle that I use the earth to communicate with the other Ularu. The energy of this circle is connected to the earth's Life-net, energies and all of the elements. If you need healing you may come to this ring of stones. This circle's flow of energy is how I was able to track you and know what you were thinking from a distance. By sitting inside these white stones, one's awareness is amplified over many mountains and valleys.

Lesson two, no being with negative intentions, may enter this circle without those negative intentions bouncing back onto them. This is due to the natural cleansing properties of this circle's energy. The same thing goes for beings with positive intentions; except the positive intentions come back to that being. You felt this cleansing when you stepped into the circle the first time. This circle's location on the planet acts like a giant amplifier and magnifier, receiver and transmitter, for the flow of energy worldwide and in the cosmos.

We are going to spend a lot of time here. The energy in this place will cut down on the time it takes you to fully cleanse, what would take six months outside this circle can be done in 6 hours within the circle, especially after consuming the right plants. Those are your two lessons for the day. Tomorrow we start your cleansing process. Are you ready?"

"More than ever," I replied. "More than ever."

18) Oma God of the Ularu

The next morning after getting a good nights rest, I walked outside to see E-Su eating from a wooden bowl while sitting on the forest floor, and I decided to join him. After stretching and communicating for a little bit, I stood up to go get some food from my backpack inside the cave, but E-Su stopped me.

"You may only drink water this morning. Today we're going to empty your head, heart, and gut of the four walls, for that, you need an empty stomach."

At first, I was confused at such a radical notion. *What in the hell did emptying my heart, head, and gut of the four walls mean?* **I thought. I contemplated this as I looked at him debating what to say and do. E-**

Su laughed, his genuine hard laughter gave off the same strange snorting grunt sound as before, causing his abdomen to move in and out.

"That's what we Ularu call it. It just means your spiritual cleansing of the things that inhibit and confine your spirit's growth. The head, heart, and gut are the places that this process happens the most profoundly." I calmed down and relaxed. "If you are ready, we should make our way to the stone circle." He said looking over his shoulder in the direction of the circle.

I smiled and said I was ready, so E-Su stood up and began walking in its direction, I picked myself up and followed at his side. We were walking for some time before I noticed he was carrying what looked like a worn down brown leather bag in his hand and I wondered what it was. Reading my mind, he said "You will see what is in my hand when we make it to the circle. It's what's we Ularu use to empty your spiritual vessel." I thought that collection of words sounded vague and I was left wondering what was inside of the bag. It looked kind of big, whatever it was; I kept looking at it periodically throughout our hike, trying to decipher all the while what was inside.

E-Su interrupted my internal deliberation by saying, "You remind me of myself when I first started on my path, with the exception of the constant mental curses." He laughed out loud, "I was always curious about every little thing my teacher had in store for me too. It was never what I expected, and I should have just learned to let it

come to me in time." he laughed to himself and shook his head as I walked at his side.

I started feeling like a small child and began to walk with my head down; E-Su patted me on the back, saying "It's okay if you feel childish, that is how we learn when and where we need to mature. Besides, many adults in your species are stuck in spiritual adolescence until they are of old age anyway, so don't worry too much about it."

I replied quickly, no longer needing to maintain eye contact to communicate I was able to keep the non-verbal exchange going by sharing a quick glance, "Sometimes you act like the Ularu are so much better than humans E-Su, why is that?"

"I don't at like we are better, I act like we are more evolved." He replied putting his hand out to signal that we stop for a moment, afterward he directed my face toward his with his hand. "We Ularu intentionally evolve through the overcoming of intense hardship and ignoring spiritually derailing desires, not many humans do this. Not striving towards your own evolution is the reason your species lives in so much comfort, yet feels so empty inside. The spirits who cling to pleasurable sensations of their flesh are not willing to perform the intense mental and spiritual work required to gain such understandings. We believe that any spirit that is not working toward realizing its full potential is doing the world a disservice. There is no greater gift that you can give than your fully realized self.

Ignorance will not be your fate if you would only recognize when you are acting childish and behave like a mature spirit. You know that you will eventually see what is in my hand if you just wait patiently. So, I ask you which is more evolved and mature. To focus on what you can't control? Or focus on what you can control? Also, if you are concentrating on what you can't control; you lose focus and energy that could be invested where you do have control. Exercise patience; instead of impatience, that's just a waste of precious energy. It is the same with all positive and negative habits and attributes."

"So what is the Ularu way of doing this? I am sure there is a method. Right?" I said curiously.

"There is a method. It is as simple as this, we Ularu always ask ourselves, 'toward what intention are my thoughts, feelings, and actions directed? Is it toward unity or separation? Captivity or emancipation? Selfless reasons? Or selfish reasons?' You must ask yourself these same things, and be entirely honest with yourself if you wish to be a good leader. Good leaders are patient, bad leaders are impatient, good leaders are selfless, bad leaders are selfish. Let things come to you in their time. Worry is imaginative wonder mixed with anxiety, and no amount of it will bring you evolution in life. So be patient and let things come to you in their time during your training. Otherwise, every mystery will inevitably lead to paranoia."

Then he turned and began walking again. I pondered on his words for the rest of the hike instead of wondering what was in his hands,

because he was right. After we both had made it to the white stone circle, we sat and got started. E-Su asked me to close my eyes and accomplish one thousand conscious breaths because he needed some time to draw. Then he walked over to clear an open patch of dirt on the forest floor and grabbed a stick off the ground. As he started drawing in the dirt, I watched him for a moment and wondered what he was drawing, then I realized I was being impatient like I had been on the walk, and so I did as instructed and performed one thousand conscious breaths. After those conscious breaths, I didn't care what he was drawing in the dirt because I knew I would see it in time. Upon completion, I stood up and walked over to where he was sitting.

After examining his earthly artwork, I saw he had carved a large circle with a spiral inside of it with a smaller circle at its center. Littered inside the larger spiral were a bunch of smaller circles, each smaller circle also had a spiral with a small circle in its center and all around the smaller spirals were even smaller circles containing spirals. So I asked him "E-Su, why are you drawing stuff in the dirt if you can just put the images in my head?"

He laughed and replied saying "I was wondering if you were going to ask me that. In all honesty I don't need to draw anything in the dirt, but I do need your mind to be cleared before we start your cleansing. So I had fun drawing in the dirt while you did your conscious breaths." He laughed again, "Not everything in my training is as it seems, but it all has a purpose. The purpose of the drawing is to allow you time to clear your mind, as well as it gives me something to

do. Now, what I am about to relay to you is one of the great Ularu understandings passed down from the ancestors, it is empowering information, but without the proper techniques to use it, it becomes useless. Listen carefully because things are about to get deep. I am going to tell you the Ularu's story of creation, and a few of the secrets we know about this planet and the life that exists on it. I am going to pass it on to you as it was passed on to me and while it is simple, it is also telepathically dense and heavy. Are you ready?" I nodded my head with a benign look and sat down on the ground as he explained further.

"All of existence is a virtually endless whirlpool of varying realms locked in a synchronous spin; we Ularu call this whirlpool of energy the sacred spiral and its spiral pattern manifests on all levels of existence, micro and macro. The first churn of the spiral began due to the primordial laws of physics manifesting from the void's paradoxical infinitude. From these initial conditions, a large spiral realm of existence emerged. As the spiral continuously spun, it eventually ended up back where it started and accreted into itself, thus allowing it to perceive its own existence. This resulted in the sacred spiral projecting a smaller second spiral into the larger spiral pattern as a physical excretion of itself; the inclusion of this new smaller spiral realm effectively expanded the sacred spiral's confines, while also acting as a conscious internally nested self-reflection. Once this self-reflective experience was accreted, it expanded the self-awareness accrued in the sacred spiral exponentially, while also creating a new spiral realm based off of this new self-reflected

awareness, accordingly expanding the sacred spiral's confines each time this accretion and excretion process repeated and completed. This constant cycling in and out of conscious awareness never ceases and is in constant flow.

By combining the expanded awareness accrued within these new spiral realms, and the initial conditions that created the sacred spiral itself, countless new smaller spiral realms were continuously created. From this process of grander and grander self-reflection, a conscious omnipresent Vortex emerged, which eventually exceeded the confines of the sacred spiral itself, while also impregnating all of the sacred spiral's realms with its conscious omnipresent self-reflection. We Ularu call this self-aware omnipresent vortex Oma, and with each accretion of the sacred spiral, Oma's vortex and all of its encompassed realms emanate farther through the excretion process, continuously bringing all of spiraling existence to a higher collective awareness through Oma.

As Oma spins, its extremities cut out new territory, jaunting through the previous path and continuously forging new ground to be retraced and expanded upon in perpetuity. In this way, Oma is constantly manifesting new layers of awareness that exceed its old layers, evolving an ever-growing consciousness. Each new realm created manifests a more intense threshold of self-awareness than the previous, producing an ever-becoming experience. As spiritual growth is made within all of the realms of the sacred spiral, both new and old, the sum total continuously deposits back into Oma, and a

new level of collective consciousness unlocks, allowing Oma to have a granderr self-awareness after each accretion and excretion process. This accretion and excretion process is called the flow of chi.

A full revolution of the sacred spiral is when a newly created realm is absorbed into Oma for the first time through the constant flow of chi. The conclusion of this process results in a novel realm of Oma's divinity being excreted into the sacred spiral. However, this process is continuously happening due to the endless amounts of realms previously created that are only now just being included.

With every revolution of the sacred spiral, Oma experiences one of two alternating states of awareness. The sleeping state, where all realms are connected, and the waking state, where they are all separated by time and space. We call this alternation process an awareness cycle. The awareness cycles of Oma may seem to take an eternity to our perception, but it is simply a series continuous flashes for Oma.

Oma's flow of chi combined with the awareness cycle manifests as an ever changing graceful and complex unfolding of events in all realms simultaneously, each emerging as an incredibly beautiful orchestra of self-aware self-reflections working in concert. Some call this conductor and its symphonies God, science calls it the multi-verse, medicine men call it the Great Spirit, it is all just Oma and the endless amounts of different symphonic spiral universes created, are called realms.

While Oma is in its sleep state, it dreams it is all the countless internal reflections within the endless ocean of realms in the sacred spiral. Inside these spiral realms Oma manifests experiential life forms who explore each realm's infinite possibilities in order to create and manifest a possibility into an experienced reality. Essentially, every spirit in all the realms of the sacred spiral are an individualized reflection of Oma's evolving omnipresent Spirit choosing a reality to experience as an actuality from the endless possibilities at Oma's disposal. Each physical body also uniquely mimics the awareness cycle of Oma to expand its individual spiritual awareness. Every spirit micro and macro, from bacteria to bugs, human to Ularu, planets to galaxies, represents a single aspect of Oma's reflection. However, conscious beings like us have the capability of being all aspects of Oma's reflection, consciously. Given enough devotion we can become a perfect reflection of Oma and thusly change reality with our thoughts and will power alone.

As each individual spirit exists within their physical body, the spirit lives, sleeps, wakes, and reproduces within their realm, all the while, their flow of chi always goes back into Oma. When the body dies, their spirit fully detaches from the vessel, and it accretes back into Oma. If it wishes, it may be born again as a different life form within any realm of the sacred spiral. This is so Oma may endlessly explore each realm of its reflection from countless different perspectives, while also continuously expanding its awareness without having to remain confined to a single vessel for the entirety of its sleep state. It

also allows Oma to manifest reincarnated spirits within the new realms for further awareness expansion. However, if a spirit so chooses, it may stay with Oma as oppose to being reborn into the spiral, or it may stay stuck in its realm until the sleep state is over.

Oma's evolving reflection is always moving inside, through and around all spirits, in all realms, through the flow of chi. And when a single change is made within of our own spirit, it affects our realm dramatically, thus affecting all other realms as well. This constant chi flow within our spiral realm is what creates the infinite amount of possibilities that our spirits have to choose from while living in this realm; for the chi also carries with it, Oma's power to create matter through the accretion and excretion process, a power which is also inherited by its individual evolving reflections. It is through the cause and effect of our conscious choices as Spirits of Oma and the implementation of the creative process that we create possibilities into actualities experienced as reality and accreted into Oma.

Oma's process of sleep induced self-exploration can seemingly take forever for our spirits, but eventually when Oma has completed its sleep cycle, it wakes up with a more profound understanding of itself than it had before going to sleep. Adding to its ability to create new, novel realms to explore and expand its self-awareness further. Once the sleep state is over all beings within the sacred spiral's realms experience a conscious oneness with Oma while living in their realm. It's as if all the secrets to life are at your psychic fingertips and all

you need do is grab hold of them. This state may seem impossible now, but it is a reality that is not too far away."

19) Oma and The Living Library

"In other words, Oma is an omnipresent, self-replicating pattern of flowing and growing awareness that takes physical form in all realms as an inhabiting spirit, and through the flow of chi, Oma is in a constant state of evolving and self-exploration. Thusly, we as spirits have been put in this realm to accrete the flow of chi into our bodies, experience Oma's evolving reflection; and emit its essence based on our spirit's chosen pattern of internal reflection of Oma; thus also interacting with all of the other spiritual reflections of Oma; whom, are also undergoing the same process within the sacred spiral.

Oma made this complex feat possible for the spirits of the Earth realm, by creating the living natural world that you call Mother Nature and the endless amounts of spirits within her bosom. We Ularu call Mother Nature, the living library. The living library is a direct physical representation of the endless amounts of spirits and realms that exist in the sacred spiral as a whole; as well as our ability as spiritual reflections of Oma to explore those realms and

communicate with all of the other spiral reflections of self.

Every spirit in our planetary realm acts on Oma's behalf as they consume plants and communicate with the living library's countless other spirits, including its plant spirits. Each spirit in the living library, both mobile and immobile, represents a particular physical vessel for Oma's spiritual reflection to flow through. When mobile organisms like ourselves eat plants, the plant spirit's unique reflection of Oma is layered onto the unique reflection of Oma within our Spirits; creating a double layered reflection of Oma within our consciousness, giving us a clearer picture of the totality of Oma, through the combination of the two Spiritual reflections being experienced as one.

There are literally countless amounts of plant spirits on this planet with vast amounts of knowledge and information housed within their physical bodies. Many of these plants you already know about, but there are countless others that are not even known to your species because they are so rare in nature and have never even touched a human tongue, it is many of these unknown plants which are used in the Shama ceremonies of every Ularu. With the right combination of plants, or just the right single plant itself, one can absorb other worldly information and perspectives that material wealth could never buy. There are several different categories for the multitudes of plants within the living library. We Ularu have condensed our use of them into five groups. Food plants, Healer plants, Death plants, Ordeal plants, and Elder plants.

Food plants or 'Spen Shesh' in my tongue, are plants that directly contribute nutrients to the body and thus primary awareness expansion to the spirit eating it. These plant spirits mostly create a more analytical mind or a stronger body and euphoric heart.

Healer plants or 'Ba Sil Shesh', are homeostatic plant spirits and when consumed they disrupt old stagnant patterns of energy within the spirit and optimize health. They can also be used to cleanse a space of negative chi.

Death plants or 'Hath Haash Shesh', are reserved for those in need of a quick death. These plants spirits are used when an Ularu would like to leave this realm and return to Oma to either be reincarnated or otherwise.

"Ordeal plants, or 'Madagash Ka Shesh', are plants that bring the spirit's body close to a painful death for a few hours, only to not kill the body but instead allow the spirit to become a more humble, loving, and caring reflection of Oma. These plants are not for the faint-hearted and are sometimes used by certain Shama to treat radical forms of selfish behavior.

Elder plants or 'Moosh Roomba Shesh' are the plants that house a chemical key to a doorway which leads to a total view of one of the many Oma perspectives available. This small group of plant spirits worked hard to survive when all seemed dead and lost on this planet, and they have helped to bring the earth back to life on more than one occasion. They are some of the oldest and boldest plant spirits on the planet. And as a reward for their courage, and enduring spirits, they

have been blessed by Oma and given a key to an Oma perspective. Inspiring all who consume the plant to ensure its protection and survival after its consumption.

These Elder plants, like all others, when consumed, merge with the spirit of the consumer, melding the two perspectives of both spirits together into one. Only, each different Oma key that the plant spirit holds, allows the observer to see the whole picture from a specific previous awakened Oma perspective; allowing the consumer to glimpse into the endless amounts of realms that exist within the sacred spiral.

However, in order to see this perspective, the plant's consumer must first converse with Oma's Key holder and Guardian, the Plant Spirit. This can often cause the consumer to experience a high wave of intense visual hallucination or feelings of terror. So I warn you, what may appear to be a demon in a vision could be an angelic plant spirit guarding Oma's key to a life-altering perspective. Remaining calm and focused on one's goal of enlightenment, without giving into pure terror is quite the challenge, but it's the only way to pin this intense illusion to the floor and see it for what it is. This wrestling between the plant and consumer's will powers is like a spiritual work out and expands the consumer's self-awareness exponentially if seen through to the end.

Upon overcoming the plant spirit's obstacle, the Oma perspective that the plant spirit is guarding can be experienced and absorbed. If over time a positive relationship is developed with the plant, then the

Plant Spirit will relinquish Oma's key to knowledge without forcing you to overcome adversity. With the right combination of plants, some of the most amazing spiritual doors can be opened, many of the spiritual realms become visible, and the most grievous wounds and illnesses can be healed. Every plant spirit looks different for everyone, but they are always there inside the plant waiting when consumed. For this is how they become perceived in a visual and communicative form that we can understand. Through the consumption and the attention devoted to the communication, we may converse with the vegetation of the planet.

All individual plants and animals have a common earth based magnetic energy pattern which corresponds to their particular body and species. However, it also connects it to all other species on the planet as well, allowing all species to subtly communicate with one another. As you know we call this common net of connectedness a Life-Net, and each species, including plants, communicates through the magnetic pattern that they share with one another in the life-net itself. Throughout each plant's life, all sorts of information and knowledge is collected and thus passed on to their offspring, this is done through the life net. All plants communicate with one another, either through the life net or inaudible pitches of sound that the human ear can't hear, or through chemicals that humans can't always smell, or even through the fungus in their roots. Just as plants have their own life-net connection to one another, so do all insects, sea creatures, and terrestrial animals.

When certain Life-threatening information is collected by a species'

Life-Net (local or global), Oma creates mutations within the spirit of the offspring through its evolving reflection, adapting the new offspring to the threat. It is through the life-net that the energy gets from Earth to Oma, and it is through the Life-Net that specific adaptations and mutations are made per each Spirit's need within their environment. These changes end up getting passed onto and manifesting in newborn spirits with greater and greater prominence as time goes on. As this mutation process continues to unfold, the new spiritual pattern becomes more permanently integrated into the Life-Net of the species.

When information gets loaded into a species Life-Net, whether it be through plant power, epiphany, meditation, hard work, or the many other means of its collection; the information becomes accessible to all spirits within that Life-Net through their spiritual entanglement. This is largely the way we are communicating via telepathy, our individual Spirits and Life-Nets are both plugged into the spiritual base of the Earth Realm itself. I know your species' spiritual frequency pattern in the Life-Net and I am able to tune my spirit the way you would tune an instrument to harmonize with your frequency pattern. Eventually, you will be able to speak on my frequency without any pain or struggle. When you're telepathy abilities get strong enough that is. And that is the end of the story of Oma the Sacred Spiral and the Living Library as it was passed on to me. Did you understand?"

His telepathy stopped, and I finally felt that I could chime in so I replied by saying, "I did. Surprisingly, my head doesn't even hurt

and these are some heavy concepts you have relayed so far. I think I am getting it more and more each day."

He grinned, then continued. "Yes you are, and I am proud of you for that, very proud. But returning to the topic; in order to empty your head, heart, and gut and get rid of the four walls, we are going to have to adjust your spirit's frequencies using a particular elder plant-spirit. The process is going to be intense and there may be parts that you will not like. The only way out of the bad stuff is through focusing on your goal. If you get lost in the intensity and believe the illusion is real it will take on a hellish nature and become overwhelmingly intense; which may cause you to act insane for a time. But if you remain calm and do not fight the process, once it's over, you will not have to do it again and you'll be able to move on. So, all of that being said, are you ready to meet a plant spirit?"

"I think so E-Su!" I replied. "Let's do this!"

20) The Cleansing Plant Spirit

E-Su pulled out the brown bag from behind his back and opened it. Inside was a wooden bowl, inside the bowl looked like a bunch beige powder of varying shades. E- Su handed me the bowl and said "Here eat this powder and drink it down with water." I was skeptical at first, and I had this overwhelming desire to ask what it was, but I ignored my old habits, and I consumed what was in the bowl. I

wondered what would be in store for me and I contemplated why it had to be in a powder form. I was pouring the powder from the bowl into my mouth, when E-Su started to pray with his hands cupped over my head, his head bowed, and speaking in Ularu tongue. The intensity of his tone and presence changed drastically and I tried to mirror his seriousness as I continued to consume the powder.

His language sounded incredible, but also very primitive and strange. It was so fast and foreign to my ears; even though I couldn't understand it, I wished I could have heard it more often. I simply tried to go with the flow as I slowly poured the bowl's contents into my mouth following it with some water. The powered tasted like stale crackers and was difficult to get down at first. My stomach was eventually full of the powder and water, and I waited, knowing that whatever it was, it would come to me in time. I was doing my best to patiently wait like E-Su suggested and it ended up making the whole process much smoother.

Eventually after a short time, I began to feel slightly lightheaded and dizzy, followed by a small amount of nausea. I decided sitting against a large white rock might help me to feel better, as opposed to sitting on the forest floor, but when I tried to stand up, I felt my equilibrium was off. I stumbled around in a daze eventually finding my way to one of the larger white stones bordering the circle. I looked for E-Su, but I did not see him anywhere. *Where was he?* **I wondered,** *why would he leave me when I'm feeling like this?* **After sitting on the ground, I rested my back against the large white stone.**

My breathing was shallow and panicked; I started to sweat profusely until I heard E-Su's voice "Breath deep. You must control your breathing; or your experience may be unpleasant. Allow the plant to cleanse you, allow the plant to teach you."

I closed my eyes and laid my head back onto the stone. Suddenly, I felt myself spin backward into the rock that I rested against. As I drifted in a spiraling tunnel away from my body, I felt slightly overwhelmed and I slowly opened my eyes again.

Everything in my vision bounced and exploded with color like a bunch of fireworks were going off inside my head. This of course, made my surrounding terrain rather difficult to visually navigate. As I felt the intensity rise after this open-eyed excursion, I decided to close my gaze for a second time and drift in mental space. As I sat there, I felt myself sink into the earth until its surface was all the way up and over my head. At that moment, I remembered that I was in the stone circle, so I followed the energy of that circle to the center of the earth.

While I continued to descend into the heart of the planet, I could feel myself becoming one with its enormity. There was a downward moving sensation followed by a growing heat and a deepening sense of time distortion as I sank deeper and deeper into the earth. I then heard a deafening internal ring that made my body feel like it was being saturated in a warm euphoric liquid. The audible warmness turned into a hiss; then it coalesced as an intense feeling of liquid fire in my veins. Instead of rejecting the sensation I chose to find its

intensity enjoyable, mainly for fear of the hellish nature that the experience would take on if I didn't learn to enjoy it. It felt like I was violently scratching an itch that once finally addressed would go away forever.

All of this registered visually as powerful surges of multicolored waves moving throughout my body's circulatory system in increasingly more bold pulses of color. My forehead began to break out in beads of sweat and my skin felt ready to bubble and boil. My reality started evaporating in front of my closed eyes in a multi-colored steam, and yet, as everything I knew dissolved, I sensed the pressure that I had felt all my life decompress. This sensation was accompanied by a deep sense of peace mixed with a small hint of real terror, so I opened my eyes yet again.

Looking down at my color engulfed torso, I saw the alien nature to my own body's primate structure and appearance. I first noticed an oddity in the shape of my hands; then I observed the oddity in the hairiness of my arms, legs, and chest, then to the stink of my deodorant free armpits. All of these experiences were accompanied by a sense of peculiarity and dizziness that I did not feel even a few seconds earlier. I decided to close my eyes and at once I fell back into my trance.

Suddenly, I saw a colorful tunnel filled with geometric patterns pulsing with light and energy form all around my closed eye perspective. I started to zoom forward through the tunnel at high speed and traveled for a few minutes in this way, feeling the G's as I

turned around sharp corners and up and down steep hills and valleys, then I noticed that there was a shimmering light at the tunnel's end. Eventually, with greater and greater speed I approached the light to see it was the spinning sacred spiral.

I was being drawn toward the light at the spirals center at greater and greater speeds, eventually passing through the light and emerging on the other side. There was a bright red flash followed by a popping sound and it was then I realized that I had broken on through to the other side. Upon looking around, I realized that I was surrounded by smoke in an arena of some sort, a very dim light a few hundred feet above my head lit the space I found myself in. While observing my surroundings, I noticed a white door had appeared off in the dark distance. So I walked up and tried to open it, but it was locked.

The knob suddenly began to shake, and then melt, instantly the door became engulfed in bright orange fire dissolving it into ash. Then from behind the ashen door in the distance, I saw a very intense looking creature with a massive muscular build. It had a bull's head which was crowned by rounded rams horns; it had two big hoofed feet and a long but thin tail with a tuft of hair at its end. When our eyes met, the beast charged at me with great speed and ferocity. I tried to run away, but every direction I turned the Minotaur was there. I soon realized as it drew nearer, that there was no running from it. I didn't know what to do, so I just stood tall and imagined what it would be like if I was made of stone and braced for impact.

I could hear the pounding echo of its hooves getting louder as it approached, then the beast made a terribly low intimidating roar as it slammed into my forehead. To my astonishment, I was not fazed. The Minotaur was centimeters from my face, its spiraling horns protruded out from its head arriving next to my throat while its stared into my soul. Its skin was stone gray, its eyes were angry black slits surrounded by bright orange fire, its teeth were sharp, bright white fangs and it had a pierced septum and a forked tongue.

With our eyes locked it asked me in a deep demonic voice "Why are you here?!"

Intense heat surrounded my entire body as I responded in a polite voice saying "Uh...I am just here to learn and be cleansed."

The Minotaur pulled backed away and turned its back on me to walk off into the dark distance. Once again, I was left in the dimly lit arena wondering what was going to come next. Then I heard its hooves pounding echo again in the surrounding darkness; it blasted from the unknown depth with its eyes glowing red and its legs moving in a blur as it charged at me like a freight train. This time we slammed foreheads, and it screamed even more intensely "Why are you HERE?!"

Despite the uncomfortable warmth of its presence I calmly respond with a respectful tone, "I am just here to learn and be cleansed." Once again, the Minotaur backed away, narrowed its eyes in disbelief, and walked off calmly to disappear into the darkness.

The large arena became fully of lit by a light source from above, and

I thought the ordeal was all over. Only then did I see the Minotaur had grown to be 30 ft tall, smoke poured from its nostrils as it was once again charging at me, full speed, and roaring with intensity. I knew there was no running from the intimidating creature; so I didn't try, I instead faced the monstrous beast unafraid.

Thinking quickly I stood my ground, and I yelled a war cry that shook the entire arena, suddenly I grew equal in size to the Minotaur, and we once again slammed our heads together. It yelled with earth-shaking intensity "WHY ARE YOU HERE?!" its forked tongue hung out of its fang-filled mouth, its eyes burned brighter than ever before and steam shot from its ears. The feelings of intensity and heat experienced during this ordeal are done no justice in my description and at this point became nearly unbearable.

I replied with proper reverence saying "With all due respect, I am not afraid. I am just here to learn and be cleansed."

The Minotaur backed up and looked me up and down with suspicion, then it snorted. After which, it looked deep into my eyes and said "I know you have not been here before, but I will allow you access to the cleansing door. You seem to wield the right intentions in order to move up to higher dimensions. Continue to visit me so we can be friends and put all of this silly Minotaur business to its end." With those words, the Minotaur turned into a cloud of smoke, and a bright open door appeared in its place. I couldn't see what was beyond the door, so I put my best foot forward and walked through.

On the other side, I saw a memory of my early childhood. I was an

infant lying naked on an operating table and a doctor wearing medical gloves, a face mask, and a surgical uniform walks up, grabs my penis and begins to cut the skin. I scream, cry and wail in agony as the man completes the circumcision and sews up my now bleeding and tender flesh. I felt the full weight that the trauma still had on my developing infant psyche as I watched this gruesome act and in a sudden rush, I felt the intense shock, horror, and disbelief that I felt at the time. While I looked at the ground in nauseous disgust, the scenery began to change.

When I looked up, I was in a park, observing my step-dad push me on a swing that was inside of a sand pit. I was only two years old, and he told me to hold on to the chains so I wouldn't fall off, but being a naive toddler I did not understand, and I let go of the chains in the midst of being pushed. Causing me to fly and fall face first into the sand of the playground. The shock and confusion I felt the moment of impact hit me like a ton of bricks and I relived the feelings I experienced in this memory too. This was my second clear memory from my life on earth, and I had suppressed it altogether.

As I looked to my left, the scene changed again, and I watched myself at age four and a half, run after a small dog through a cramped, messy apartment with clothes and bedding on the floor. My parents and their friends were sitting on the couch watching the TV. Eventually, they asked me to stop running, and I sat down with them. As I watched the TV, I saw an action figure commercial, and I immediately wanted the advertised toy. The commercial made the action figure look like so much fun; I remember wanting it so badly I

asked my mom for it right then and there. She replied that she didn't have the money to buy it right away, but she would see about getting it for Christmas. This was very disappointing; the commercial made me feel as though there wouldn't be any more left and I had to get it then, or it would be gone forever. For the first time in my life, I felt disappointed, inadequate and deprived of something I thought was essential for my happiness, all because I didn't have the action figure that I saw on TV. This was my third strong memory from childhood that I had almost also entirely forgotten, as I relived the feelings of disappointment and confusion.

While I looked at myself crying over this perceived loss, my body dissolved and when I looked up, I saw myself a few feet away, at age five laying it bed asleep. My mother came into my room and told me "Hey Will, you have to get up for school. Today is your first day." I woke up but was not used to getting up that early and went right back to sleep. My mom re-entered my room a short time later and woke me up again, repeating the same instructions. I remembered not understanding at all why I had to get up so early. Even though I was crying, I knew my mom wasn't going to let me sleep, so I finally got up and got ready.

When I got to school, I did not realize that I was going to be staying there without my mom and when she left I began to feel a deep state of fear and panic. After I was assured by the teacher that my mom would be back soon, I calmed down. However, almost every one of the rules in the classroom went against my imaginative exploratory nature. I didn't want to stay in my seat, I wanted to play outside, I

didn't want to write my name I wanted to draw a dinosaur, I didn't want to stop playing after recess was over, I wanted to continue to use my imagination. I was miserable all day until my mom was there to pick me up later, but I felt an even worse dread than I had felt the day before when I had to get up the next morning and go back to school again for the rest of the day. I had thought it was just a short adventure at the time and did not understand that I would have to keep going back there for years and years to come. It wasn't until a full week of school was complete that I realized I would have to keep going back whether I liked it or not. This whole experience was very traumatizing for me, and I had never really fully gotten over it. This was my 4th clear childhood memory that I had also repressed. As I looked to my left again expecting to see another version of myself through memory, I saw another being entirely.

The being was a humanoid of a varying silvery shade which contained every color. The entity was bald, had slightly pointed ears, cat's eyes, and no eyebrows. Its nose looked like a serpent's nose with two small nostrils above its large plump silvery lips; it also had very sharp canine teeth and a forked tongue. It appeared to have on the equivalent to a pajama onesie, which was also the same hue as its colorfully reflective skin. One other funny thing I noticed was that its shoes were curled around and came to a point. I made eye contact with the being, and it looked right into the depths of my soul when it spoke.

"Now, with your mind open and free, are you able to see? Fear and pain are the obstructing walls contained within thee. These four

experiences from early life have shaped you more than you know. Before, they had always held you back, only now they can help you to grow. Eventually, these hurt feelings will kill you if you do not let them go, so you must release them all in order to restore your energetic flow. While here with me in the bright bejeweled palace of the plants, you are free from these fear-based illusions of death and blind chance."

I was speechless as the caricatured spirit encircled me in a pause of silence and then posed an inquiry. "Shall I continue my rhythmic rave? Or is this something that I should save?" I nodded with affirmation for it to continue, and the spirit ceased its circling, and stopping right in front of me. It gazed deep into my eyes and began speaking once again.

"I have brought many of the strongest beings to their knees, simply by displaying for them the truth's harsh realities. I help spirits evolve through relaying direct and specific instructions, then I leave each spirit to spiritually create a new pattern's construction. Listen to me close if you wish to remain among that group, otherwise my words may become an incoherent loop.

Each human has an Earth pattern embedded in their spiritual field; and throughout their lives those patterns change their flow through the chi that they wield. The pattern can be added to or remain the same as it was; it can change over time, or in seconds, based on what the spirit does.

Many people create harmful knots in their fields by clinging to the

past or their fears. Countless humans unknowingly cope with these knots in their spiritual field for years. These tangles disrupt the flow of energy in the body, the heart and the mind; many beings go mad as they ignore their knots, which creates a more complex bind. To ensure negative patterns do not stay in places within the spirit for too long; elder plants expose each of the harmful patterns' traces, while teaching spirits to be strong. By working to remove all of these spiritual knots, you become so much stronger in all of your weakest spots. You will continue to shine brighter and brighter as you grow, converting the darkness more and more the brighter you glow.

Once complete peace has been attained and then consciously maintained within your head, heart and gut; that is when your spirit is most powerful, most creative and its toxic ties are cut. Most people have lost sight of their unity with the planet's Spirit and their Oma self-reflection; hence why humans search for peace through objects, drugs, and fleeting pleasures, instead of Oma's core connection.

The wisest of beings never consume more than they actually need, always being reverent and giving back, they never behave with greed. For, they live with Oma's peace as the basis for the self which they're creating, they give and they take with each choice that they make, while planetary peace they're maintaining.

By consistently choosing to absorb the knowledge which the living library holds, you can keep your vessel free of cultural illusions, while retaining gnosis of gold. You must simply ask the plant if it is willing to be consumed, if its spirit agrees then the consumption may

soon be assumed. Bless the plant and sincerely thank it for its body's sacrifice. Show its spirit respect and reverence; for this is the plant's asking price. After eating the plant, just sit, watch, listen, smell, feel, and taste. Use your intuition and all your senses to ensure no knowledge is missed in haste. You will be illuminated within if you treat the sacred as such. For being thankful and of good intent, the plants will share so much.

Real food supplies your body with nutrients, bringing more energy into your life. Food should never cause disease, obesity, disorders, neurosis, death, pain, or strife. You see now how it is true, that you are what you eat; so take care to never be fast, processed, fake, microwaved, or cheap. An enlightened Spirit is not profitable, nor easily enslaved; making the living library a major threat for those seeking to keep human spirits caged. One spirit's complete inner transformation can change the entire Earth-realm for the whole human race. Once achieved, this cues a new age of humanity's state of conscious oneness, in everlasting grace.

Most members of your species are ignorant to some basic truths about reality, as well as to their own influential roles in its creation and its finality. All of your life before you had grokked this knowledge, you were among that vast group of people. Now knowing the truth, are you happy simply peering through another Oma door's key-hole?"

With that the being dematerialized in pixels of multicolored silvery dust that were wisped away by the wind, its words left a lasting warm

ring in my head, heart and gut as the world around me began to rumble and crumble under my feet. When the floor gave out below me, I saw that I was falling back through the same tunnel and space full of geometric patterns. As I descended the ball of light had relocated to above my head and seemed to get further and further as I plummeted toward my physical body. *What was happening to me?* **I wondered.** *What was going on? Who did I just communicate with?* **Then I remembered I was sitting in the forest with my head leaning against a rock inside the stone circle with E-Su.**

I opened my eyes to see the setting sun and everything else in my reality was waving and vibrating; my head felt like it was made of Jell-O, and my limbs felt as heavy as anvils. Every move that I made seemed to be a move closer and closer to nausea. As I lifted my head up from the rock, I felt all the powdery plant matter in my stomach travel up my esophagus and project out of my mouth onto the ground in between my legs in front of me.

Instantly I felt much better, almost as though everything that was negative in my life had been drawn to the plant powder in my stomach and came out of my mouth in one cleansing shot. Peering down into my vomit, I saw all of the four walls of personal inhibition from my childhood that the plant spirit had shown me. Each scenario played out in beautiful blue and violet hues inside of the liquid on the forest floor. The images started out very bright, but eventually faded away into the soil. I had not realized how much those four memories had constricted my spirit, until they were finally gone. As the images faded into the soil, I felt my head, heart and gut finally let the energy

of those incidents go completely. It was then that I felt the entirety of my consciousness return to my physical body, and with that sensation came the feeling I always got throughout my body when an elevator stopped suddenly.

I was fully back, but this time my body was an empty vessel as E-Su had promised. I had not had my world rocked so hard before in my life. I had never felt so free, or so elated. When I looked around, I saw every plants spirit as clear as day, the trees and bushes either had faces or they looked like strange alien creatures, this would have normally been terrifying, but they all seemed to be happily conscious of me and the fact that I could see them. The ground was breathing along with my lungs, and the sky had all sorts of kaleidoscope-like colors and patterns in its dusk. Then I heard footsteps coming from behind me. I looked over my shoulder to see E- Su walking up with a smile. "How did you like meeting the plant spirit?" he asked.

"That was fucking trippy!" I said with excitement, "I had no idea this world was so magical E-Su! Thank you SO MUCH for being willing to show me these things! I am indebted to you forever! I feel like a man who was born blind and just got to see for the first time!"

E- Su laughed and said, "Your excitement reminds me of my first plant spirit encounter."

“It's not just that E-Su, I can see the plant spirits all around me, and they can see me, everything is alive and conscious!” I said in astonishment.

E-Su laughed out loud and said, “It’s incredible when you see the

truth for the first time isn't it? Now try to understand, that the way you see the world now, is the way all fully initiated Ularu Shama see things all of the time. Unfortunately for you, your ability to see the plant's spirits won't last for but a few short minutes this time. After your spiritual rebirth, however, it will last for a full moon cycle. Then, after you become a Shama you will see the plant spirits and all other disembodied spirits, all of the time, everywhere you go. Now, here, drink some water, your body needs it."

E- Su handed me a water bottle he had taken from my backpack, I happily grabbed it and drank the whole thing without stopping for a breath. I was sweating profusely, I did feel rather dehydrated after throwing up but, I had also never felt more liberated in all my life. The emotional and mental weights which I had been carrying around with me for twenty-something years were finally gone. It felt like I had just taken off a heavy pair of tight shoes, except I felt like that all over my body. This feeling gave me a sense of freedom that exhilarated me! Whoever William Sage was, that was not who I was anymore, I felt like I was just pure Will.

As I looked back at E- Su, he seemed to be reading my mind, his eyes were narrowed, with his head nodding, he seemed to be affirming what I was thinking. "Now that your spirit is clean and empty of the four walls, we can fill your vessel with highly concentrated amounts of the truth about reality." He said very matter of fact. "I hope you're ready. Tomorrow we start the process. It's going to be intense and unpleasant at points, but I assure you, after this you will be ready to learn the ways of Shama from my teacher."

21) The Sacred Spiral

I woke up the next morning inside the cave to the sound of birds chirping and E-Su's telepathic voice saying, "Good morning. Come eat and drink with me."

I came out to see him sitting on the forest floor in a meditative position across from a fire that was mostly ashes and smoke; he handed me a wooden bowl that he was eating from. It was half full of freshly picked thick spongy dark green leaves and some dried brownish red vines. He smiled, motioning for me to eat the rest. I didn't want to eat any of it, but regardless, I ate the rest of the contents of the bowl without question. It felt light and fluffy in my stomach, but also hearty and filling. He handed me a wooden cup saying "This is a mixture of the two plants you just ate into a tea, drink it. Now that you know what the sacred spiral is, you will meet a plant spirit who can show it to you and how it affects everything in our realm."

I did as I was told, I quickly swallowed what was in the cup with a few large gulps. The liquid's thick warm texture mixed with the tart tongue-twisting taste was nauseating and it saturated the inside of my mouth and throat for several minutes causing me to almost throw up a time or two. When I finished, he stood up took the bowl and cup from my hands and rubbed the top of my bald head. Throughout E-Su's interaction with me, I got a feeling of loving friendship which I

had always wanted to get from my step-dad, who was always either working or drinking. My mother was usually there for me when I needed her, but my instinctual desire had always gravitated me toward finding a positive male role model. While looking at E-Su, I began to see that only he, thus far, had touched that fatherly nerve in my heart in the way that I'd always hoped someone would.

Shortly after I drank the tea, we both began to walk toward the stone circle. The hike was a little more strenuous than I remembered and when we got to the white stones, I was already exhausted. I set down my backpack and sat on one of the large rocks with my feet in the circle. E-Su patted me on the back saying "Starting now, you are breathing consciously. Perform one thousand five hundred deep conscious breaths, count each of them as if they were your first and your last, be in the moment. After you are done, come talk to me."

E-Su stepped outside the circle and went over to grab a twig off the ground. He stepped back in the confines of the stones, then started clearing the same spot on the forest floor as before, to expose the fresh soil below. He began to draw in the dirt again while I did my one thousand five hundred conscious breaths. Afterward, I walked over and saw E-Su had drawn a perfect spiral in the dirt. When I sat down, I felt the leaves and vines I ate and the tea I drank begin to take hold in an intense expansive rush.

E-Su read my mind and said, "Close your eyes and do not fight what is coming. Otherwise, your head will hurt a lot afterward." So I laid down on the forest floor and closed my eyes, then every nerve in my

body relaxed and I let go of mental control.

Before my closed eyes lay a blackish blue abyss, followed by a rising tone which sounded like a group of very low horns being played inside my head, it rose with intensity until it surrounded and filled every fiber of my being. As the sound rose to its climax, the dark abyss I was floating in became increasingly more unstable, eventually shattering before me like glass. As it fell disappearing out of view, a rainbow waterfall emerged in front of me. In wonder and awe, I passed into the waterfall, and countless rainbows ricocheted off of my body and shimmered in the air all around me as I was enveloped by the endless hues of soft, warm colors. Curious as to what lay beyond this amazing waterfall of colors I walked through to the other side of the rainbow's flow to see a cave full of alien bioluminescent life all over the walls and ceiling. As I walked and looked around in wonder, I didn't see the black pit in front of me, and I unwittingly fell into the deep dark hole.

Screaming as I fell, I looked below my feet to see that I was descending toward a huge roaring fleshy mouth full of sharp jagged teeth each covered in blood and puss. From inside its gape, it had long slimy tentacles that emerged to reach up and constrict me as I was pulled into the mouth. I began trying to free myself from the binding force, but the tentacles squeezed me so tight I felt like my eyes were going to pop out of my head. Then the tentacles let me go, and I began falling face first toward the open mouth full of eviscerating teeth. As I descended, I realized that there was no avoiding the horrifying fate that waited for me at the bottom of the

drop. My internal heat began to rise, then the dull sound of the roaring horns echoed louder than ever before. Suddenly amidst this chaos, I remembered that I had consumed a plant and I realized that my experience was all a part of the plant spirit's test to guard its knowledge. As I passed the threshold of the teeth into the monstrous mouth, I assumed the cross-legged meditative positions while the jaws began to close around me.

I did not panic, I kept calm, the dull horns reached their crescendo as the mouth closed around me, turning everything black once more. There were no tentacles wrapped around me or sharp teeth piercing my skin as I had suspected would be the case. After a short time I, realized I was floating, suspended in the dark. Then the mouth slowly began to open, only, what were once bloody puss covered teeth had turned into the beautiful pink petals of a lotus flower. When I looked down, I realized I was sitting in its magnificent yellow pollen filled center. I looked up and saw a plant spirit surrounded in swirling streams of glittering pollen descending from the top of this blooming lotus.

When the plant spirit was finally floating right in front of me, I only saw it as a shifting blob comprised of varying shades of green, blue, and pink. Then its form began to emerge, starting with a long cone-like hat under which a small head comprised of four faces materialized, below it emerged a second larger head, also made up of four faces. Each of the face's eyes was made of large glittering green emeralds, its noses looked very sharp but appeared to be human, and led down to mouths full of pointed teeth. Below the two four faced

heads emerged a long thin neck and long slim torso. As the process unfolded, it became apparent that its torso was covered by a large robe made of changing colors, patterns, and designs. Then four sleeves emerged on each side of its body, running from the top of its shoulders down the lengths of its torso to near where its hips would be. Each of the eight total sleeves suddenly became occupied by long thin arms, which ended in skinny five-fingered hands accented by razor sharp fingernails at their tips. It did not appear to have feet, for I followed the robe as it stretched touching the golden floor of the flower's center and no feet appeared. When I looked back up, I noticed the plant spirit was cupping something in its bottom two hands; it then extended these two hands toward me. When I looked inside of the spirits colorful palms, I saw a black sphere. Suddenly I was sucked into the sphere, and the plant spirit's secret was imparted.

I was in darkness when I saw what looked like a giant white orb of light appear in front of me. From this Orb, other little orbs of light began to emerge on all sides in a spiraling disk like fashion. As each new white light emerged, it became evident that the central orb was spinning and this emergent spiral pattern was the result of this continuous spinning process. I then realized in that instant that I was witnessing a galactic birth.

Suddenly I was launched forward into this bright galaxy toward one particular sphere of light. Flying deeper and scaling down, the central light at the core of my vision remained in the center of my vision, but my position had changed, I could see that all of the bright

orbs around me seemed to be spinning in a spiral fashion and performing the same process as their larger galactic center. Getting closer to the bright luminescence I was approaching, I made out two spiral arms, to see it was, in fact, an enormous spiraling galaxy in and of itself.

The notion of a galaxy made of galaxies instead of stars had never occurred to me, and I was spellbound by the enormity of the vast timescales I was observing in that moment. After assimilating this understanding, I was blasted forward into the bright light once more. The speed I traveled was unparalleled; I started my astronomical observations at the center of a galaxy only to suddenly find myself whizzing by stars at such speeds they looked like a streak of light passing my observing eyes. Then I was on the galaxy's outer arm, the objects that emanated from the light's center changed with the size and scale.

I continued to magnify forward and ended up reaching one of the smaller stars on the outskirts of the galactic arm. I recognized the growing semi-orange spinning luminescent orb was actually our sun moving at high speed through time and space, around it each of the planet's orbital paths looked like they were a different portion of our sun's spiraling comet-like tail.

I gravitated near a planet close to the sun and realized it was the rotating Earth. While in the earth's upper atmosphere, I watched spiraling clouds turn to into tornados on land and hurricanes at sea. When I reached the planet's soil, I saw all planetary life emerge from

the dirt and grow in a spiral fashion: plants, fungi, insect, invertebrates and animals alike, all were formed, grew and moved through space and time in the same spinning spiral fashions as all of the galaxies and other solar bodies I had seen in the vision prior, and all had the same spinning light emanating from their center as I continued to zoom further down in scale.

I zoomed into the physical bodies of these organisms and was shown the spiral shape to the double helix of all DNA. The plant spirit was showing me that the sacred spiral's pattern remained the same on the molecular level as well. The structure of the microscopic looked very similar to the structures of the macroscopic, and I naively thought that this was the end of my adventure, but then I saw atoms and electrons flying through time and space in the same spiraling fashion which our planets used to move around the sun. The orbiting electrons were the size of planets as they pulsated with electricity and whizzed by my observing eyes. Then I turned my attention to the center of the spinning atomic nucleus, and I realized that from afar, it looked just like our sun.

I continued zooming toward the atomic center and emerged on the other side to see, the same massive spiraling galaxy made of galaxies that I had first observed at the beginning of the vision. Only after the process was completed the first time, the same zooming process repeated again and again, along the exact same path as before. Only I traveled faster and faster after each cycle, repeating the entire process over and over again until I realized the truth; zooming in deep enough in scale, was the same thing as zooming out far enough

in space. Eventually, they meet on the same common ground of neither big nor small. Once I grokked this understanding, the zooming ceased. Then I zoomed outward in scale as opposed to inward and I observed that this massive galaxy made of galaxies, was but one of the billions of others just like it. Each and every one spiraling as they orbited at incredible speeds around what appeared to be a gigantic ball of light made up of endless spiraling energetic clouds of titanic proportions affecting all of the near infinite spiraling galactic realms within its grasp.

Stunned by the enormity of this spiraling colossal sun, I realized that within its orbit was contained countless spinning galactic fields, each galaxy being compromised of rotating stars which were orbited by countless twirling planets. These rotating planets contained spiral forms of life, who's DNA is made of up of spiraling double helixes, comprised of molecules, atoms, and subatomic particles. All of which moved in the same spiral fashion as the spinning Galactic center. It appeared that all things physical and non-physical alike were moved by the same cosmic tide, just as all pebbles on the ocean floor are affected by the same planetary movement.

After this, I was instantaneously pulled out of the immersive vision inside the black orb held by the skinny hands of the plant spirit. It then cupped the dark ball and pulled it back toward its long changing colorful robe and spoke,

"When you open your eyes and looked at the natural world, you will see how the Sacred Spiral in all creation is twirled. From the way, a

cactus arranges its thorns, to the way the mountain goat grows its horns, from the way branches bloom on trees, to the way the wind blows its billowy breeze. Even in the way water flows in open streams, life is always deeper than its spiraling surface seems. I now grant you the ability to use the spiral pattern for your own creative means, may its form channel your intentions, and ward off evil beings." Then with a rumbling explosion of glittering pollen from underneath its robe, the spirit shot up into a bright orb above my head that seemed miles away from the base of the lotus flower.

Suddenly the flower disappeared leaving me in darkness again. I began to fall at incredible speeds and was immediately slammed back into my body. For a while I had forgotten where I was and who I was with, then I opened my eyes, and E-Su was looking at me smiling. I wanted to say something, but he just waved his hands over his eyes in a gesture to close them. I took a deep breath and closed my eyes as he instructed.

E-Su then telepathically put the image of the spiraling titanic galactic sun that all the cosmos was orbiting, and place it in the center of my spirit and over my heart. I felt tears well up in my eyes, for the beauty of what I just witnessed, and the profundity of the message overwhelmed me. I had not felt or understood things so clearly in all of my life. As I tried to say thank you I felt a painful knot form in my throat, and it was followed by a tightening sensation in my chest, leaving me unable to speak. Then I heard the call of the raven followed by the sound of thunder, and my mind was completely shocked while my heart was filled with wonder.

22) Preparing for My Spiritual Rebirth

The day of my spiritual rebirth was approximately a week after the sacred spiral experience; we waited because E-Su insisted that it be a full moon for my spiritual rebirth. I woke up on the morning of its arrival slightly nervous, but still carried out my morning routine; I brushed my teeth with some water from a bottle, and I meditated facing the sun as it rose.

What I had learned while meditating in the time I spent with E-Su was how to use paced thinking to direct my raw emotions, creating a harmonious balance between the two, as neither took full control of the other, but rather fed off one another. Having already personally discovered a few techniques for centering my mind, I began experimenting with these new techniques in different ways to center myself more quickly and efficiently. On this particular sunrise, I had a significant breakthrough. I focused on the truth of my energetic connection to all reality, then after a feeling of deep connection to all living things, I felt an incredible love for all forms of existence as I saw in my internal reflection, the central core of all creation. When I did this, I suddenly felt the omnipresent bond of Oma within all of life, and I did so without the aid of any plant spirit, only it was gone as quickly as it had arrived.

Using my mind and memory, I tried to create the same feeling again. However, by creating a similar feeling using my ability to

imaginatively recall my previous experience, I only created an experience vaguely analogous to the original one that I achieved without seeking. I soon realized the experience wasn't a whole complete feeling itself because it was an attempted mental copy of an experience that I had at my spiritual core.

After several such mental attempts to re-experience the same euphoria, I came to find the only way I could consciously create the feeling, was by allowing a new experience of the connected ecstasy to fill me in every moment. And if this were accomplished, my spirit would be evolving with Oma's ever changing reflection through the constant flow of chi. I came to discover that attaining the Oma experience is not about obtaining it once and clinging to that one experience.

The truth of connected ecstasy was something I must already know is the state of things, only then can it consciously be embodied as a physical experience of my senses. Seeking that state of being only pushed it away from me. Acknowledging what is and experiencing that as truth, is always possible for any and every spirit, especially if their concept of self is not associated with their body, but rather their spirit. For this kind of experience to be attained in every moment, it must be perceived as the true nature of reality without force or ulterior motives, including the seeking of the experience itself.

The only times I was able to feel the euphoric ecstasy within myself was when I was at peace with my Self as a spirit, not just seeking peace out of a passionate body bound desire. Desiring peace keeps it

from you, Being peace makes you the peace, so there is no need to want it in the first place. After some time of oscillating back and forth from the peace of Oma to my clinging ego, I finally got to a point of attained and sustained peace with the Oma connection. However I could only have it when I didn't try to keep it, and I could only be it when I didn't try to think it.

Then E-Su's voice startled me as he said: "You're making progress I see." My whole body jumped at once, and E-Su laughed out loud. "Sorry. I couldn't resist. Eventually, sudden telepathy won't disturb your internal peace. Eventually, you will see and feel it coming before it even hits your body."

I turned around to look at him, shaking my head with a smile saying "Yeah, I was starting to make some progress."

I stood up and walked over to E-Su, he looked at me and said "You are ready for the next step, but before we go to the stone circle, I want you to take this with you." He handed me the black stone my mother had given me before I left. It had been tucked away in my backpack, and I forgot about it entirely in the months I had been living with E-Su. "You're going to tune that stone to your body today, believe it or not, that smooth black stone is going to play an instrumental role in your spiritual evolution. It has been in your family for many generations has it not?"

"It has, yes. How much about me do you know? I mean how can you know so much about me by only reading my mind? In all honesty, I am starting to feel slightly violated."

He interrupted me and said "Relax your tension. Let's go to the stone circle, and you can see for yourself how it is I know what I know. Maybe one day you will end up having someone ask you the same thing. I didn't violate your privacy; I only observed what was lying around in your spirit's flow of chi. But that wasn't how I knew about the stone's history. I apologize for going through your bag, I felt its power ever since you brought your things here and my curiosity got the best of me. I had to see where the energy was coming from. When I picked the stone up I saw its entire past in a flash and for this reason, I now know something about that stone that you do not."

"Oh yeah, what is that?" I asked skeptically

"When I touched it I saw its past, it is meant to repel dark spirits, it is a very powerful stone, and if you learn the ways of the Shama, it will relay unto you intense and great power."

"Really? That's cool. Why is that?" I asked curiously.

"Because it has had a lot of positive energy put into it by many powerful warriors in your bloodline and you share in their DNA. You can wield the stored power they put into the stone if you learn how to channel your chi properly." E-Su paused for a moment and said "I don't like to show off, but I will show you one of the many uses of conscious Chi channeling, then I will explain it. I have been waiting for the right time to show you, and I think now is that time. You have enough understanding of the sacred spiral, Oma and the flow of chi at this point to comprehend how they empower the creative process."

I put the stone in my pocket and we walked out of the cave. While I was sitting on a rock I watched E- Su quickly gather some kindling and wood together to make a fire. Then he stacked the wood in a cone shape and got on his knees to pray with his eyes closed and palms together in front of his chest. Following the prayer, he opened his eyes and whispered some magical words into his praying palms. Then he separated them and lifted them up to the sky. After holding them there for a moment, he put one palm on the ground and one palm over the cone-shaped pile; he closed his eyes and concentrated as he moved his hand up and down slowly over the wood.

Pushing his hand down quickly, he held it directly over the cone-shaped pile and as his hand began to shake violently, smoke rose from the center of the woodpile, followed by a small flame. Then E-Su rapidly pulled his quaking palm upward, and the whole cone shaped wood pile caught on fire instantly. Which I thought was an incredible display of power, but E-Su said: "This is a very small achievement when it comes to what you can do with the potentials of chi. Because chi takes on all forms, it can be used to manifest miraculous events. If the flow of chi is mastered it can be used in many ways, it can be absorbed, used strategically to heal, poured into objects like your stone or simply accumulated within one's spirit for a longer life, or later use. What you saw me do was the use of my understanding of the way chi flows; combined with the conscious use of my reflection of Oma within my spirit. It's more technical than that, but for now, it will do. "

"What exactly do you mean? How is that possible if the chi is always

flowing?" I asked

"Everything is made of chi, your body and the air that it breathes. Only, your body is like a standing wave of chi. A standing wave is when two equally powerful currents meet to flow into one stream, when this happens it creates a standing wave in the middle where the two currents meet. Your spirit's standing wave is made of chi flowing from the past and chi flowing from the future, meeting in the present. Everywhere your standing wave travels, it changes the flow of chi in that area. From there it goes on affecting the flow of the chi throughout this whole realm. Learning how to consciously use the movement of chi, both in and out of our bodies, can end up making our standing wave much stronger than others. How powerful the standing wave of a spirit can become, is determined by the conscious focus of two sets of polarized intersecting forms of awareness. The intersection of these forms of awareness in the body is in the heart, and it is through the use of these intersecting forms of awareness that our chi pattern is created. These dual intersecting polarities are Projection and Perception as well as Intention and Attention. These forms of awareness, act like four reflective walls, each mirroring a different aspect to our spirit's reflection of Oma. How we use each of these mirrors to manifest our spiritual desires is up to us."

"I think I get it, but could you elaborate more please?" I replied

"Of course!" E-Su replied, "The spirit's personal internal reflection of Oma, expands upon the chi absorbed, and afterward, it projects the perceived chi out of the body through the hands and the top of

our head. This chi is then taken to the grander Oma reflection for accretion and excretion. We can consciously control this outgoing flow of chi by first becoming aware of its existence. Then by using focused intentions, we use the imagination and senses to create the chi pattern of the reality we desire within our spirit and body first. Afterward, that chi pattern then projects out of the body, affecting Oma's evolving reflection within the larger sacred spiral. After this projection process is completed, we focus our mind's attention on perceiving the reality we intended on creating. By knowing that the possibility exists, it can be manifested into an actuality by employing Oma's ability to create matter based on its own evolving reflection.

This is how our spiritual understandings and abilities broaden, it is also how the current of our standing wave of chi becomes stronger and more powerful. By becoming closer to Oma and being more like Oma's reflection, we draw more chi into our spirit. Through the conscious use of the Oma reflection within one's spirit to manifest possibilities into actualities, we attain grander realizations of self, allowing our individual spirit to become exponentially more like Oma's each time."

Getting excited I asked, "Is the flow of chi in and out of our spirits how miracles are created in the human world? Like miracle healings and stuff like that?"

"A miracle, is nothing more than Oma's omnipresent spirit being used to manifest one of the infinite possible realities that exist within our spiral realm of flowing chi. Through the creative power of chi,

we can do far more amazing things than light fires, heal broken bones, or invert massive trees. Through chi, we can channel the creative powers of Oma's reflection within our spirit to manifest the most magical and miraculous events imaginable. In this same way, all spirits are creating a new reality based on the constant flow of chi, but they are not conscious of this process.

The stronger the spirit's conscious reflection of Oma, the greater the amount of chi drawn into and expelled from the physical body's standing wave of chi, creating a more drastic effect on the chi around the spirit itself; this is one of the many understandings that come with learning the way of Shama." he replied.

I was spellbound by this understanding; then my stomach grumbled, and I was instantly distracted by my hunger. I was about to go into the cave to get some food, then E-Su read my mind and said "Don't bother eating; you're not supposed to eat today. Besides, we should get heading to the stone circle anyway; we should start earlier rather than later." So we put out the fire he had just made with some dirt and left to the stone circle.

We were talking and laughing like old friends on the walk over, E-Su for some reason was talking about the wonderful feeling all beings experience after a satisfying bowel movement and then he randomly asked me, "Do you believe in reincarnation Will?"

To which I replied, "After some of the stuff I have experienced so far, it would only make sense that life continues outside the body. I mean, where was life before it was in the body? Right?" I said

laughing

He only said "That's right." then oddly chose to remain silent. I wanted to know more of what he was thinking, but my telepathy was nowhere near strong enough to pry into his mind, so I didn't even try. We arrived at the stone circle, and once I stepped in, I took off my backpack and sat against a large white stone bordering the circle. E- Su unzipped my backpack and pulled out his brown leather bag.

"Inside this bag is a very special liquid concoction and a special pipe and plant blend to smoke" E- Su said holding it up in front of me. "They have been a part of the Ularu culture since the beginning of our arrival on this planet, the tea is made from a rare fungus that my ancestors were shown by the light being that brought us here, and the smoke blend is a recipe that they were given to use in combination with the tea. By using these tools, you are being trusted with immense power and perspective. This plant spirit has not been encountered successfully by a human for millennia; this is the part where Christine's initiation ended up taking a tragic turn. This Plant Spirit guards several Oma experiences which have been combined into one deep and complex experience of spiritual rebirth. Things are going to get really heavy and very high pressure for a time, but the only way out of it is through it. Keep pushing forward during the rough times, they are only there to prevent you from getting too comfortable. Unlike the other journeys you went on, in this one, you can get stuck inside of an ethereal paradise until your body becomes an empty vessel, like what happened to Christine."

"Um, ok..." was all I could think to say as he opened the bag in silence and pulled from it a small stone cup, plus a strange type of leather like drinking pouch that was full of a thick liquid, he was looking at his hands as he poured it into the cup, and communicated without the need for eye contact.

"As you are being pushed further out of your body you will feel less connection to it, you will still be attached to your body by a very thin energetic thread that keeps you connected to this realm, we call this the cord of fate. The cord of fate is the energetic cord that connects your spirit body to your physical body. During this time you will be paralyzed, and your breathing will get very shallow. Don't worry, I am going to be here to make sure you do not get hurt while you are away from your body." he stopped the pouring process and looked up at me. "There will come a point when you reach what we in Ularu call the dome of dimensions. This is the place where all physical realms within our universe converge into a higher non-physical realm within another grander dimensional layer of the sacred spiral. To pierce through the dome of dimensions, you're going to have to hum inside your spirit at the same frequency you hear all around you.

Once you do that, the harmonics will sync up, and the veil will dissolve, allowing you to pierce through to the other side. Once that happens you won't even remember having a body, at that point, it's going to be up to you as a conscious being to remember to come back to this realm using your spirit's chord of fate. If you drift too far from your body for too long, your chord of fate will get so

energetically thin that it will snap and you will become lost while your body becomes open for demonic possession like Christine's."

He handed me the cup, I looked at it, then back at him concerned and asked "How am I suppose to remember to come back if the liquid is designed to make me forget? How did you remember under such intense pressure? Is there any technique to trigger the memory? Something? Anything?"

He smirked and put his hand up for me to be silent. "Just listen." He replied, "The moment you remember you have a body; the chord of fate will act like an elastic band to bring your spirit back to this place and time. When you return, you will be a spirit that came as close to death as anyone can get without actually dying. Like I said before, I will make sure that your body is safe; you just worry about getting back to it. Just don't get lost in the beauty or the terror and you will be all right."

"Is this the initiation ritual for an Ularu who is 28 winters old?" I asked quickly trying to get a word in before he told me to drink the tea.

"Yes, that is correct. The reason for this experience is to fill your spiritual cup with a potent experience of Oma, as well as your own personal history. This is done by showing you how your physical body ccame into being, thus also showing you that you are not your body but are your spirit. After this experience you will be able to see the world as it actually is, you will see the Truth. But only for a moon cycle, after that, it fades away rapidly."

E- Su could sense the doubt in my heart and so he said "You can do this Will. Every path in life may lead to our death. There is power in accepting this and moving forward unafraid. This is the first step one must take when creating an extraordinary life, it is the first step onto the path of adventure and wisdom. By staring the darkness of our own death in the face without fear, our spirit may grow. Fear is the first step to doubt, and doubt is the first step to failure. So believe fearlessly, and you will achieve endlessly."

He rubbed my head with his massive black hand, and I agreed to move forward unfazed. I knew when I tried out for the Special Forces that their training could be deadly. *What was the difference here?* **I thought. I just had to be super intense about my focus and determination. I wanted to believe in myself, and I wanted to grow as a Spirit, I just had actually to put in the work and effort to do so!**

23) My Spiritual Rebirth

I quickly drank the concoction E-Su had poured in the cup; it was the consistency of whole milk and tasted of burned plant matter with a hint of lemon. The strange aftertaste lingered for minutes afterward. E- Su laughed at the look of disgust on my face. After about an hour and a half of singing and praying in the stone circle with E-Su, he pulled a long wooden pipe from his brown bag and a small cloth pouch containing some dried green plant matter. After packing the unknown green dried substance inside, he lit the pipe

with a lighter from my backpack, and began to smoke from it profusely. He handed me the still smoking pipe, and I took a few enormous inhales of the rough gray smoke deep into my lungs, it tasted like licorice and the herbal blend crackled, then hissed as it smoldered with a bright orange glow. After my exhale, I looked at E-Su and passing him the wooden pipe I asked: "What is supposed to happen next?"

Then as I asked the question, I realized I was watching myself ask the question, and unexplainably time stopped entirely. I sat in awe as I saw a grasshopper floating in the air mid-jump, pine needles were suspended in the air on their descent, the smoke from the pipe remained motionless, and my usual perception of time had stopped altogether.

Then, from deep within the woods, I saw something green moving gracefully like lace through the trees. It looked like a giant piece of green tissue paper dancing with the wind as it weaved through the woods. I only saw that it was interlaced and intertwining vines when it gracefully floated above E-Su and morphed its transient structure into a single bald human head with one face. After this, the vines started moving amongst one another rapidly inside of the head's structure. Suddenly, the head grew eyes in a line across the back and sides of the head, linking with the two eyes in front, below the eyes sprouted human noses, followed by open mouths full of sharp teeth and forked tongues.

The vines had created a series of interlocking faces, each sharing

mutually linked eyes and cheek bones. Then the head began to scream a high pitched wail as it rotated in the air. Vines fell from the base of its head creating a neck, followed by a massive chest and torso. From its pronounced shoulders, four strong arms were forged and from these four muscular arms came hands containing two sharp fingers and a thumb. Two large wings burst from its back, and it completed the bottom of its torso with a long serpent's tail that hung near the ground. When the head stopped spinning, vines burst from the top of its crown and moved around like live snakes. Then all of the eyes lit up with a bright red light, and the vines growth ceased. The plant spirit had turned from a gracefully floating green lace into a massive twenty-foot monster made of interwoven vines flying in the air.

It roared a deep thunderous roar, shaking the earth and trees, still frozen in time. Then the plant spirit suddenly reached out with its huge green tail and grabbed E-Su. Wrapping around him in a knot, it squeezed his body into a squirting bloody pulp of organs, broken bones and hairy skin with its tail. I was appalled as I saw the blood covered vines unravel the gory mess and drop his remains onto the forest floor.

Then the tail reached its bloody vines toward me and wrapped around my body in an instant. The sensation of its sudden grip felt rough and abrasive in some spots and slick and warm in others; I assumed this was because of E-Su's blood. My panic mounted and I began to fight the process, then the plant spirit yelled in a deep voice " You dare challenge ME?! Who do you think you are?!" then it

threw my body up and into the sky. As I plummeted face first back toward the earth, the plant spirit opened its front facing mouth and swallowed me whole. After landing inside its esophagus, I traveled downward and felt like I was being asphyxiated by greasy latex all over my body. I struggled all the way down its throat fighting to free myself while I suffocated. Eventually, my hands found a place that was open and warm. So I pulled myself down and inside of its more spacious confines.

After I had fallen inside, I discovered it was full of some warm gel. As I floated fully submerged in the goo, my body began to tingle all over. Then the sensation got increasingly more intense, and eventually it felt like millions of needles were being pushed into my skin from everywhere around me. I began to scream and at that exact moment I was regurgitated back into my location of the forest floor.

I looked up to see the massive plant spirit say in a deep, commanding voice "Quit fighting me and just accept the truth! You are MINE NOW!" I looked at my hands and body still covered in the strange transparent gel. As I tried to wipe the gel from my arms, my skin began to melt off my muscles and fall onto the forest floor in large bloody chunks; I looked up at the plant spirit shocked and appalled.

"Keep fighting me, and it will get worse!" it declared begrudgingly.

I looked back at my melting flesh in disbelief and terror to see that below my missing skin, all of my muscles had turned into mingling maggots and worms. I opened my mouth to scream, but roaches

began to crawl out from inside of my throat. Then my whole body which was still made of worms and maggots, fell apart, dispersing inside the dirt of the forest floor. I followed the worms, maggots, and roaches that made up my dissolved body underground and into the earth when everything became black.

I waited for about a minute wondering what was to come next when I heard a very deep painful moan in the darkness that sounded like an old man dying. I looked down to see I had a body again and began to wonder where I was and what the hell was going on. Then I remembered that I was with E-Su and was in the process of my spiritual rebirth. So, I decided to stop fighting the plant spirit's sifting process and remained calm in a meditative position. After I came to this conclusion, a legion of rotting corpses and deformed demonic humanoids emerged from the darkness moaning and groaning as they reached for my meditating body with their blood soaked hands. I decided the best course of action would be to sit and meditate, unafraid as the group of ghouls advanced toward me. They all lunged at once toward my body, but I remained unmoved. Then the undead monsters began to bite my face, neck, arms, legs, fingers and torso, while I still remained in the meditative position. There was a sensation to the experience of being bitten, but not a sensation of pain, for I did not fear the illusion being created for me. In fact, I closed my eyes during the process I was so unconcerned, then I felt the sensation of the biting stop.

When I opened my eyes I was back in the forest, and time was still frozen, only the monster made of vines was now shaped to look

exactly like me in every way, only if I were made out of vines. The plant spirit was sitting between me and E-Su, who was actually fine and not a bloody pulp on the forest floor. Looking at the plant spirit's replica of me was astounding; it had a frizzy beard like mine made of moss and it even kept the top of its head bald while giving more moss like hair around the sides and back of its head. It had my same muscular build, was the same height and even had beautiful vibrant green flowers for eyes.

I stared into its gaze, and then it spoke to me. "Your body is too courageous and pure for me to eat; I only consume cowards for their delicate self-absorbed meat. When you look at my spirit, I want you to see your reflection; this is done to create a longer lasting spiritual connection. You passed my test and are worthy of rebirth, don't hold on tight to your body with fright, for your spirit is about to leave earth."

Then large angelic wings emerged from its back, and it flew into the air, pulled my spirit out of my body and shot up into the sky about a hundred feet above the trees and mountains. I saw the chord of fate which was attached to my body, still sitting below frozen in time. Then I watched as time reversed while we hovered in the air. The sun began to rise in the west and fall in the East countless times a second like a strobe light. Trees that were dead rose up to return to life and then back into seedling inside the ground, I saw countless generations of animal bodies rapidly recompose from the earth's soil, and then reverse in age. Flashes of green grass, bushes, and trees, being covered in white snow, appeared and disappeared everywhere. Then

the tree covered landscape of northern Arizona began to shake and change dramatically without making a sound. I watched in awe as the entire mountain range was flooded with water over and over again, then all the surrounding mountains turn to lava and ashes and flew back inside a massive volcano.

Suddenly I was thrown out into space and watched as the earth was covered with ice and water several different times. The continents reformed into the giant continent of Pangaea, then, as we panned away further, our sun grew dimmer and dimmer. The plant spirit and I floated in space with time moving backward at such a quickened pace; I watched our solar system become un-forged. Then I began to hear a constant drumbeat start to rumble all around me; it got increasingly louder, and faster and faster as I continued to pan away from our solar system. I did not if it was the sound of my increasing heart beat or a auditory hallucination brought about by the plant, but either way it grew in ferocity and speed.

I panned away for our entire Milky Way galaxy, as the beat became thunderous and very fast paced. I watched as all of the countless stars within our galactic disc were pulled toward a massive black hole at its center. The bright star filled mass of the galaxy was getting increasingly smaller, while the black hole at its center grew ever larger, the plant still having its grip on my spirit, flew us toward this growing black center. The pounding got intensely more rapid as I neared the core, it was then followed by an increasingly louder ringing sound that echoed throughout my being. When we finally approached the massive black hole surrounded by a small number of

stars, I felt the plant spirit drop me into the growing void. I looked up at it in confusion as I fell and was sucked into the black hole. I was afraid at first, but when I turned around to observe my fate, I passed the event horizon and heard a loud popping sound. I noticed that beyond the illusion of darkness perceived from outside the black hole was an incredibly bright light whose intense presence is only comparable to being stretched paper thin, baked in a convection oven and pounded on like a drum.

Once fully inside of the confines of the black hole, I felt the gravity of the gigantic ball of light at its center. It felt like the weight of the entire Galaxy compressed into one massive ball of light had been placed on my chest. At that moment I completely let go of any concept of self or spirit that I had before, and there was a feeling of connectedness in the oneness of that light which I had not thought was possible. The feeling was the most intense unbearable ecstasy that I had ever experienced. I can only describe it as an overwhelmingly intense orgasm all over my spiritual being. The euphoria was so extraordinary that it almost felt too good!

As I neared the massive, heavy light I observed that it seemed to be spinning, ringing, and pounding with waves of vibration. It appeared to be turning so fast it looked to be standing still. Then out of nowhere the memory of E-Su's instructions hit me all at once. The intense feeling of pressure and weight I felt, must've been what E-Su meant by things getting really heavy, I thought. Then the massive dense ball of light started to descend on top of me, brining the drumming and ringing to a new unbearable level.

Once the sphere was a few feet above my head, I saw it open up into a dome of endless spinning bejeweled shapes of every size and color, each of the endless geometric forms and hues representing a different realm in our universe, the dome was also crowned by a bright light in its center. I knew this was the moment that E-Su had spoken of, so I began to project the same high pitch that I heard all around me, which wasn't difficult to do without the sensation of having a mouth or ears ironically enough, it was simply a matter of willpower. As the dome spun all around me, I matched its harmonics. While making the strange high pitch mechanical wail deep inside my being, I ascended toward the domes luminescent center, and after a tremendous pressure wave, I pierced through the center of the dome, then shot upward at great speeds.

When I looked down, I witnessed with my own eyes how all of the realms in the known multi-verse were contained in a single simple multi-dimensional structure of the sacred spiral. I watched as all of the realms rotated together as one flow, and I became entranced. I lost all touch with any and all experiences I had prior to that moment. I did not remember having a body, nor did I care. The peace and serenity in that place was so all encompassing that I lost all track of my individuality and all concepts of Self.

As I drifted for what seemed like an eternity, I had four questions cross my conscious mind that changed everything. Who am I? What am I? Where am I? And how did I get here? In that instant, I briefly recalled that I had a body and back into the center of the spiral I zoomed. Time began to race forward instead of backward, at an

incredible rate. I saw galactic bodies form in a spiral fashion, upon zooming into a single galaxy, I saw it was creating gigantic rotating Red stars within its confines, orbiting these red stars were smaller and smaller stars very similar to ours, followed by planets orbiting those smaller stars. Zooming in further and faster, I passed by each of the planets and understood that all of them were sentient spirits of Oma. I perceived each planet as a God-like being that was not yet grasped in its totality by most of the spirits within their terrestrial elements.

As I got closer and closer to our planet, I understood the earth too was a living being and a magnificent representation of Oma, just like everything else. Then I saw the viney plant spirit that looked like a replica of me floating in space above the earth not too far away from my location. It flew over with its massive wings, grabbed my back and flew toward our planet.

As I watched the Earth from space, I saw all the life on its surface as a massive swarm of genes, moving through highly permeable membranes, almost like watching bacteria under a microscope. The earth looked like a chaotic gene pool and appeared to be full of what looked like microscopic life forms. As time continued to zoom forward, I followed my specific ancestral lineages. Suddenly, the time slowed down enough for me to watch my mother and father change from genes in the gene swarm, to individual human bodies meeting for the first time; I watched them stay together for a short while, then break up because my mother caught him cheating on her.

Afterward, I watched their divorce, then my birth, and all the in-between. I watched my step-dad get introduced into the picture, then I watched my entire life and all my decisions in it play out right in front of me. I saw and felt everything I had ever felt in my whole life at fast forward speeds; seeing, tasting, smelling, feeling, and hearing everything I had ever perceived in my life throughout the course of my experience.

I humorously enjoyed watching myself run away frightened after spraying E-Su with bear spray, but I couldn't wait to be done with the trip. I felt like I had several millennia worth of experience in that short time and was looking forward to being a human perceiving time normally. I remember thinking that the whole process was taking so long and was so full of knowledge that there was now way I would remember every detail. Finally, I got to the time in my life when I drank the tea E-Su gave me and smoked from his long wooden pipe.

I thought that was the end of the experience as I watched myself ask my question after blowing out the smoke. Then as the plant spirit and I once again floated above the forest and my body, the plant spirit dropped my spirit off at that place in time. I expected to fall back into my flesh; however, I remained approximately ten feet out of body watching myself lay motionless in that stone circle. E-Su laid down a blanket, picked me up, and laid me on the blanket. Then he pulled the black stone from my pocket and put it into my hands then placed them on my chest. Afterward he put my sleeping bag over my body; I assumed this was to keep me from being eaten alive by flying

insects and it was from this point on that time passed as normal.

I floated as a disembodied spirit that was anchored to my earthly vessel for three days. E-Su was sitting next to me the entire time ensuring I was safe. I strangely did not feel any sense of panic or fear during my dislocated paralysis, but rather, I felt calm and transcendental. I felt I was a spirit from another dimension obtaining otherworldly knowledge that somehow kept me from being able to fully re-enter the confined realm of my body. It also helped me to understand and affirm the idea that I was not a body that possessed a spirit, but rather I was a spirit that possessed a body.

While I floated above my motionless vessel on the forest floor, colors unseen to the human eye and dimensions unknown to the human imagination unfolded before my spirit in patterns not comprehensible by any rational mind. These patterns flowed inside of themselves while also expanding their reach outside themselves. Simple patterns converged into an endless colorful, complex matrix of geometric shapes, patterns, and dimensions interlinked in all directions.

There was a slight hiss to this strange metaphysical place. Then I heard the plant spirit speak its final words to me. "I grant to thee, the ability to see, the constant flow of chi. Focus on creating chi in a pattern you desire and your standing wave will grow stronger, wider and higher."

Then I slowly started to re-enter my body and I realized E-Su remained by my side for the entire experience. Finally, after three days and three nights of floating disembodied in a multi-dimensional matrix, I returned to my body and sat up slowly.

E-Su heard my movement as he sat next to me and stopped in the middle of meditation to put his hands out attentively. I grunted out loud as I moved my feet and removed the sleeping bag from my face.

E-Su asked quickly "What? What is it?"

To which I replied, "I can hardly stand...and I really have to pee."

24) The Void

After my spiritual rebirth, I was able to see the chi in the world all around me, as well as all of the plant spirits that existed in nature; I could even talk to bugs and animals if I wanted to. It was astonishing, and I wanted to talk to someone about it. I vented to E-Su, but he just allowed me to talk and would not answer any of my questions. In fact, E- Su did not say much at all in the days after my spiritual rebirth. He made it clear that I was to absorb my experience without his input. It was no coincidence that a butterfly happened to cross our visual path during the explanation of his silence. E-Su said that the butterfly was Oma's way of reminding me of the independent nature to the spiritual growth process and the damage done by helping an aspiring spirit mid-metamorphosis.

Later that night E-Su made a fire the way he had before using his

hands and chi, only this time, thanks to my spiritual rebirth, I got to see how he used the chi to create the fire. The continuously flowing Chi all around me looked like a flowing grid made of infinite layers of energy piled on top of one another, each layer was about an inch thick and looked to be bordered by a thin transparent line that segmented each individual layer. Each layer moved from the ground, all the way up into a massive ever-changing geometric pattern in the sky. I watched as these chi layers were pulled into E-Su's body, changing the flow and pattern of the layers surrounding him, like a massive rock disrupting the flow of a smooth stream. Then I watched the layers of chi leave his body, each one containing interconnected symbols resembling, Arabic, Sanskrit, or Hebrew. The symbols were strung together in an ever-changing pattern that emanated from his body. In this way the chi carried E-Su's spiritual pattern inside its layers going back to Oma as the waves continued to rise very quickly into the sky and out of view.

When E-Su started praying and spoke into his hands, I saw a tiny orange symbol that flickered like a flame emerge at the base of both of his palms and the top of his head. When he lifted his hands toward the sky, several orange fiery symbols continuously poured from his hands and head, becoming intergraded inside of his chi pattern in the sky; then the fire symbols stopped flowing from his body and were taken upward in a massive orange cloud into the sky and out of view. E-Su knelt on the forest floor and put one hand over the woodpile and another onto the earth. To my astonishment, the fire symbols that rose into the sky came up through the earth in near endless

quantities and were pulled into E-Su's body through his feet. He poured these symbols from inside his body into the woodpile with his shaking hand. When the symbols accumulated at the base of the woodpile, a visible flame emerged, causing all the symbols to turn into flames and the wood pile was ignited in an instant as he pulled his hand up quickly. I was in awe, even though I shouldn't have been, I should have become accustomed to being astonished by E-Su and the application of his sacred knowledge.

The fire felt warm and comforting against the cold night. I heard a wolf howling somewhere in the near distance; apparently, word had gotten around the forest that a human being was learning the Ularu way of Shama, and the wolf was congratulating me on this accomplishment from a respectful distance, knowing I could comprehend his howls in my enlightened state. The world was so alive and full of respectful kindness, it was most certainly a magical place of unending beauty. I looked up at the waning moon in the sky and wondered what the moon's role was in that magic and mystery. Its dull shine combined with my heightened state of awareness lit the dense surrounding forest surprisingly well. As I looked around, I could clearly see several details like never before, including E-Su coming out of the darkness of the cave carrying more wood.

Even though I had fasted for three days during my spiritual rebirth and was feeling weak, I still felt elated to be back in my body. I had never known how amazing and euphoric having a body was until I went three days without being able to enter mine. My old views of reality were totally obliterated after my spiritual rebirth; the only thing was I didn't remember much of the experience after I returned to my body—except for brief flashes. Nevertheless, in some profound way I was changed down to my core. I felt as though I belonged to some higher cosmic order of understanding or at least that I was the participant in something far more extraordinary than my brief life on earth. I felt as if I had reached beyond the limits of physical reality itself and into an unknown dimension of mystery and spontaneous illumination.

I looked at E-Su while he poked the fire with a stick, and in a similar way to how I felt about my mother before I left for the forest, I felt a very deep sense of gratitude for all the blessings that E-Su had brought into my life in the few short months I knew him. I was so grateful to have the perspective I had, but it's funny how getting what you want can remind you of what you had; because at that moment I thought of home and I wondered how my mother might be doing considering I was never found. I wondered about how my sudden disappearance was affecting everybody, including Isaac and my brothers, I even wondered about Monique.

More than anything, I wanted all of them to share in my incredible experiences. I wanted to tell them all how the world isn't what it seems on the surface in any way. But how could I do that without giving away vital details that E-Su asked me to keep to myself?

Then I heard E-Su's voice "Even if you told them, they wouldn't believe you. The ones you love would think you had gone mad, and if they did believe you, they would want to meet me for themselves."

I tried to reason with him by saying “I don’t know E-Su; my mom would probably believe me and so would my grandpa. Besides, most people are good hearted and open to paranormal phenomenon, if it is introduced in the right way that is."

He looked unaffected by my words, "Allow me to tell you the story of the panda; then you tell me what you think." he replied, taking a deep breath. "During the British colonialization of China, there was talk amongst the local Chinese of a black and white bears that lived deep in the forest and ate bamboo. For quite some time none of the British believed that this rumor was true, calling the Panda a myth and legend. Until one day an English explorer arrived on Britain shores baring the skin of one of these sacred bears. After having proof that these beautiful, rare and mysterious animals existed, it became the new fad of these selfish, simple-minded consumers to own the skin of these animals. The panda is almost extinct right now because of these atrocities." His face was very stern and serious; his eyes did not lie.

I suddenly became very sick; I felt the pain and sorrow of the panda species as I momentarily tapped into their portion of the Life-Net. It was so tragic and overwhelming that I had to regain my mental bearings as he explained further, "If humans have proof of the Ularu's existence, we will meet the same fate as the panda or worse. For that reason alone, we Ularu usually stay on the move. I am only remaining in one cave for your sake, I found out the hard way that having predictable behavior makes you easy prey. As I said before, I had a son once Will, he was...." A tear began to show in E-Su's eyes.

"He was..." He paused for a moment and took a deep breath. "When we were walking back to the cave we called home, he and I were abducted by a flying metal disc vehicle, inside were evil humans dressed in white coats. They used otherworldly technologies I had never seen before when they bound and tortured my son and me."

He paused for a few moments, I was going to ask what happened next, but I saw tears were flowing from E-Su's eyes as he covered them with his hand; he was very obviously emotionally upset, so I decided to stay quiet. He continued speaking after his tears stopped "My son and I were forcibly restrained by our hands and feet with an electric rope that would shock us if we moved and they put these rings on our heads that didn't let us use telepathy. Then they shocked my son's head with electricity to knock him out while they restrained him on the metal operating table."

Streams of tears started to pour from his eyes again, his sad face began to turn angry, and his eyes turned glowing red as he lifted his fist up and smashed it on the ground "And I could do NOTHING!!!! Nothing, but lay there helpless and watch as they skinned him alive on that operating table. They said they wanted to study the living anatomy of this newly discovered species, and then they laughed..." He roared out loud, "They LAUGHED, as he screamed restrained and in pain on the examination table. I did not believe he was conscious of the experience until I heard him wail. He kept screaming for me to help him! I tried to break free, but I couldn't, so I roared so loud it shook every sharp surgical object in the examining room. One of the men walked over and electrocuted me with the ropes,

leaving me conscious enough to watch in silence as they removed my son's eyeballs to see where they attached to the brain, then drew all of his blood and bone marrow while he was still alive. I have never been the same since."

I relived the experience with him through our telepathy, and I was crying as well after seeing and feeling everything E-Su communicated. "I am SO sorry E-Su," I said, I felt such a strong connection to him and his son at that moment I felt as if I were there as he told me the story by the light of the fire.

He continued by saying "Thank you, even though it is against the way of Shama I got my vengeance. I waited patiently, remaining calm, as I was determined not to have the same fate as my boy. I allowed the men to think the electric shock to my head knocked me out and I remained limp while they took off the electric ropes and worked to put my heavy body on the cold metal examination table. I bided my time, so they did not restrain me right away, and when all of their backs were turned preparing the tools to skin me as well; I rose up and released my wrath upon each of their small, fragile bodies."

"What happened?" I asked entranced by his story.

"Well I don't like to speak of it, but I might as well finish the story. I crushed one man's skull with my hand, then one of the others hit the alarm button on the wall. As the alarm siren sounded, I ran over and grabbed the man by his arms and kicked him in the chest, ripping both of his limbs from their sockets as he flew across the room

screaming. Another man reached for a weapon, so I threw the bleeding arms at him to slow him down; giving me enough time to race over and grab him by the ankles. Then with one strong pull of both of his legs in opposite directions, I tore him right in half as he wailed in pain and showered me in his blood. Afterward, I moved on to the last remaining human in the operating room. He was screaming for help while cowering in a corner like a scared child. I silenced his screams by picking him up by his feet, uncurling him from the fetal position and wrung his body like a rag. The crunching sound of the bones combined with his horrible screams of pain is something that is burned into my memory.

The alarm and all of the screaming attracted much unwanted attention and to survive, I had to release a vicious storm of rage on the rest of the humans in that air vehicle, causing it to crash in the desert where they were taking us. My escape was so horrible and gory that I don't want to speak of it further. I will just say that I made it home soaked in the blood of my captors with my son's body in hand and my life was never the same. This is why I don't want you to tell anybody about me. It's bad enough for me that there is rumor of a Mogollon Monster living in these woods. It is a good thing that people don't believe that it is true. If enough people know that it is true and word reaches the dark lords, those who want peace with us Ularu will be outnumbered by those who wish to hunt us, experiment on us or use us for work purposes."

"That is so awful E-Su! I am so sorry to hear that you had to go through that. I wish things didn't have to be that way between the

humans and the Ularu. Wasn't there a time when the Ularu and humans got along?" I asked curiously.

"Yes, as I told you before there was a time when the Ularu and humans lived in harmony, we spent much time conversing with your medicine men and helping them to understand the truth about reality. However, with the European's migration and thus the spreading of the dark lords influence, your species has seen much death and pain. We Ularu have avoided much of that because for countless winters my kind has lived a free, peaceful life in the forests and jungles. I will not see that jeopardized by the loose lips of a human I chose to trust. I will not appear before others if you ask me to. I hope you understand. I do not care to say much more for the night. I am going to sleep, rest well Will." E-Su stood up, rubbed my head with his hand and walked into the cave.

I remained sitting in shock for several minutes afterward; I fully understood E-Su's reasoning and I felt a real profound sense of sorrow for him and his son. I also had a profound feeling of honor that he chose to reveal himself to me after such a terrible thing had happened to him. *What an incredible heart he must have to be willing to take me under his wing after all of that,* **I thought. Such compassion was not something I was used to in the human world. My culture taught that it was either kill or be killed, that only the strong survive, and it's every man for himself.**

I began to wonder what could have led us to such heartless and selfish conclusions. Then I thought about our cities, their crime, their

poverty, their pollution, and I saw where the dark lord's way of using our world led. It led to everyone fighting and killing one another in wars over the illusion of scarcity. *If more people were like E-Su and the Ularu themselves maybe the world wouldn't be in the condition that it is in, maybe we should adopt the way of a Shama, for all of life's sake,* **I thought. Then after putting some dirt on top of the fire, I went into the cave to sleep on my bed of foliage.**

Upon waking the next morning, I went outside to stretch and meditate. I had grown more than I had ever thought possible during my time with E-Su. I began to get so comfortable for the months that I was there, I lost track of the days of the week and the month I was in, however, I was able to keep track of the time, and the days by using the sun and moon cycles. I was consciously using the creative process in combination with the influential power of the sacred spiral more and more often in my thoughts and daily practice while I lived in the wild. This caused my senses to become more enhanced and I felt I was in touch with the earth and the natural world as if I were born in the wilderness. When I came back into the semi-darkness of the cave after completing my morning routine, E-Su was smiling with a subtle disappointment.

"You have grown so much from when I first met you. Your Spirit is truly reflecting the Oma within. I wanted to tell you, that you alone have restored my faith in humans and helped me to get over what happened to my boy.

My teacher told me when those men killed my son that something

exactly like our interaction would occur. I didn't believe it at the time; I was in too much pain and it did not seem possible. Especially with the way the dark lords have control of your species. Then a few days before your arrival at my prayer tree, my son came to my mind during meditation and so did my teacher's prediction. The Oma at my core told me that you were coming, but I still doubted. Until I suddenly felt something delicate touch my nose. I opened my eyes to see a beautiful butterfly had landed on my nostrils and I could not deny the omen.

You remind me of my son in a so many ways, including the hook-shaped birthmark on your chest being exactly like the one he had on his chest, and in the same spot too. All of these things my teacher told me to look for after almost 100 winters. That was why it was just as strange for me to meet you as it was for you to meet me, because I was told you would be there and I could not believe it. You've helped me to come to the next step of my healing process, and thus to the end of my old life and the beginning of a new better one; a life free from the torment of my son's torture and untimely death. For that, I thank you for helping me as much as I have helped you, and it has been an honor to have interacted with you.

For today I have a special tea potion that will help you to regain strength very quickly and retain the memory of your spiritual rebirth. You should feel your internal vigor come back to you over the course of the day and you will wake up tomorrow feeling completely refreshed." I did my best to remain silent while he communicated with me, for among the Ularu I learned you do not

wait for you turn to speak. You are to really listen to everything the other being is sharing.

He handed me the stone cup from my spiritual rebirth, this time; it had a greenish-black tea in it. I drank the brew without hesitation. It tasted like burned chocolate and old orange juice while having the kick at the back of my throat like cayenne pepper. Despite its unusual taste, I felt its power begin to work immediately. The liquid seemed to get soaked up by my body, like water to a sponge. I felt every single cell become supercharged with high-intensity energy and in the process; I felt a strong connection to my previous experience of the heavy light at the height of my spiritual rebirth. I got to see it again for a brief but magical moment; this profound flashback allowed me to remember every bit of my spiritual rebirth in vivid detail. The peace of this sudden rush caused me to close my eyes.

Upon doing so, I saw a light at the end of a colorful tunnel like I had seen before. Feeling on the verge of ecstasy, I suddenly felt myself drop from this experience into a black void below my feet. My energy plummeted and I became freezing cold while I fell downward. I tried opening my eyes to stop the experience, but it did not matter, everywhere I looked was black, which freaked me right the fuck out. I started sweating profusely; my breathing became shallow and my heart rate became rapid. My windpipe was closing up, and I found it increasingly harder to breathe. Eventually, I couldn't move my body at all, and I felt like a cold dead statue falling through an endless pit of despair.

Then there was a sudden impact, and I knew I had returned to my body. I knew this for sure because I could feel a warmness shoot up from the base of my spine and protrude out of the top of my skull, causing the sensation to fall like colorful drops of rain onto my spiritual perspective. With this feeling also came a high pitched ring that no human ear can hear. Inside of my body, this frequency was every piece of my experience as a human encapsulated into one sound, every memory I ever experienced in my life was compressed into one mentally accessible stream of energy within my spirit, allowing my memory bank to remain open for absorbing massive amounts of new esoteric information. Somehow thanks to this special brew, I could also instantly access any moment from my life with photographic memory. I opened my eyes and looked over at E-Su. His physical body was no longer visible. However, the chi that flowed through his tremendously wide and tall spirit was clearly visible.

Then I came to the shocking realization that I too was one of these spiritual beings flowing with chi. This was not all dull thought, but rather it washed over me like a tidal wave of gnosis and wisdom in a matter of a few moments. I was enveloped in a radical new way of seeing the world and my role in it; physical objects were no longer just objects but physical manifestations of the invisible fields of chi that created them. Upon realizing this, I threw my head back and laughed at the sky. Little did I know, this entire experience only spanned less than a few minutes.

E-Su began to chuckle while he read my thoughts and psychically watched my experience, saying "I just gave you the cherry on top of

your transcendental Sunday. The potion you just drank was a very special one. That mix of herbs and spices did not contain an Elder plant with an Oma key, but it was meant to do several other advantageous things. That potion is meant to catalyze highly improved cognitive function, add massive amounts of memory space and make all other memories accessible at will in every detail. It also temporarily removes all recognition of the physical realm allowing you to perceive only the flow of chi for a brief time span. The brew is given to an Ularu after they have returned to their bodies following their spiritual rebirth. This is done in order to lock the experience of the spiritual rebirth in the memory of the physical body. By showing you the Void you got to see the yin and yang of the galaxy itself and the intensity of the places that exist within our galactic realm. There are all sorts of places you can go in the psychic space.

The experience of rebirth is often too intense for any physical membrane to retain, but its memory is retainable in the chi pattern of the physical body if this brew is drunk in the proper amount of time. Now, kneel." As I slowly kneeled he continued, "You are now officially one of the Ularu and your name shall be "Juh Kah Bu", which translates closest to "Will and Power". This is your Ularu name because only a Human Spirit of undying will can make it through the intense initiation process of the Ularu and because you are being shown the ways of chi power; you as a spirit, are a combination of the two. Let it be known if only to the trees of this forest alone, witnessed by the pine old and new; you stand before me and these woods an initiated Ularu. Rise Will and Power stand a free

spirit and be empowered!"

I stood up proud and smiled in a bashful way, then he said "In a matter of minutes you're going to fall into a very deep sleep, and you're going to stay asleep for a full day while your body recovers entirely from fasting, when you wake it will be night again and then we're going to go to the stone circle to contact Yeti in order to see if he believes you are ready. Do you have any questions before you fall asleep?"

As funny as it was only one question was on my mind, so I asked him "Isn't Yeti the Abominable Snowman?"

E- Su looked confused then laughed out loud, shaking his head back-and-forth; he said "You humans are so strange. No, Yeti is the name of the last earth dwelling Ularu elder, he is one of six Ularu elders left in the Galaxy, and he currently lives in the Himalayan Mountains. He is also the oldest of all Ularu elders. No one knows how old he actually is, but his DNA, like all Ularu DNA, are much like the earth's sea turtles, our DNA doesn't degrade over time. So we Ularu only grow larger and more powerful as we age. Yeti has disappeared for centuries at a time and then re-emerged more powerful than ever before, a feat many did not believe was possible. Besides, Yeti looks nothing like what your species calls the abominable snowman.

What you know as the abominable snowman, we call the 'Moo Laka' which means 'gorilla bear.' That beast is actually a massive mammal from the Ice Age. It hibernates for ten years and eats in mass

quantities for ten years. It is a gigantic white-haired monster that towers over twenty feet tall and is bigger than any Ularu. It weighs approximately thirty thousand pounds, and it looks like a blend of a bear and gorilla, hence the name. Their fur is all white, but their skin is black, their roar is often mistaken for thunder, and it's movement is often mistaken for earthquakes. The primary distinction between the males and females of the species is, females just have small spiraling horns on their forehead, while males have spiraling horns on their forehead and large sharp antler-like tusks that protrude from each side of their jaw. The males use these antler-tusks, their massive claws and the sharp points of their teeth to fight over females. They migrate over thousands of miles of land, and sea to mate. Only a handful of humans and Ularu have survived an encounter with one of them because they are carnivores and eat whatever they catch raw within a few quick bites. There are only a few of them left in the world though, one lives in the Himalayas, two live in Antarctica, one lives in northern Russia, and one lives far north in what you call Greenland."

I was shocked that any creature lived through the Ice Age. *How many other legends were true?* **I wondered. How many other beasts and creatures actually existed on this planet that industrial society had written off as fantasy or had no idea even existed? If the Sasquatch existed as the very real Ularu race, the abominable snowman was real and plants had conscious spirits that I could communicate with, then what other mysterious creatures of ancient lore lurked in the forest, jungles, caves, oceans, and lakes of the earth. That was my**

last thought as I collapsed and fell asleep while standing and talking. E-Su caught me before I hit the ground, and laid me down on my bed, then he placed the black family stone inside of my hands on top of my heart and let me sleep.

25) From: Hello to Yeti to Goodbye to E-Su

I woke at night as E-Su promised, I walked out to a star filled sky and a waning moon to see E-Su sitting on the forest floor, meditating in the dark. I sat beside him and meditated feeling entirely recharged and filled with vigor as he had promised. Then, I heard his voice. "Are you ready to go to the stone circle?"

"I am," I said. Despite enjoying everything that I had experienced, I felt it was time to go back to my people, back to my home.

"You don't feel hungry do you?" E- Su asked

I replied in confusion. "No, not at all. Why is that?"

E- Su smiled and said "That's the tea I gave you doing its magic, it's keeping your spiritual energy high, so there is no need for food. You won't feel hungry at all for a couple of days, but it's probably best that you eat something small before we hike to the stone circle." E-Su looked around and pulled up a couple of dandelion plants from the soil and handedd them to me saying "Here eat these, flowers, leaves, roots and all; they have all of the essential vitamins and nutrients

your body needs." Then he went back inside his cave. I had grown past my queasy nature while living in the bush with E-Su and ate them without question. They didn't taste good, but I ate them all before E-Su came out of his cave. I looked up to see he was holding a large black bag and a long, thick gray wooden staff with a crescent moon carved out at the top.

"What is all that stuff for?" I asked curiously.

"You will see when we get to the circle." he said as he smiled, then we made our way to the stone circle.

After reaching the circle, E-Su leaned his staff against a bordering white boulder and insisted that we both meditate. After we both had cleared our minds, E-Su stood up then pulled a tribal drum about the size of his hand from the black bag and handed it to me. "Play this drum at two beats per second while I use my staff to call to Yeti. The magic to call to him requires a specific vibration that this drum houses when beaten. Do not stop playing no matter how tired your arms get. Okay?" I nodded my head; then he walked over to grab his staff still leaning on the stone.

I began playing the drum as instructed while sitting in the middle of the circle. The sound waves emanated off of the drum and into the air above the circle in large rings of sound which enveloped the surrounding white stones. E-Su walked over to the eastern quadrant of the stone circle and spun the front of his staff in a spiraling motion through the air while speaking in Ularu. His words sounded something like "Noom Tom Bockee Ehh Somba!" the intensity in his

voice rose each of the four times the words were spoken. Chi emanated from the tips of the crescent moon on his staff leaving a spiral tracer of his words in a pattern of black symbols made of glittering chi in the air.

Then he thrust his staff up through the middle of the spiral he created, and the symbols were shot into the sound waves of the drum, blending them both into a single circular wave of chi moving up into the star lit sky. Suddenly the wind began to noticeably spin and swirl all around the circle.

E-Su moved to the next quadrant of the circle and repeated the same process of with his staff while saying his magic Ularu words, this time creating new symbols of chi with his different words which manifested as white in color. "Eeth Coola Rem Haki Eeta!" Once again after repeating this phrase four times, he thrust his staff through the spiral's center sending the symbols into the drum's sound waves and up into the heavens. Immediately following this action, a loud distant clap of thunder echoed, the wind blew even harder, and the borders of the clear starry sky rapidly became covered by masses of gray clouds.

Next E-Su moved to the neighboring quadrant and repeated the process over again, this time creating red symbols by saying, "Heetha Hoola Deh Nala De Na!" When he shoved his staff into the air and the symbols were thrust into the drum's sound waves, the wind blew with hurricane force, the clouds swept over the entire sky above our heads, and lightning began to strike everywhere around the circle.

We were enveloped in a dense fog and thick fat globs of rain fell from the sky. I got nervous for a moment, and my drumming slowed just slightly, then I heard E-Su say "Don't worry, keep drumming and don't stop for any reason otherwise the signal will not work." I could hear E-Su's footsteps move to the last quadrant as I continued my drumming.

I assume he repeated the same process with his staff a fourth time because I could not see in the dense fog, but I heard him shout in Ularu "Com Vel Dah Hana La Com!" The rain poured harder and faster, the fog got thicker and the lightening began lighting up every quadrant of the circle with streaks of bright electricity. I felt the thunder rumble in rhythm with my beating of the drum; then I heard E-Su yelling out loud, as he sent his message to Yeti in the peak of the storm.

"Chom Patha Wallo Yeti! Kee Sheembe Weshee, E-Su! Sak Tom Cooshoo, Jaah Ka Boo...Umba Et Aki Etaah Ularu, Toom Blah Kasha Haba Waksa, Moosh Roobahs, Et Ah...Boo Shoo Boo Washka Shama! Ra Blah Plah Blah, Woo Foo Shama...Esh Tib Whibb Levaah...Bogaah Nagaaah Wathaaaha!"

E-Su howled magnificently loud, and as if the sound wave from his lungs pushed it away, the storm rose from the circle in a massive spiraling cone shape of rain, fog, and wind. The lightening that weaved through it carried the spiraling storm into the upper atmosphere, and then it dissipated completely.

I was still drumming until E-Su walked over to me with his staff and said. "You can stop drumming."

"Okay." I replied, "So now what?"

"Now we wait." he said.

"Wait for what? What did we just do?" I asked still perplexed.

"Wait for a reply from Yeti. It's kind of like your digital web of computers only we use the life-net of the planet to send the message. We use the flow of chi and the elements as our medium to house the message and the magnetic grid of the earth to transport that message. We will get Yeti's reply in the form of a storm. We Ularu speak telepathically when face to face, but we use the earth to carry our messages a great distance. This circle magnifies my telepathic abilities only so far, if I want to send a message all the way across the planet, I must use the earth and its elements as the means of relaying that message, and I am only able to send such a message from within this circle. When the storm gets here, it will house Yeti's reply."

"How will we know what he says?" I asked

"You won't because it will be in Ularu tongue, but don't worry I won't keep you in suspense about it." He laughed. Then to my surprise an enormous bright streak of light descended from the sky toward the circle.

"Wow! That was a fast reply!" E-Su said standing up looking at the streak of light coming toward us.

"That's a reply?" I asked as the bright streak traveled closer and

closer to our location.

Bracing for impact with his staff, E-Su said: "Hold on, here it comes!"

The moment the bright streak of light reached the sky above the circle it exploded in a clap of thunder, sending out a shockwave that nearly burst my ear drums. There was a very deep drumming sound that grew louder and louder as a massive spinning grey cloud descended on top of us, lightening struck the ground everywhere, thunder echoed in rhythm with the drumming, rain poured hard and with the falling rain Yeti's words echoed in the storm. His voice was far deeper than E-Su's as he spoke in Ularu.

"Cromb Lom E-Su...Tog Wog...Hatha Tob Kemba Jaah Ka Boo...Ra Blah Plah Blah, Woosha Fooshoo, Oma Shama...Toma Oom Eskaton...Noma Trob Blob Nom...Eshkee Teebee Womba...Crok Tomba Deeth Beedee Nooth." Then there was a deafening roar that sounded far superior to E-Su's, which sealed the message. All of the rain and clouds fell to the ground becoming absorbed by the earth, and the lightning and thunder stopped completely.

E-Su turned around still soaked in rain holding his staff, he shook off the moisture like a dog and afterward he said "You must leave right away. Your heightened state of Spiritual Rebirth is only going to last until the next full moon. Even though its memory is locked into your spirit, the freshness of the experiences fades and so does the view of chi within our spiritual realm. You will need to be in that state to see the path to Yeti's cave. You must leave today."

Taking my hands off the drum and putting them in the air I replied "But I have no money, how am I supposed to go anywhere? And how am I supposed to get to the Himalayas of all places? That's just ridiculous E-Su!"

He grabbed the drum from my lap and put it into the black bag. Then he reached inside of the bag and pulled out a thick gold coin. Handing the large heavy coin to me he said, "I'm giving you this ancient gold coin, it should be worth enough money to get you food, water, plus enough camping and hiking equipment to make it to Yeti in the Himalayas." Then he began to walk toward his cave, and I followed quickly after while examining the coin with my fingers.

"If this coin you gave me is an ancient gold coin, how old is it?" I asked curiously

"I found that coin and many others like it several hundred years ago inside of a cave." He replied, "I am not sure of their origin, but the cave was in this forest, I will take you to it one day when you return." He motioned all around us with his open palms. The coin had carvings and markings on it that I could feel with my fingers but couldn't read in the dark.

"Where would I even turn this in for money to buy supplies in the first place?" I asked

"You're going to have to go home to the city for a time Will, but going into the city may make it difficult for you to remember everything you experienced out here. When in the forest, you are in the bubble of life. While in the city you are in the industrial bubble

which is manufactured by the dark lords to imprison your spirits. Nature's bubble has natural, healthy frequencies emanating from it; these frequencies increase your spirit's ability to perceive Oma and the flow of chi through your body. But, when you go into the city, there are all sorts of unhealthy, unnatural frequencies emanating all around you, these are the dark lord's spells of oppression. Your phone towers are like invisible prison bars all around you; they create a net of frequencies over your entire city that obstructs your spirit's ability to perceive chi and the presence of Oma. As long as you stay in the heightened state of awareness from your spiritual rebirth, you will not be affected by these poisons or frequencies. You will remain untouchable by their spells, and it will not be as difficult for you to remember the truth."

"Wow!" I said, "Is there anything else I should know about going back to the city?"

"Yes, I would recommend that you only eat food which is poison free. Do not eat food that comes in a package, and if you can, try only to eat raw fruits, vegetables, and nuts. Those other foods in your stores are low resonance foods; they dull your mind and make you more susceptible to the spells of the dark lord's. If you eat those food products, they will take you further and further out of your heightened state much more quickly. This will make it even harder to return to your state of euphoria. So on your way to see Yeti make sure to only eat raw foods not polluted with poison to kill insects."

"But, how will I know what to do when I get to the Himalayas? How

do I find Yeti?" I asked confused.

He put his hand up and said, "If you let me explain all questions will be answered." I collected myself and tried to remain focused on what he was saying, "When you get to the Himalayas you will make telepathic contact with one of Yeti's most daring and courageous apprentices. He will conducting a stealth mission to retrieve you and will be waiting for you at the airport. He'll remain invisible to everyone else accept you. His name is Sot, he has an interesting sense of humor, so try to get out of the city and away from people as fast as you can because he enjoys toying with humans when he can. He is a part of something like your military's special forces for the Ularu. The only way you can see Yeti is if you bring him an offering of his favorite hallucinogenic honey. Sot will take you on the path to find the hallucinogenic honey. It's only made in the Himalayas and it is very dangerous to get, but if you can accomplish it you can meet Yeti and receive his training to become a Shama.

Once you have the honey comb, you need to find Yeti's cave. In order to see the path to Yeti's cave you must be an initiated Ularu, and in order to meet Yeti, you must first travel the hardest path to his cave with the honeycomb in hand. Once at the cave, you must leave the honeycomb on the stone altar at the entrance for Yeti to find. You may have to wait quite some time, maybe even days for him to arrive. It all depends on your patience level, which Yeti will telepathically know. Sit and wait patiently, and he will arrive far quicker. I personally had to wait three days and nights, because my patience level was not right.

Yeti will test you more than you have ever been tested in your life. I often wondered during my training if he was the most evil Ularu alive. He pushed me so far beyond my mental, emotional and physical comforts that I thought he enjoyed my suffering. All I can tell you is this, everything is a test, you must have courage, and nothing is what it seems."

While I contemplated his words, we walked until we came upon the entrance to the cave. E-Su walked into the cave for a moment and walked out with my backpack. It was then I realized I was going to miss him a lot. As he handed me my bag we shared a grin, then he randomly spit in my face, covering my eyes, nose and lips in his thick gooey saliva. I was shocked, disgusted, angry, and confused, all at the same time. Feeling highly disrespected, I wiped my face with my hand and said, "What the fuck was that for?"

He laughed at me hysterically for a minute and then said "That is a custom of my species when someone has to leave. It might keep evil spirits away, or it may just be gross, I figured it was better to not take any chances." I was grossed out, and I know I looked as such as I wiped my face clean. E-Su laughed again and said "Hey, at least you will be protected; besides you threw up all over me when I healed your leg."

I didn't know if he was serious or wanted to play a joke on me before I left; so I smiled, rolled my eyes and put on my backpack. I put the coin in my pocket next to my family stone, then I started the long trek toward the dirt road. Before leaving I turned around and asked,

"Will I ever see you again E-Su?"

He replied with a slight grin, "If you survive Yeti's tests you can be certain of it! So be sure to survive so we can converse again sometime soon! I love you Will and Power, and I thank you for everything my son!" he laughed, turned around and then disappeared in a ball of light as he had before.

26) A Life for an Eye

All of my flashlights were dead, but my heightened spiritual state allowed me to have better vision while I walked through the forest in the semi-darkness before dawn. As I hiked back to the road, I wondered if everyone I knew had forgotten about me. I wondered if they had a funeral, then I wondered what my grandparents would say when they saw me on their doorstep? *Would they be in such shock, that they would have a heart attack? What was my mother going to think?* **I figured she would probably freak right the hell out and cry like a ten-year-old girl. My mind raced a million miles a second as all of my closest friends and loved ones came to mind.**

While I did look forward to seeing them again, I was strangely more excited and eager to meet Yeti. From what E-Su said he was the real

deal when it came to mystical beings and was far more powerful than him. Yeti was a sage almost as old as the Himalayan Mountains themselves, what a privilege it would be to meet him.

I touched the gold coin sitting next to the black stone in my pocket. If anything else that coin was proof to me that E- Su existed, and that despite the extraordinary circumstances, I wasn't crazy. And despite what seemed to be the insanity of my experiences, the past few months had been just as real, if not more real, than anything I had ever experienced throughout my life in the city. My mind raced and raced as to what I would tell everyone had happened to me out in the forest.

The gold coin and the scars from the witch on my arm were proof that my journey had been exciting and anything but uneventful. But I still wondered, *how would anyone believe the scars on my arm were from a crazy old witch who got lost in the forest? And that the gold coin was from an Ularu who took me in to show me the ways of his species and show me the secrets of the conscious living earth?*

While I was walking and thinking about all of these things, I occasionally heard movement behind me, followed by a strange feeling of being watched. As I walked further south through the forest toward the dirt road, I could tell something was off, there was a negative presence of chi in the air, and I knew someone was following me. That was when I heard a strange aggressive deep growling in the bushes behind me.

Things got quiet for a moment and something was thrown at me from

a bush ahead, it bounced off of my chest and onto the forest floor. I thought it was E-Su throwing a rock and playing a trick, so I stopped and smiled. After picking the object up, I could scarcely make out what it was, but it felt strangely familiar in my hand. It felt as though it was a stone of some sort, but it had a slightly rough black dry mass stuck to one of its ends. I brought the object closer to my eyes and used my heightened senses to focus intensely on the material in my hand. To my horror, I realized it was the smoky quartz crystal I had stabbed into the witch's eye. I instantly dropped the crystal from my palm and shouted out loud in disgust. Then I heard the witch's demonic laughter in the dark forest surrounding me.

I was about to run when I saw a single blue luminescent eye appear ahead of my position. The mass of the witch's body came into view through the darkness; its silhouette was surrounded by several floating demonic faces. A very distorted and chaotic pattern of negative chi symbols surrounded the body's mass, distorting the surrounding chi in a chaotic manner.

The demons spoke through multiple hellishly intense voices layered upon one another, as it raised a sharp fingernail at me. "A LIFE FOR AN EYE!" it growled.

After quickly receding into the darkness, I looked around as it sidestepped me, striking with a debilitating stiff forearm to my chest, knocking me to the ground. I saw stars, and for a brief moment, while laying disoriented on the ground, I forgot where I was. The witch jumped on top of me, pinned my arms with her hands and

began sucking the life right out of my mouth. It felt like all of the moisture from my throat and lungs was being pulled away from my body in a never-ending exhale. I could feel my spirit slowly being sucked of its essence and I struggled to free myself in vain. The feeling of helplessness was becoming overwhelming and I feared the worst.

I tried to work my legs in front of her chest to kick her off of me, however, as if it were perfectly timed, the black family stone fell out of my pocket and onto my chest. It instantly exploded with light, like it was a holy hand grenade, shooting the witch up into the air and onto the ground. I picked up the black stone which was still perfectly intact and pulsing with a fading light on the forest floor in front of me. The moment my hand touched its smooth surface, it emanated a light so bright it lit up the forest around me. The witch got up and roared out loud as I followed her around my perimeter with the stone's light.

I suddenly remembered that one of the plant spirits granted me the power to use the spiral pattern to ward off evil spirits; so I swirled the luminescent stone in a spiral around me, enveloping myself in a bright swirl of protective light while I scanned the perimeter to locate the witch's position. I spotted a single pale blue eye emerge from behind a tree and immediately swirled my light bearing hand in its direction. As she tried to run from the bright streak, she was stuck in the back by the swirling light, knocking her to the ground. The demons let out a deep roar, bounced up from the ground and receded into the darkness beyond my light's reach.

The spiral of light that shielded my body was gone, and in a panic, I didn't think to do protect myself with it again. Instead, I focused on locating the witch for another attack. While looking around the dark using the bright luminescent black stone in my hand, I could not see her at all. But I heard movement in the distance all around me; her speed was superior to my detection techniques to say the least.

When I thought I saw her in front of me, I ran toward her, but she blindsided me using her entire body to tackle me to the ground like a linebacker. A very sharp electric sting ripped through my spine and torso, followed by a brief ringing sound as I lay in the dirt. The terrible tackle forcefully knocked the luminescent stone from my hand onto the ground, causing its protective light to extinguish. Her devastating blow left me in enough shock to forestall my fighting nature. So the witch pinned my biceps with her iron grip, and leaned toward my ear to whisper in a soft woman's voice "A life for an eye," followed by a sadistic laugh.

Then her one eye turned black, and several dark demonic faces poured out of her open mouth. As I began screaming in terror, the demons entered my mouth and traveled into my throat. It felt as if I was trying to breathe from the hose of a high powered vacuum. I tried to fight her off, but could only remain paralyzed while the invading darkness crept deeper into my lungs.

She was in the middle of sucking the spiritual chi out of my mouth when she was suddenly struck by a bright orb of light; causing her to fall to the ground instantly. She screamed as the light turned into

binding electric waves, crackling and electrocuting her entire body pinning her to the forest floor. The woods all around me were illuminated for a brief moment by the wave left behind by the bright impact.

When I looked to see where the electrified ball of chi had come from, I saw it originated from the crescent moon at the end of E-Su's wooden staff. Electricity emanated from each tip of the moon, meeting in the center, creating a pulsating ball of electrified chi; as E-Su approached the witch, he began roaring in Ularu. "Whoo Boo Noo Hoo Shoo Boo Pola Tee Shan! Una Tomba Wonta Tonga! Roo Be Ularu Shama! Oma Whaanah Toonka! Ularu Sha! Oma Sha! Shama Sha Lamaha, Heeloo Rees!" I remained in shock as he approached her raving in his magical native tongue and using his staff to keep her bound.

Once E-Su was near her body, he put the ball of chi emanating from the crescent of his staff, directly onto the witch's heart. The demons tried to fight E-Su's electric spell of binding chi in vain, the Witch's body writhed on the ground, as the demons began speaking all manner of curses on us both. E-Su roared with intensity and continue his chanting in Ularu tongue. Oddly enough, amidst all of this chaos, I noticed what E-Su meant by a spirit's thoughts being open to telepathic view; for in order to exert his extraordinary power, E-Su first had to open his spirit to release some chi which his Spirit had stored. This allowed me to see into E-Su's mind for the first time, and I could see and read the chi symbols of his thoughts all around and through his body while he exorcised the demons; allowing me to

translate his Ularu words.

"You demons have been evading me and feeding on innocent hikers for far too long! Now, you are no longer able to run and your time has come! By the power of OMA, I command you to be GONE!!" E-Su yelled

"NEVER!" The demonic voices roared intensely, "This vessel is OURS! It BELONGS TO US!! Leave us ALONE before we kill you BOTH and eat your hearts!"

E-Su pushed the crescent of his staff directly on top of the witch's chest and he raised his voice to a booming volume "Through the life-giving power of the elements! And by the Collective Omnipresent Spirit of OMA itself! I command you to leave this demon's tool! Be banished from these realms of life and light! In the Name of Oma and all living beings of the cosmos, I command all of you to be gone from this world!"

Immediately the chi ran throughout the witch's body with a bolder, thicker intensity. Her face looked overwhelmed, and her breathing became panicked. Her skin cracked and spilt all over her face and body while dark streams of blood poured from the wounds in gory excess. Dark demonic faces started spiraling out of her mouth and moving toward the borders of the electricity surrounding her body. Seeing that his exorcism was working, E-Su increased the intensity of his chi even more; maximizing the electricity's thickness and rapid movement, and overpowering the demonic faces still spiraling out of the witch's mouth. While E-Su finalized the exorcism, blood poured

from all over the witch's convulsing body only to be flung into the air and onto the forest floor as she roared in pain that was unbearable to the human ear.

"I banish you dark spirits from this world forever!" E-Su yelled in Ularu, "Allow this body to rest in peace! As an Ularu Shama, I command you in the name of OMA, to go into the realms of light to be absorbed and depart from this vessel NOW!" As he released a massive amount of chi into her chest, I saw how E-Su used a small portion of the incredible amount of chi that he had stored in his spirit; I watched the flow of chi travel from the center of his body down the staff and surge through the witch, filling her quaking body with even more convulsive exorcizing energy.

Her soulless screams of pain and anguish echoed throughout the endless trees for miles then ceased suddenly as all of the dark demonic faces stopped pouring from her mouth and became broken apart by finer and finer veins of white electricity. The combo of the two evaporated in a plume of gray dust, and Christine Wellington's body was no longer pouring blood, but instead had become entirely dehydrated. Her dry blood covered delicate corpse remained frozen with its face wearing a look of pain and terror. I walked up and kicked the dry mass, the texture was that of burned wood and ash, then the body suddenly disintegrated onto the forest floor and becoming a fine black dust.

E-Su looked over at me as I looked up at him in shock, "Intense stuff huh?" he said. Then we both laughed out loud, contributing our

chuckles to the sounds of the post dawn bird chatter.

"Thanks for saving my life," I said, "I thought that I was done for to be honest, luckily I had that stone in my pocket."

"I told you that stone was going to be vital to your growth." He replied with a playful grin, "I am proud of you though, you have come a very long way in quite a short time. You almost fended the witch off on your own; that's very admirable as you are not even a Shama yet. But I must confess that I used you as bait."

I looked at him confused "What exactly do you mean?"

"Well, I decided to follow you just in case the witch wanted to get revenge, and it was a good thing I did too. I have been trying to perform that exorcism on her for over a decade. She didn't see me coming at all when she was entirely focused on absorbing your spirit. Sorry, her exorcism came at your expense, but that was the only way I knew the demons would leave her body vulnerable to my powers. I am never there when she finds the lost hikers; I just find their dry, withered bodies sucked of all their spirit, like hers was before you touched it. Anyway, seeing as how I used you as bait I brought you something special. Here, drink this." he said as he handed me a small pouch full of liquid. "That will restore the chi you just lost to the witch, it won't taste good, but it will feel amazing. And you don't have to worry, it isn't an intense elder plant, it's a very particular combination of food plants and healer plants to help boost your chi level."

I downed the liquid quickly, it tasted very earthy, which I didn't

mind, but when I felt the effects immediately, I looked at E-Su with wide eyes and looked back at the empty pouch still in my hand. He laughed and said “You will learn how to make this potion and much more when you receive your training from Yeti. After you get back from that part of your journey, you will be able to use your chi much in the same way that you just saw me use mine."

"So I am going to become that powerful?! How is that even possible? I am just a human, and you are a powerful Ularu?"

E-Su smiled and said "You humans are so smart yet you choose to think so simply. That kind of thinking is based on the spells of the dark lords, it’s meant to limit human’s spiritual growth, and keeping you un-evolved. Humans are incredibly powerful spirits! It is possible for all humans through the creative power of Oma's evolving reflection being channeled through their body as Chi and directed outside of their body to eventually become matter. Yeti will train you in all of this far better than I ever could. Now that the sun is up and the witch is gone you should get going to your elder's home. It has been an honor and a pleasure Will and Power. Until we meet again, take care son." I ran up and hugged him, he embraced me for a moment, then pulled away to bow and vanished into a ball of light as he had before.

27) Back Home But Not at Home

All of the events of my incredible otherworldly experiences weighed heavy on my mind as my exhausted feet pounded on the wooden steps to my grandparent's cabin. I hadn't even come up with an excuse for being gone for so long when I knocked and waited. I saw a shadow walking toward the door. When my grandfather skeptically looked through the window, I got to see what his eyes would look like if he had seen a ghost. The astonishment was unlike anything I had ever seen on his face before.

He opened the door immediately and gave me a hug with watery eyes, "WILL?!? I thought you were dead! Thank God almighty! Come inside, come inside. Nana! Nana! Will is Alive! Will is here, and he is alive!"

From the bedroom near the back of the cabin, I heard my grandmother's love filled yell "WILL!?" She ran to see me faster than I had ever seen her move before. She hugged me so tightly my back popped; I had no idea that she had so much strength. "Oh, thank God! My prayers have been answered!" she exclaimed.

They took me into the dining room and gave me some food and water. I ate and drank like it was the first time, throwing all manners aside as I stuffed my face with a sandwich from their fridge, and some chips and salsa.

"So what happened to you Will? Did you get lost? Were you abducted?" my grandfather asked.

My grandmother was wiping tears away from behind her glasses as I replied.

"I, uh..." I didn't know what to say, I wanted to tell my grandfather that I actually made contact with the Mollogon monster, but I knew E-Su had asked me not to. I was feeling very torn by the desire to be honest, while also remaining true to my promise to E-Su, so I lied and said "I was hiking going north in the forest, then something started chasing me. So I ran and got lost for weeks out in the wild. I only made it back because I walked south until I found a road."

My grandfather looked skeptical, and I began to read his mind similar to the way E-Su had read mine. I could see as I focused my attention more on my grandparent's chi, that their thoughts were floating around their bodies in symbols which displayed exactly what they were thinking. I could already tell my grandfather didn't believe my story before he said "You look like you have a bright glow around you Will and you don't look like you have starved at all. How did you survive out there?"

I didn't even know I had a glow around me, but he was right, I wasn't deathly thin; in fact, I was in better shape than when I had seen them a few months prior. After reading their minds, I realized they both thought that I had played an enormous, elaborate prank on everyone. They continued to doubt me, so I stopped my mind reading and said. "To be honest, my army training saved my life a lot

while I was out there grandpa," My grandfather was always proud of my military service, so I figured mentioning it was a good way of convincing him it had paid off. "I hunted and lived like a wild man until I eventually found the dirt road."

He looked skeeptical at my answer; he knew I wasn't entirely honest with him, and I didn't want to read his mind to see what he was thinking. "Well, I am just glad you are okay Will." He replied, "I am going to call your mother; this will cheer her up for sure! She almost fell apart completely when you turned up missing." In those moments I felt so guilty for leaving everyone the way that I did that I began to resent myself for my decision.

My grandfather picked up the phone and dialed, but my mother didn't answer. After hanging up he said, "Well, she didn't answer, but we will take you down to Phoenix, she needs to see that you are alive."

My grandparents let me wash a small load of clothes, and use their restroom the shower, shave my beard and buzz my head before the three of us got in their car and drove down to Phoenix. On the ride down the hill to the city, they explained that after my lease was broken at my apartment, my mother had collected all of my things and put them in her house as a keepsake, including my car. We made the trip to Phoenix in an awkward silence, my stomach began to gurgle, and I continuously had burps that tasted like vomit. The drive lasted a little more than an hour and a half, and as we

approached the city, I could smell the pollution in the air. Eventually, I could actually see a large gray net of wireless signals over the entire Phoenix Valley from a distance. As we drove into the city limits, I began to hear this strange underlying tone that eventually gave me a headache; but I did my best to ignore it until we arrived at my mom's house.

I knocked on the front door, but there was no answer, so my grandparents and I went around to the wooden gate into the bark yard and found it was unlocked. We walked past the back porch and up to the back door where I knocked before turning the unlocked knob to go inside. We walked through the kitchen and heard the TV playing in the living room at the end of the hall. We walked in to find my mom passed out drunk on her love seat with empty cans of beer everywhere. My grandfather gently shook her shoulder, and she slowly opened her inebriated eyes. When she saw I was standing behind my grandfather her eyes widened, and she freaked out.

"Oh my God WILL!" she jumped up quickly moving past her dad and hugged me so hard she brought me to the floor. She squeezed me so tight I almost couldn't breathe. "I have been praying for this moment so hard and for so long! I knew you would come back! I just knew it!" She kissed me all over my cheeks and head, then she hugged me again, squeezing me very tight. This lasted for at least five minutes before she calmed down and started to cry hysterically. I felt so bad for how horribly I affected my mother while I watched her cry. After a while, she stopped her sobbing and looked around teary

eyed to say "I am so sorry for the way things look around here. Obviously, I haven't been the best housekeeper recently. Are you hungry Will? Do you want something to eat?" she asked in an attentive manner.

"I appreciate it mom, but I am actually feeling so full I am kind of feeling sick," I replied. Then my stomach gurgled and my mouth filled with saliva. I knew I was going to vomit within a minute and I had to get to a toilet. "Actually, I have to use the restroom I am sorry to say, please excuse me."

I moved quickly down to the hall to the bathroom. After lifting the toilet seat, I threw up all of the food I had eaten at my grandparent's cabin, and I instantly felt better. I realized then why E-Su suggested I not eat any processed foods filled with chemicals. My body had been fully cleansed and putting those chemicals into my body would only cause an adverse reaction.

After getting out of the bathroom, my mom asked me what had happened and why I had disappeared for so long. I gave her the same story I had given my grandparents, only as I read her mind, I saw that she was much more willing to believe me in her half inebriated state. I could tell by briefly looking into all of their eyes that they wanted more details on what had actually happened, and where exactly my several month long excursion in the wild had taken me. I assured them that I would tell them more in the coming days and

ironically more than anything I needed my alone time again to process everything I had gone through.

That night, I slept on my memory foam bed for the first time in months. Oddly enough, over time I had come to find more comfort in the bed that E-Su had made for me and in that moment I missed him. So I pulled out the gold coin he had given me from my pants pocket on the floor and began toying with it in my hands. It was then I noticed, that instance, was the second time E-Su had come to mind since I left to go back to Phoenix. I deduced it must've been the food that I ate at my grandparents that made me forgetful, after all, it did make me vomit and give me give me a bunch of awful burps.

Once E-Su came to mind the memory of everything else I had experienced came back in a flash as well. Then was when I fully remembered why I had come to the city. I was supposed to take a plane to the Himalayas after turning in the gold coin for cash. Although at the time, it seemed so much easier just to stay there. I could have easily used the money from the coin to get myself back on my feet in the city if I wanted. The Shama training sounded like a lot of work, and after everything I had experienced I was exhausted, and emotionally overwhelmed. I wondered if I had to leave right then or if I could wait a little bit, and just leave in a few weeks. Laying there staring at the ceiling, I began to reason with myself that it would be okay if I left in a month as opposed to within a few days, then I fell asleep.

The next day I went about my city life and tried to live the normality experienced by an average American citizen. At around noon, Isaac and I met up at a fast food joint; he offered to pay for my food, but I, knowing it would dull my mind and make me sick, chose to respectfully decline.

After telling him the same story I told everyone, I read his mind and saw that he didn't believe me either. Then he said, "Well if you had come back looking like skin and bones then I might believe you, but you have a glow around you that I have never seen around anyone before, except for in paintings of Buddha and Jesus and shit. Actually, you look healthier and happier than ever. So, I know you well enough to know that there is something you're not telling me, and I don't know why. If you can't tell me, then who can you tell?" He looked hurt, confused and slightly angry as he made his point, then he bit into his delicious smelling fast food burger. The odor made my mouth water profusely, but I knew it was a trap, it was a scent based coercive spell, designed to look like food, but if absorbed into my spirit, would result in mental suppression and spiritual repression. So I looked away and tried to ignore my hunger.

"Listen, I am not going to lie to you." I said trying to level with him, "There was a lot that happened out there that I am not going to talk about with anyone, ever. It is not because I don't want to tell you in particular because believe it or not, I want to tell everybody! But, because I gave my word that I wouldn't tell anyone ever, so, my lips are sealed."

"You gave your word to who?" he asked quickly.

"I can’t say." I replied, "I have probably already said too much as it is." I rubbed my forehead to relieve some stress. "Isaac, I need you to trust me now more than ever. I know my excuses are lame and I know my answers only leave you wanting more, but I just can't give you the answers that you are looking for bro, I am sorry. I just can’t."

He looked upset and confused, and as I read his mind, I saw symbols that stood for fear, anger, and confusion. They all united into a single string of symbols before he spoke aloud saying "You can't tell me? Or you won’t?"

"I can’t and I won't, it’s just too important that I keep my word," I replied sincerely.

I already knew what he was going to say before he said it, but I was shocked at how accurate my telepathic mind reading was when he spoke in the tones of the symbol I was seeing all around him.

"Whatever bro, if you ever decided to actually open up about what happened to you then let me know." he packed up his half-eaten burger in the wrapper and put it into the bag as he stood up saying, "I’m gonna to get going, come on, I will give you a ride back to your mom's place."

“Dude, come on, don’t be like that,” I said. But he simply walked away and went out the door to his black two door car. I followed after him and realized as I read his mind that it didn’t matter what I said to him at that point. So, we made the five-minute drive back to my mother's in silence. I tried to apologize to him through the open window of his car after he dropped me off, but he interrupted me in a perturbed manner.

"It’s whatever bro. You don’t see me for months; I think you are dead, and then when you resurface, you refuse to tell me the truth about what happened! It’s all good though; I will just see you whenever you are ready actually to talk." Then he sped off while flipping me off out of his window, and I didn’t know if he meant it in a friendly way or not.

I felt awful for being so distant and lying to everyone, but I refused to break my word to E-Su. When I went inside, I laid down to watch some TV and get my mind off of everything. Only, when my eyes were on the screen, I felt as though the new understandings I had obtained in the wild become so incomprehensible and overwhelmingly odd that I wondered if I had just gone mad in the forest.

Only, the kind of experiences I had in the forest, were the kind of experiences most human beings craved throughout their lives. I had a euphoria after my contact with E-Su which was similar to the

euphoria I had when I believed in Santa Claus or the tooth fairy and would wake up to a surprise under the Christmas tree or my pillow. Only that natural high was stolen from me when I was told the truth about Santa Claus and the Tooth Fairy. I had not had those feeling again until my encounter with E-Su.

Except, whenever I became fixated on a screen, it seemed to be easier put this mystical point of view to the back of my mind. I didn't like the feeling that my addiction to the screen gave me, after enough time of sitting stagnant, I felt like I had nasal congestion, except it was in the center of my brain and went all the way down my spine.

The strange effect that the screen had on my psyche illustrated for me how the perspective I had acquired in the forest was as much a responsibility as it was a blessing. Inclining me to see how things would go with Monique before I fully made up my mind on whether I was going to leave to train with Yeti. After everything, I still felt a deep love for her, and it was that love that made me want to stay in the city.

After reactivating my phone I sent Monique a text, she had apparently deleted my number, because she responded with "who's this?" When I told her who it was and I got no response, I tried to call her, but she didn't pick up. So I decided to go over to her apartment complex and knock on her door. Surprisingly she opened it very quickly, charged with emotion. Then she hugged me right away and began to break down in tears.

Turning to dead weight in my arms she pulled me to the ground as she slowly sank to the concrete outside of her door. She kept sobbing and talking at the same time. All I could make out was "I thought you were dead." and "I'm so sorry." After calming down enough to speak clearly, she eventually said "I am sorry Will, I am glad you are not dead, but I can't see you anymore. I got back together with my Ex, and he will be home soon, so it is probably best if you just go." Even after all of that time, her words were quite the emotional blow.

"I understand," I said in a calm but disappointed tone. "I just wanted to let you know I was alive and well and that I wish you all the best." I gave her a hug and walked away trying not to let the anger, pain, and sadness get to me. To say the least, I was heartbroken once again, and I left her apartment knowing that my heart belonged in the Himalayas. That afternoon I turned in the gold coin for cash at an antique store totaling five grand in cash pay out. Then I bought a plane ticket to the Himalayas, got the gear I needed for the hike, then I packed all of my things and was ready to leave the next morning.

My flight wasn't until the next night, but I couldn't wait to leave. I could feel the toxicity of the city, it was filled with chemicals and frequency spells of suppression and depression. Eventually, the negative chi patterns began to have an effect on my psyche; it was only when I ate some organic fruits and vegetables from my local farmer's market that I felt the negative effects wear off. The plant's

chi and spiritual perspective helped to restore my heightened state of awareness, and I felt euphoric once again.

By that point, I had seen the pattern; while in front of the television, on my phone or the Internet, it was much easier to doubt my intuition and set aside the truth that I knew about reality. The wireless frequency spells emitted by the cell phone towers, combined the hypnotizing power of the colorful screens all around me eventually became intolerable. Their low vibrations were moving all around and through my body, the whole city smelled of toxic fumes, and I felt every time I breathed in I was inhaling a bunch of deadly chemicals. Eventually, I began to wonder how I ever got used to such a thing. The feeling was so overwhelming, in fact, that after only a short time, I felt the starving desire to connect with nature and leave the confines of my mother's comfortable air-conditioned home in favor of the wide-open skies of a nearby preserved mountain range inside the city.

I could not ignore the urge, and I decided to leave the house and go on a hike, I was very thankful that my mother had not sold my car, as it got me around while I was in the city. I drove to the mountain preserve quickly and following a brief stretch to warm up my muscles, I began my hike.

When amidst the mountain preserve, I noticed that the lava rocks had faces, then they began to whisper to me as I walked by saying "Leave the city! Save the planet."

I noticed that the tree's faces looked distressed as they urged me to leave, saying, "Go, you must see Yeti! You must not ignore the path of Shama!"

All of the tall Saguaro cacti cried out to me "The whole earth will die! Go to Yeti! Do it for all of us!"

I became overwhelmed as everywhere I went I was urged by nearly every spirit in nature to leave the city and learn the ways of Shama. Feeling the pressure, I asked out loud "Oma, if you exist answer me now in a way that is irrefutable. Should I leave to train with Yeti? Is that what all of this is about? Should I continue down this path to become a Shama? Should I try to save the planet from the dark lords?"

Suddenly I heard a raven call from behind me, and as I looked up, I saw its enormous black silhouette fly overhead and land on the arm of a giant Saguaro cactus in front of me. The Raven looked right at me, cocked its head to the side, woofed its wings, and said "Go! Go! Go!" afterward it looked up at an airplane that was passing over the mountain range. Then it jumped off the cactus and flew in the direction of the local international airport. I knew then that raven was my personal omen, and the longer I stayed in the city the harder it would be to remember E-Su and everything I had experienced. As I gazed up in my spiritually awakened state, I saw the dark gray net of negative chi in the sky was connected to a tower on top of the

mountain which I was hiking. So, I climbed to the top of the mountain to get a better look at the tower and the origins to the net of negative chi itself.

From the rectangular metal structures mounted on the tall gray towers, I saw the negative chi of the dark lord's spells spewing forth and permeating the entire valley. After closer inspection I noticed that the chi was made of varying dark symbols; each one standing for a different negative feeling. Among the net of symbols racing across the sky and raining down on the city were: hate, death, fear, destruction, disease, anger, scarcity, sadness, confusion, duality, pain, depression, separation, suppression, segregation, dominance, racism, and sexism. All the feelings that caused pain and problems in the human world were represented in the frequencies and their symbols flying through the air and raining down from the net in the sky. I found it interesting I could discern what each of the symbols meant just by looking at them in my awakened state.

When I focused enough, I could see that some of the symbols were going to my phone, and surrounding my spirit in their dark spell of negative feelings; except the symbols couldn't penetrate my spirit field due to its heightened vibration. It was then that I saw these waves of symbols assaulting my spirit were, in fact, the origins of the intolerable feelings I felt all around me while in the city. I began to understand what E-Su meant about the towers being invisible prison barrs. From the top of the mountain, I clearly saw how the whole city was being drenched in these streams of negative symbols and

frequencies, each stream going to a cell phone or another kind of hypnotic colorful screen device. I realized then that E-Su was correct about many things that I just didn't understand and I knew it was best then that I didn't tell Isaac what actually had happened, despite my very real desire to do so.

I hiked down the mountainside and into a dry arroyo and found a nice little human size cave like dwelling. I made a bed of foliage as E-Su had done for me and I said a bed blessing spell over it before lying down. As I lay there, I thought about how I had changed more than any of my friends or family had ever fathomed possible. I also realized that I was about to go on another journey to transform myself even more radically. However, this time, I didn't care if it made me incomprehensible to the dark lord's brainwashed nitwits of the world. I was done with my life the way that it was and I was determined to be the master of my own destiny. For the sake of every life form in the world I was going to craft my own fate by making the hard, but right choices in my life; while also not allowing any fear or doubt of others to hold me back. I knew by making the right choices at the right times I would be put on the path to my fullest potential. These were my final thoughts as I fell asleep.

I woke to the sun rising above the mountain ranges, followed by the sound of birds chirping. There was something holy about the early morning; that time of the day always felt so fresh and newly pregnant with possibilities. Only I felt terrible in those moments, for I knew I planned to disappear again and I knew it would leave a bad

impression with everyone that cared about me. I mostly felt sorry for my mom because I knew she would be hit the hardest, I was just glad she knew that I was alive. I decided that before I got on the plane, I would send her a text explaining that I had gone to the Himalayas to find enlightenment and that I loved her very much, then I would throw my phone in the trash because I didn't want to keep receiving the dark lord's spells.

After some internal deliberation, I decided to walk to the airport instead of taking my car. So, I drove it back to my mom's place and began to walk alone to the airport in the early hours of the morning. As I walked with all my camping supplies and food in the pack on my back, I was given several good reminders as to why it was I was choosing the path of Shama. Being forced to breathe the polluted air all around me and seeing the way my species had been exploited by the dark lord's culture made me sick.

As I walked I looked around at people while they hustled by or surfed the web, I watched as the negative symbols from the towers rained down from the sky to their cell-phones. Everyone's phone emitted a frequency which encased them with these negative signals and symbols. I also noticed that there were cell phone towers by every school, grocery store and church in the city, undoubtedly dousing everyone that entered those buildings with spells of negativity. Everyone was going about their day as the negative symbols merged with their thought and feeling symbols produced inside of their spiritual field. The negative chi symbols affected their

flow of chi dramatically; mostly by entangling every person's feelings with the negative chi I had seen pouring from the grey net in the sky. I watched in horror as I walked through the city and only made it to the airport without freaking out, by telling myself that each step I made was a step toward a better future, not just for me but the planet as a whole as well. I was making this decision for everyone not just myself. I had apparently met E-Su for a reason and my heart knew this was it.

While at the airport I got a further reminder of the invasive nature of the dark lord's culture as I was poked, fondled, and forced to be drenched in X-Rays by airport security. The X-Ray machines also carried symbols and frequencies of fear and depression. These X-Ray machines drenched everyone in their symbols before going to their terminal, affecting everyone's moods and spiritual state of being dramatically before their travel. Only I got through this process rather unaffected, because of my heightened state.

I made my way down the aisle of the plane and to my cramped window seat in coach. As I sat with my eyes closed I prepared myself mentally for what was to come next, I pulled the black family stone from my jeans pocket and began looking through the blackness using the distant light of the sun in the window. I thought about the path I had chosen and what was in store for me in the Himalayas. Then suddenly, through a swirling pattern of light inside of the stone's illuminated center, I saw myself, standing with a stronger muscular build than I have ever had, while holding a long white staff. I took a

closer look and saw that my face had a solid black vertical line tattooed down the right side of my forehead, going over my eyebrow and my right cheek, ending in a point at the base of my jaw bone. Then the image became unclear and dissolved as the plane engines started. I briefly looked at the engines for a moment, and when I looked back into the stone, the image was gone completely. I looked up in confusion and wondered if I had just seen my future inside of the stone, then I felt the plane begin to move forward and start to take off.

30) My Story Continues

The hologram suddenly stopped and the polished stone promptly dropped on the little silk pillow at the top of the altar. I felt a low level of shock, as if I had experienced a whole other lifetime in that night. My brain felt boggled, scrambled and fried; after so much information input my mind was spent. Even still I was upset that the story was over. My father stood to his feet and rolled up the cloth in front of the doorway to allow the morning sunlight to shine on the black crystal.

I stood up and looked at my father and said "Why did you have to end it there? It was really starting to get interesting!"

He laughed and said "Well I was hoping the whole thing would be interesting." Then he laughed again, "Only a little bit at a time sweetie, I don't want you overwhelmed. Otherwise the knowledge might not stick in your mind." He covered the stone with the white cloth then faced me with an anticipatory smile.

"Wow!" I said, "So, that is the same stone that your mother gave to you way back then?"

"That's right!" he replied with a smile. "And now I have gifted it to you for your birthday. However, I am going to ask that you leave it here with me until the other seven stories are done and your training is complete, that way you know how to use it properly. Okay?"

"Of course dad, whatever you think is best! I still can't get over how all of what I saw is even possible. I mean it was all done with chi and that stone?"

"Well that and the creative process being consciously implemented for countless hours, upon countless hours. You see, without the observer to use the tools of the body, mind and spirit, the tools themselves are useless, I just used my tools to create something with chi and words." He replied using an informal tone.

"Wow! My mind is just blown dad; I don't even know where to start with the questions that are running through my mind right now." I replied excitedly, more than anything I just wanted to hold and look into the crystal again.

“Why don’t you start with can I hold the crystal again?” he smiled mysteriously with a raised eye brow.

“That’s a great idea!” I replied, “It’s like you are reading my mind…Dad!?” He started laughing hysterically, “Have you been able to read my mind my whole life?” I asked inquisitively as he kept laughing, “No wonder you just let me talk and talk and only offered advice when I actually wanted it! How much about me do you know that I don’t know you know?”

He was still laughing and I had to wait far longer than I would have liked for an answer. I stood there entirely flabbergasted for I saw my whole life in an entirely different light after those moments. Then he spoke, “I never invaded your mental privacy, I tried to allow you to be as free and private in your mind as I could. You have no idea how hard that is to do as a concerned and loving father though I assure you. Bbut you will know what that’s like one day when you have kids and are able to read their minds.”

“I am gonna learn to read minds too?” I responded in excited anticipation.

“Yes, that will be part of your training.” He replied with a patient grin. “Everything that I know, you will learn, everything that I have mastered, you will also master. Now, you wanted to hold the stone again, I think that is a good idea. I am curious to see what happens when you put it in your hand now that you know what you know." He replied with a slight grin.

I walked over to the stone and looked at it for several seconds; I looked back at my father for reassurance. His eye brow was raised as he waited leaning against the wall smiling. I channeled all of my intention and attention on becoming one with the life force within the stone. I projected the reality that I would immediately feel a profound and life changing surge of energy when I made contact with its smooth surface and tried to perceive that reality's existence before I ever touched it.

Only when I picked it up, I didn't feel much of anything. I held onto it for several seconds with my eyes closed, but nothing happened. I was rather disappointed with such results. So I tried to put it back, except when I attempted to set it down, it would not drop from my hand. It was stuck to my palm; I thought my father had put some sort of adhesive on it until I felt the heat begin to grow inside my palm. In a panic I tried to pull the crystal from my hand but it wouldn't budge.

Something told me to stop fighting its power and look into its center. As I gazed into its depths I became hypnotized and memorized by an image that began to surface from the abyss. It was a feminine face made of light, colorfully decorated with ancient looking make up. Atop the head was a golden crown filled with diamonds and rubies. It took me a moment of staring to realize that the face I was looking at was my own. Suddenly the vision encompassed my whole reality.

When my eyes locked with the eyes of the woman inside, the stone started to glow and I immediately felt everything that the woman on the inside of the crystal felt. With this feeling I imbibed the woman's entire history; she was the inheritor of a vast amount of esoteric knowledge and had chosen to place all of that knowledge into the stone. She carried the stone with her every time she went to learn the art of creating reality from her great sorceress mother. Whenever she learned something new, she would place the knowledge inside the stone so she would never lose it. Before she died she gave it to her son, on the condition that he passes it on to his first born for protection. As she died she blessed the crystal with a piece of her spirit so she could always protect and guide her loved ones through its power. I was that woman, and I saw how history was repeating itself while also digressing from its previous path simultaneously.

The feeling of being in that psychic space was very pleasant; however as I felt another hand touch the top of the crystal, the pleasant feeling was soon interrupted and replaced by another vision. I was immersed in a thick snow covered forest with the cold winter wind blowing hard against the bleak dark night. In the distance a small fire burned with two people circling around it.

Upon running over to the light of the flames, I saw my father shirtless and bleeding with a massive hunting knife in his hand as he backed up around the right side of a nearby tree. Seeing he was wounded and retreating from something I ran over to his aid, but for some reason he couldn't see me standing in front of him. He looked above my head terrified and raises his knife as a display of aggression.

When I turned around I stood below a ten foot tall, half decayed beast with lanky arms and long legs ending in long razor sharp claws. It had a long wolf like snout that snarled, showing its large bloody saliva covered fangs, it stared with eyes as black as night at my father. Its heavy breath left a cloud of moisture in the air, gooey saliva visibly poured from its mouth, steam rose from the several lacerations on its chest and arms, dripping blood stained the snow with dark near black drops as it approached my father.

It leapt over me and on top of my father, the creature bit into his shoulder as he stabbed it over and over again in the ribs with his knife. They both roared and screamed at each other as they rolled on the ground, flinging blood into the air and all over the clean white snow. Suddenly the vision stopped and I was back in my father's ceremony room. He had the stone in his hand and was placing it back on top of the altar's pillow.

"Dad? What was that—that—that thing?!" I stuttered.

He sighed and looked down as he said, "That is something you were not supposed to see yet. That is another story, for another time Maria." He replied coldly.

"No dad! You need to tell me now. What was that—that—that thing?" I retorted.

“Maria, even if I told you right now you wouldn’t understand. That monster is my burden to bare, not yours, so you don’t concern yourself with it one bit sweetie.”

“Well I am very concerned, how am I not supposed to be! That was absolutely terrifying! Did that really happen? Was that a memory?” I said in a panic.

”I promise I will tell yoou everything in its time; you just have to let me tell you when I feel it is time. Okay?” he said reassuringly.

“What makes you think I won’t understand now?” I replied smartly.

“Do you trust me?” He asked raising his eyebrow.

“Of course I do, but that still doesn’t explain why you can’t just tell me now?” I replied in frustration, “That vision was awful dad! I am worried about you! The feeling I got was of pure dread and disgust!”

“I will be fine; the bigger a light gets inside someone’s spirit the larger the darkness it has to conquer grows. Try not to worry about things that your mind isn’t ready to comprehend yet. All that worrying won’t change what the next step is going to be for you.” He said as he smiled.

I could tell he was trying to change the subject. Which I knew meant I would get nothing more out of him in regards to the vision I saw, so I did my best to mentally move on, convincing myself I'd sort out the details later.

"Ok dad, I'll ask, what's the next step?" I said reluctantly.

"Let me show you instead of tell you. Come down stairs with me." He said. And with a hand around my shoulder we walked out of his ceremony room and down the staircase as he continued talking, "So, now that you understand the flow of chi and the creative process, wouldn't you say that my little home here is one fine piece of craftsmanship?"

"What do you mean? You mean you made this whole thing using chi and the creative process?" I asked skeptically.

"That's right, from the ground up; if you want I can show you how I did it when you get back?"

"Get back?" I replied confused.

He smiled and laughed and said "Yeah, you didn't think that was it did you?"

"Actually, yeah, I did." I said sheepishly.

He laughed then yelled out "E-SU!" at the top of his lungs.

Inside the entrance stepped E-Su from my father's story! He looked exactly the same as he did in the hologram. Amazed that it was him, I said "Wow! E-Su?! I can't believe it's actually you!" I put out my hand out to shake, but he grabbed me and gave me a big hug. He stunk like a skunk and I had to hold my nose to keep from gagging after he let me go.

E-Su and my father shared a laugh and my father said "E-Su says you will get use to the smell during your training."

"Training?" I asked, "I thought I was training with you dad?"

"You are sweetie; E-Su is just going to introduce you to a couple of plant spirits while I do some final preparations for your lesson on the next full moon. You are going to have your spiritual rebirth during tonight's full moon, so you should probably get some rest. I hope you are ready!" he looked up at E-Su and stared for a brief moment, "I told him to take good care of you while you are away from your body and to telepathicallly keep me posted on your progress."

"Tell him I want to hear him try to communicate with me telepathically." I replied.

As I said those woords, I felt and heard and internal voice whisper *"Maria..."* I looked up at E-Su, he put his hand on his chest and bowed then I heard the voice more pronounced say *"E-Su."* I immediately started laughing out loud. My ffather and E-Su shared another look and a smile. E-Su telepathically said "Follow me Maria" and he walked out of my dad's home. I gave my dad a big hug and a kiss on the cheek then said "I love you dad! Thank you for the best birthday present ever!" And I quickly ran out to catch up with E-Su.

Made in the USA
Las Vegas, NV
06 December 2021